The Nazi Connection

The Nazi Connection

F. W. Winterbotham, CBE

Weidenfeld and Nicolson
London

Weidenfeld and Nicolson
11 St John's Hill   London SW11

ISBN 0 297 77458 1

Printed in Great Britain by
Redwood Burn Limited
Trowbridge and Esher

To Petrea

Contents

1
Convictions

Modern films, books and television serials have made spying appear a dangerous, glamorous and romantic job in which the objective is always obtained. A spy may have found the site of a new type of rocket launcher or unearthed secret plans to blow up the planet; he may have tracked down the master mind behind some devilment or rescued a scientist from behind enemy lines, but once he has accomplished this objective, the job is finished. In real life spying is infinitely more interesting and much more complex. It has many more facets and far more problems, and it is often slow and laborious, involving a great deal of work for a small return; it can also be tough, demanding and bitterly disappointing. For Intelligence work at the highest level is not always a matter of the mechanics of collecting and collating information; more often it is concerned with people, with what they may do and how they may do it. When I was a member of the British Secret Intelligence Service during the thirties, working in Germany on and off from 1934 to 1939, I frequently found myself playing a game of bluff and double-bluff with the upper echelon of the Nazi Party, each of us trying to assess the other's strengths and weaknesses.

Despite being head of the Air Department of M16, I found it extremely difficult to discover all I wanted at long range from London. So, frustrated by sitting at a desk, impotently waiting for answers to my queries, I decided to go out and discover for myself; to become the master spy instead of the spy master. For the job I had set myself was to find out all I could about the new Air Force which I suspected the Germans were busily creating; how it was being set up; its framework, growth and potential.

Over the years I was able to find out practically everything I wanted to know about German rearmament in the air between the wars, and indeed a great deal more besides about their vast new mechanised Army and its future strategy. I was able to make personal assessments of the character, competence, stability and future behaviour of the German leaders themselves; and from them I gained an overall knowledge of what the Nazis were intending to do and how they hoped to go about it.

But to my surprise this was not my hardest task; much the most difficult job turned out to be trying to convince the British politicians and the military that what I had seen and what I expected to happen was really likely to come about. Impressions, concepts, judgements had to be backed up by facts, but no amount of buttressing was any good if in the first place no one would believe me. I sometimes felt that the methods I used to get the information were sufficiently bizarre to convince even the most sceptical and unimaginative politician that the details were genuine, but this did not turn out to be the case. My own side appeared most obtuse and were often unwilling to accept what seemed to me to be the most obvious conclusions. The Air Force chiefs, no doubt under pressure from their political overlords, seemed unable until almost too late to take action on the information which I had obtained with such care.

It was particularly daunting trying to persuade people in Britain about German rearmament before 1935. Then, in that year, at long last the politicians were forced to believe my figures, for the growth of the new German Air Force was visible for all to se. But even when they had seen it with their own eyes they seemed unable to grasp the scope, the magnitude and the potential power of all this might. Too many British political and military overlords were still thinking in terms of the First World War. It was then that I realised that explaining the potential enemy's strength in aircraft, the number of bombers he had and the type of fighter aircraft he was developing was not in itself enough unless I was also able to get across at the same time what this would mean when it was unleashed against us. I had to be able to drive home the fact that such powerful new weapons would lead to a complete change in the conduct of future warfare. I would have to be able to make my Chiefs of Staff envisage how this Air Force might be used; to make them see the likely number of civilian casualties that would ensue from dropping vast quantities of very large bombs; the tremendous destructive power and the moral terror mass bombing would unleash. Obviously you cannot persuade people to take suitable precautions against new strategic warfare methods unless, in the first place, you have convinced them of the dangers.

A high-grade Intelligence officer must be able to do much more than collate information. He must be able to give a general impression of the mood of the country he is working against; he must be able to assess the leaders' will to carry out war, and to evaluate the competence and characters of the generals.

Hitler told me personally at great length exactly what he intended to do. It was then up to me to assess whether this was fact or just one of his fantasies; was he boasting or being enthusiastic? Was it wish-fulfilment or hot air? Both he and some of his senior generals gave me a very detailed account of the kind of *Blitzkrieg* attack that they proposed to use. When I had found out what this meant and what it involved, then I had to assess whether the German Air Force and Army could use it. Would they have the planes, the men, the machines and above all the necessary rapid communication network and all the back-up that would be required? I was left in no doubt as to their intentions, and from what I learned they would certainly seem to have the hardware to carry them out. But where would the first attack come? Would it be on the French, the Belgians or the Russians? When would it come? In order to answer such questions and to complete my observations I had to try to visualise the result of such a *Blitzkrieg* on our rather out-of-date methods of warfare.

I made many visits to Germany during the thirties and slowly, bit by bit, I built up a detailed mosaic of a nation preparing for war. Reading about my activities now, in the 1970s, it may seem as if some of the information I collected was obvious for all to see. Alternatively it may seem as if I am inventing, with all the knowledge that hindsight has given me. But what I want to explain is how unclear it all was at the time; how unlikely it all seemed to most people and how many resolutely refused to believe what was happening. I hope to convey in this book the challenges that I met with at the time; the difficulties of establishing the truth of what was happening and the enormous problems of convincing highly intelligent leaders of what I saw and found out. I had to learn as I went along, discover what to look for and where the solutions lay, find out how to put my views across and how to interpret my own impressions in convincing language.

It would have been a most daunting task had I not had a most sympathetic and helpful boss. Each time I returned to England after a trip to Germany, I would arrive at M16 and explain to him exactly what new information I had gleaned and what my general impressions were. I did not find him difficult to convince, nor were the Foreign Office permanent staff for long in doubt as to what we should be up against. It was the military and political leaders who were so sanguine.

I first went to Germany to spy out the land in February 1934. I was able to make close contact with Nazi leaders who, at that time, were desperately anxious to get what they called "English connections with influence". These leaders were most anxious to impress upon me that Hitler did not want to involve Britain in war; he was personally obsessed with the notion that Britain should keep out of his future campaigns. Would I please explain this to my superiors? By pretending to show great enthusiasm for their régime and by exploiting their obsession for a neutral Britain, I was able to come and go in their country without any difficulty.

The Germans knew only that I was a member of the Air Staff with evident connections in *important places* and that when I came to Germany I was on leave. They felt that I was sympathetic to their cause and they hoped that I was putting their view across to the Chiefs of Staff. So whenever I was in Germany I had to play a part and I had to be extremely careful to play it well. At times it was dangerous, especially in the later years when they saw no positive reaction to all that they had divulged to me. I was really playing a dangerous confidence trick, a game of double-bluff, but I always hoped that it would enable me to obtain such detailed information that I would be able to convince the Air Chiefs of what was going on so that they in their turn could persuade His Majesty's Government of the likely outcome.

This book is an account of my work as an Intelligence officer and how I carried it out: how I had to behave like an ordinary person on leave enjoying the wonders of the Nazi régime; to praise the work of the Nazis to their faces in order to get them to talk with uninhibited enthusiasm about their plans for the future, which in fact they did, and yet at the same time to appear serious in my intentions to influence important people in London on the Nazis' behalf. This was the *quid pro quo* which allowed me to see and learn so much. The Germans would tell me all I wanted to know if in turn I would convince the British Chiefs of Staff how powerful the new Germany was, because the Nazis believed that might was right and that if the British knew the strength of the forces ranged against them, they would not fight: added to which of course they knew very well that we had nothing to fight with at the time.

I was in the strange position of seeing both sides from a very high vantage point all through the thirties. I caught glimpses of the evil behind the Nazi philosophy and I watched them prepare for war while back in England people talked of "peace in our time". The Francophiles in the Cabinet looked the other way; generals prepared their defences on the outcome of battles of the First World War and 'bright young things' chattered and danced. Again and again I wondered how I could persuade those in power to anticipate what was to come. The Germans wanted me to convince them so that we would not fight, and I wanted to convince them so that we would be prepared. It was impossible to mix with the top Nazis and their generals without absorbing information on the growth and formation of the might of the new Germany. As they grew stronger the Nazis even started boasting openly about their invincibility, so it was doubly frustrating to see how little attention was paid to my information in London. Was the answer that the English did not know what to do, so therefore they did not wish to know?

Why then did I persevere in my task? What kept me digging away all those years in the face of such vapid response? It is hard for me to explain this, but perhaps my attitude and personal viewpoint towards a potential English enemy in general and towards the Nazis in particular can best be understood if I give some idea of the influences I was under earlier in my life and if I explain how I came to have my job in the first place.

When the First World War broke out in 1914 everybody believed it would be over in twelve months. Most young men of spirit rushed to join the colours in case this excitement might fade before they had a chance to take part. I myself went straight from school at the age of seventeen to join the Gloucestershire Yeomanry, my own county cavalry regiment. Later I transferred to the Royal Flying Corps. There was a quick period of training on Salisbury Plain and then I found myself in France as a scout pilot with Number 29 squadron.

On Friday 13 July 1917 I was sitting on a hard wooden chair in the mess tent of our small aerodrome in Belgium drinking a cup of hot cocoa, having returned with my flight from an uneventful dawn patrol over the enemy lines, when my Commanding Officer came in and told me that my flight would have to act as escort to a photo reconnaissance which the Army had required at 10.00 a.m. The Army seemed blithely unmindful of the enormous wastage of trained pilots and good aeroplanes in their insatiable appetite for air photographs of the enemy's positions: the big Paschendael push was imminent and they wanted the photographic aircraft to dive to 2,000 ft. over the German guns. I, with my flight of five small scout aeroplanes, was to protect it. It was quite evident from the excessive air activity that the enemy knew the 'push' was coming. I knew at once that this would be a hot assignment and in addition the sun would be in our eyes. I think that few people who have not flown fighter aircraft in battle realise how quickly one type of aircraft becomes obsolete at a time of rapid development of aeronautical design. By mid-1917 the little French-built Nieuport aircraft, with which our squadron was equipped, were virtually out of date. We were completely out-classed both in speed and gun power by the more modern German fighters. The little Lewis guns mounted on the top plane of our aircraft were constantly jamming and could not compete with the two Maxim guns fired through the propellers of the newer types. There were of course no parachutes in those days and the Germans had the advantage of fighting over their own territory as well as choosing the precise moment for their attack. There was little one could do about it, and I now know that these somewhat suicidal photographic sorties made a deep impression on me at the time. It was unfortunate too that on this Friday the 13th my own Nieuport aircraft had to undergo a small overhaul after the dawn patrol so that I had to borrow somebody else's. In 1917 there was something very personal about your own little scout aircraft. It was wise to look after the unreliable gun, even personally inspecting each round of ammunition as it was fitted into the drum in order to see that there were no misshapen or dented bullets, and checking that the seat was just at the right height for optimum operation of the rudder bar and the joystick, the gun sight exactly adjusted to one's own eye level. Now with a borrowed aircraft everything was in the wrong place and I was without my purple garter mascot. I suppose every airman has his superstitions. I think I might describe myself normally as bold but not foolhardy, and I always considered that strict attention to detail was one of the safeguards of flying. I've never yet discovered whether it is the family genes which have, over the ages, produced the family mottoes, or vice versa. My own family motto, which has come down to me through many generations in a direct line from that forward-looking monarch Edward I (who in the thirteenth century not only called together the first Parliament but hammered 'Scotland' into Great Britain), roughly translated means: "Look before you leap". This may account for the care with which I prepared my aircraft and later prepared myself for my mission into Nazi Germany, where carelessness would have been unforgivable and quick-wittedness was essential.

The dog fight over the Paschendael area was short and vicious, with odds of 3 to 1 of some of the newest and best German fighters against us. My left winger went up in flames in the first half minute and after a short burst, which sent one of the enemy down, my gun jammed. I felt bullets ripping into the fuselage; there was a smell of burning as bullets tore the leather boots off the inside of my legs; my engine spluttered and died. I did a falling leaf movement to escape a further attack and tried to turn my nose to home but it was hopeless; I was losing height too rapidly. Eventually I managed to get the aircraft down on a straight strip of shell-torn ground without too much damage. I suppose I had acted automatically during the fight, but now with my aircraft turned upside down and my head jammed between the top wing and the ground, I was angry; angry at having to fly such a mission in an out-of-date aircraft; angry at the unavoidable lack of preparation for the mission and the virtually impossible job we were supposed to do.

A young German officer of the anti-aircraft battery near which I had crashed pulled me out from beneath the aircraft, suffering nothing more than a bloody and broken nose, and looked after me. It was lucky that I had managed to come down so far behind the infantry lines, otherwise I should have been shot out of hand. (It was only when I published my book on wartime Intelligence in 1974 that I had a letter from a resident in Texas asking if I was by any chance the young Captain he had pulled out of a crashed aeroplane near his AA battery on 13 July 1917. I was, and at last was able to

thank Mr Viegers.) I was taken away to a field Intelligence
centre some few miles further back where a 'matey' officer
who described himself as a polo-playing sportsman questioned
me, or rather told me all the activities of my squadron since
it had come to Poppering. As I sat on the terrace outside the
Intelligence building sipping some Rhine wine I watched the
whole of my Number 29 squadron, obviously led by the Commanding Officer, fly a morale patrol over the lines. My interro-
gator, watching through immensely powerful mounted binoculars, pointed to the leader and asked me casually, "How old
is Major DeCrespigny?" I too had a look at the squadron
through the binoculars. He was flying my very own little aeroplane. Later the ebullient sportsman acted as interpreter as I
talked to the pilots who had fought us and learned how well
all their operations were planned. They did not keep up any
particular patrols at stated hours as we did, but waited until
they knew a certain formation was due over their front line;
then they would send up a squadron of aircraft to attack it,
manoeuvring themselves so that the sun was always behind
them. They also told me how they had worked out very carefully the method of disrupting our photographic reconnaissances. They found that an intense anti-aircraft barrage between the photo machines and the escort confused the whole
issue and at that moment they were able to strike.

It was impossible not to be impressed by the logical and
highly effective methods the German Air Force used, not only
to preserve precious fuel and save the lives of as many pilots
as possible together with their valuable aircraft, but also to
achieve the same results as we did by our constant and often
useless patrols at given hours over the line. These were, I had
been told, largely for morale purposes and to protect our aircraft doing the artillery spotting, but the Germans managed
it a different way. I asked them how they got their information
for counter-artillery work and they said it was quite simple,
knowing the precise hours at which our patrols went up, to
sneak across a photographic plane and take low-level pictures
of our artillery positions. These were then watched by their
balloon observers while directing their guns on to the target.

As for the method they had evolved to disrupt our own photographic reconnaissances, they had in my case worked absolutely perfectly since I had not experienced it before nor been warned of it. The moment the photographic machines had started to dive down from 8,000 to 2,000 ft. to take their photographs, an intense anti-aircraft barrage had been put up between them and my escorting scouts. My attention had obviously been rivetted on the photographic machines which I could now hardly see, and I had to make up my mind whether to stay up or go down through the barrage to protect them. It was at this precise moment that out of the sun came some fifteen German fighters to attack my flight. The German pilots to whom I was talking said that provided the timing was good, it never failed to work. They had obviously given much more thought to air strategy than we had. In addition they had the advantage that nine times out of ten if any of their aircraft were damaged they would come down on their own side of the lines. Forward Intelligence posts too kept a detailed record of every Royal Flying Corps (RFC) movement; they knew precisely where every squadron was stationed and even the Commanding Officer's name. I was naturally duly impressed; it was I suppose my first lesson in Intelligence and in the thoroughness and efficiency of German organisation. Later that evening the young pilot who led the German squadron and who claimed me as his special victim brought along the cushion from the seat of my borrowed aircraft. It was riddled with bullet holes. Laughing, he said, "Just one more inch and you would have been a soprano." Was it perhaps the 'weeping angel' of Amiens that had looked after me that morning in the absence of Lulu's garter? There had been a gentle nun who had given me a small metal token of the famous stained-glass window in the cathedral, where I had gone for a few quiet moments, and I had worn it on the chain of my identity disc.

Next day I and some other RFC casualties were taken to a prisoners' cage close to a German aerodrome for about a week until a sufficient contingent of prisoners had been collected to warrant our transfer to the basic transit camp at Karlsruhe. Then we were herded into a cattle truck in a very slow-moving train with a batch of Russian prisoners who were obviously too weak to continue with their forced labour on the Western front; they were indeed too weak to stand and lay about on the floor in heaps; their almost unseeing eyes peering out from their drawn, bony faces gave some indication of what the rest of their filthily-smelling bodies must have been like inside the ragged clothes that they were wearing. No longer resembling human beings, they were probably destined to die anyway. I was to recognise now the utter brutality and complete disregard for human life which seemed to form a part of the make-up of the professional German soldier in World War I. Somewhere along the line amongst the more moronic Germans was a sadistic streak of cruelty which became so evident later amongst the thugs who joined Himmler and his black-uniformed private army, and the picture of those miserable bits of Russian humanity was so deeply imprinted on my memory that it took little imagination to realise what was happening in the Nazi extermination camps some twenty-five years later.

We were all turned out at Cologne station where pathetic, square Teutonic women spat at us as we moved off to a dungeon below the platform. Here again for the whole night we were packed in together with miserable scraps of Russian humanity; the stench was appalling and as they were infested with every form of lice and bug we soon began to scratch ourselves and realised that nothing but a hot disinfectant bath would get us clean again.

It was an itchy but better journey in a proper railway carriage with our individual German guards up the Rhine to Karlsruhe, to the large collecting camp where we inevitably met a number of those pilots who had trained with us in England and gone through the same experiences in France. Here we were duly disinfected and every stitch of clothing sterilised.

It was here, too, that I received letters from my mother and father and my sister. I had, unknown to myself, been reported killed in action and my poor family had gone three weeks believing I was dead. They were very private letters which I have kept until this day and I really never knew what a splendid fellow I was until I read my own obituary notice from the local paper some eighteen months later. Writing home, I had great difficulty with the bossy little German censor when I tried to explain to him that 'bastard', referring to the man who had shot me down, was really a term of endearment in England. However, he looked it up in the dictionary and made me write the whole letter over again.

Looking back I suppose it was my eighteen months in prison camps in Germany that taught me most about human nature; not only about my British colleagues but also about French officers who shared a camp with us at one point and more especially about the Germans themselves. The German Commandant in Trier was a delightful old Colonel who had acquired a very big and expensive red nose on English port when he was a military attaché in London. He called all the British prisoners up one day and told them quietly not to escape from the tunnel we had been digging because he knew where it was coming out, but on no account to tell the French. It was a very different proposition when we were moved to a camp at Schweidnitz in Silesia, that home of Prussian arrogance, where the camp Commandant, who only visited us occasionally, confiscated the cricket net and the bat and few balls we had so carefully had sent to us from Holland, just in case we might get any pleasure out of them. On the other hand the camp Adjutant, Hauptmann Schmidt, who came from Bavaria, was a most charming fellow and did his best to see that we were as comfortable and as happy as possible. He was also a very brave man; he'd been wounded earlier on in the war and when the end of the war came and there was red revolution in the town, the townspeople started to march on our camp where they knew we had a store of tinned food. It was Hauptmann Schmidt who set up a machine gun opposite the gates and threatened to open fire on any of his compatriots who dared to come through; it was Schmidt too who taught me the rudiments of the German language when, as British camp Adjutant, I had to deal with him over matters of camp welfare.

It was not until January 1919 that I was finally repatriated from the prisoner-of-war camp. I was 'forgiven' by the Government for having been taken prisoner, thanked for my services with the Royal Flying Corps and released from any duties with the newly formed Royal Air Force.

I had missed those years between seventeen and twenty-one in which most young men try to find their feet in the world. Instead, I now found myself more in sympathy with men of twenty-seven or thirty. I had grown both older during the war and in my prison camp than the years warranted and, I think, also wiser. However, I was still puzzled about the German people as a whole. There seemed to be two distinct types. Those from the western half of Germany, who were more like Anglo-Saxons, were kindly people such as our Colonel Commandant at Trier; on the other side of the coin were the brutal ones, who seemed to take a joy in being unpleasant and whose pastime was war, killing and conquering. I began to wonder whether in fact it had something to do with the failure of Roman civilisation to penetrate very far beyond the Rhine, while further East the tribes must have been subjected to, and mixed with, the Mongols of Genghis Khan and Attila and his 'Huns', and that their façade of civilisation merely covered their mixed ancestry of savagery when war was just an excuse for looting, rape and kicking around your victims.

What did make a lasting impression on me was the arrival back in the town of Schweidnitz, in Silesia, of the local regiment; they marched into the town after their defeat on the Western front with bands playing and colours flying, their officers strutting as if in victory. At that time we the prisoners had been allowed access to the town and countryside, as we could no longer legally be kept behind bars, and it was the arrogant young Prussian officers from the area who told me in no uncertain terms that they were not a beaten army, but they had been betrayed by their politicians and would have their revenge, "make no doubt about it", they said. These were the young men who were waiting for an opportunity to have a go at the Allies once more. This was the nightmare that stayed with me right from the time I came back to England until later when I was to go into the Nazis' den.

I had been shot down because the Germans were applying logic and versatility to their job as well as spectacular organisation and efficiency. They were clearly not the robot-like figures depicted in English cartoons who always obeyed orders and never questioned. What I had seen of their Intelligence work showed it to be marginally cleverer than ours, yet despite their superior Intelligence information they had not won the war. Would they have done so if their leaders had been better trained and their political figures had backed them up more? What, I wondered, might the Germans not be capable of if given greater drive?

My time as a prisoner of war had shown me their ruthless side, their attention to detail and their curious brand of latent fanaticism. It had helped me to understand how much they disliked and distrusted the French, and had encouraged me to think that they did indeed rather admire the English: not the individual man so much as their ideal of a perfect English gentleman. Later on in the 1930s all this experience helped me to be a great deal less surprised than most of my contemporaries by the turn of events.

2
MI6

I found that it wasn't too easy to settle down after my teen-age war and my time in a prison camp. I took a law degree at Oxford but couldn't resign myself to working in an office. I had an urge to get married, produce a family and try to live off the land. I'm told that this is natural after a war: the thought of an outdoor life with hunting and sport after being cooped up in a prison camp for a year and a half was strong. However, I soon found that with a growing family, the profits from farming in the 1920s were meagre. I looked at farming in Kenya and Rhodesia, but Africa offered no more hope than Britain. The shadow of a slump hung over all primary pro-duction so I returned to England and decided to look for a job.

At a time like this, one automatically turns to friends. I real-ised that I should probably have to work in London so after mulling over various offers, I heard of one that seemed to have considerable potential at the Stock Exchange. An old friend was a member of the firm and he wanted someone of my calibre to help with overseas clients. It wasn't what I had in mind but I was feeling poor.

On my way to my first interview in London I took an old girl friend out to lunch. She was a dear, intelligent person who expressed considerable surprise at my choice of employment. Had I been reading about the situation in America and was I aware that there was extreme nervousness already in the City? Taken aback, I asked her advice as to what I should do and she suggested I meet an old friend of hers called Archie Boyle who was trying to build up the Air Staff now that the Royal Air Force had fully established itself as the third fighting arm with an assured future and a proper peacetime role. This sounded much more up my street.

One should never underestimate the ability of a charming and very beautiful girl who can accomplish over one luncheon what it might take months for a mere male to do. She was extremely discreet and gave me no precise indication as to what Archie Boyle was actually doing.

A few days later she arranged for us both to have lunch with Archie. We talked amicably about the world in general from India to Africa, from sheep farming to lumbering. Nothing was mentioned about the RAF on either side. I went away filled with an excellent lunch, inspired with much good talk from a man of wide-ranging knowledge, but in no way conscious that I had been scrutinised for possible employment. "Be patient," said Cicely. So I went back to Gloucestershire and thought no more about it.

Ten days later, just before Christmas, I received an invitation from Archie for a further lunch. This time we were alone. Again the conversation flowed over men and world affairs. It was not until the very last moment that he casually remarked that I should be receiving a letter asking me to come to the Air Ministry early in the New Year where a job awaited me if I would care to take it. Still no mention was made of the job itself.

Just after Christmas 1929 I received an official letter from Archie asking me to call at his office on 3rd January. So on a wintry morning I dug myself out of the snow at my Cotswold farm and caught the train to London. I was sad to leave my country life behind but at least I would be able to return home at weekends, and the unknown nature of the job intrigued me. Archie Boyle took me along to meet Charles Blount, the Director of Intelligence, and together we all proceeded to the office of the Deputy Chief of Air Staff, Sir Cyril Newall, who explained the whole Air Ministry set-up and how Lord Trenchard, Chief of the Air Staff, had left it in his hands to decide on my appointment. He then told me that the Air Staff had decided to have their own section in the Secret Services.

So at long last I discovered what my new job was to be! I was to operate an Air Section in the British Secret Service alongside my colleagues in the Navy and Army. Dear Cicely had helped me into a job in a million. I just happened to be the right person in the right place at the right time. My qualifications as an ex-pilot plus my ability to speak reasonable German and good French had all helped. I had kicked around the world a bit, was of an age supposed to be of discretion and they wanted a civilian for the post, so I was in. My name was to be shown on the Air Ministry list as a member of the Air Staff and my duties would be listed as liaison, which gave me a wide scope and yet made me appear innocuous should anyone get too curious.

Sir Cyril warned me that he expected no miracles but he emphasised that a small amount of accurate information was worth far more than a large amount of nonsense. He had been assured by the Chief of the Secret Service that I would be given every possible assistance, and he wished me good luck. My two sponsors, Charles Blount and Archie Boyle, then took me off in a taxi to "somewhere in Whitehall". We entered the portals of what looked like a rather down-at-heel office building and were escorted up four flights in a large, slow lift by a blue-uniformed Government messenger. There we were met by a smartly dressed blue-uniformed type, obviously ex-service who, unknown to me at the time, carried a revolver in his belt. We were guided along a richly carpeted passage to a thickly padded door, beyond which lay the office of the Chief of the British Secret Service, Admiral Sir Hugh Sinclair. The post of Chief of the Secret Service had been retained by the Admiralty since World War I, but the Service's history and activities go back for many years to the time when Lord Walsingham made it an effective part of the security of the state in the sixteenth century.

As the Admiral got up from behind his large carved mahogany desk to greet me, I saw a rather short, stocky figure with the welcoming smile of a benign uncle. His handshake was as gentle as his voice, and only the very alert dark eyes gave a hint of the tough personality that lay beneath the mild exterior. I learned later that the vast desk had originally been housed in the old Admiralty in Whitehall where it had been used by the great admirals of the past, but had now obviously become the property of the head office. We talked a while and I saw myself being quietly assessed, much in the same way as I had been looked over by Archie Boyle at our first luncheon; again I evidently passed scrutiny. I remember one of the first pieces of advice that the Admiral ever gave. "If," he said, "you can listen to someone important telling somebody else equally important about some event of importance and, knowing the story to be quite inaccurate, you can keep your mouth shut, you may in due course make a good Intelligence officer." He assured me that I should have the full co-operation of all my colleagues. Whereupon he put a bowler hat, which was rather too small for him, as firmly as possible on his head and went off to see the Prime Minister.

So this was my new Chief and I was being accepted as a member of his staff and of the Secret Service. Admiral Sir Hugh Sinclair (Quex to the Navy) was not only my Chief, he was to become my friend and advisor for ten crowded years. His absolute personal loyalty and fairness to his staff were qualities which were rarely found in his successors after his tragic death in 1940.

I found my colleagues very willing to help me, but it was obviously not going to be easy to get inside information on aviation matters. I discovered that people who had the required technical knowledge and were willing to sell it to a foreign country were hard to find. In addition, our funds in those days were extremely limited. The sort of people I required were a considerable cut above the run-of-the-mill agent whose job was primarily to report on what he saw and seldom on what he knew. I soon realised too that I should not only have to find the right people but also train them in the sort of Intelligence I required. Then from knowledge of the motives of the agent involved in selling me the information, I should have to assess its accuracy. This was one side of the job, but I must also know and understand all the varied requirements of the Air Staff; the technical and operational performances of new aeroplanes made overseas; the organisation of foreign air forces; the efficiency of their pilots and their staff. Finally I needed to have the ability to give the people to whom I sent the information some guidance as to the reasons for my assessment. I recognised very quickly that it was no small job to start from scratch, but it was a tremendous challenge and it was not long before another side of my work became evident: that of studying the politics and the military ambitions of those countries which might at some time prove potential enemies.

In London, despite the financial crisis which had resulted from the American slump, I found a rather smug complacency. Russia seemed to be the chief topic of conversation where foreign affairs were concerned, but Communism there was settling down after its orgy of genocide, and with a crude but partially effective propaganda machine Russia was telling the world what miracles she would achieve with five-year plans and vast armed forces. There were those who argued that Russia would become normal after another fifty years in the same way that France had done after her Revolution, but people who knew Russia better wondered what would happen if ever the Russian millions were really well organised.

However, in the early 1930s it gradually became evident from the information which we were receiving that the Russian military menace, far from being imminent, was a carefully contrived bluff and it was estimated it would take at least ten years before the Russians could build up the vast armies and air forces that they now proclaimed. At this time the Americans were actually trying to teach the Russians how to make aeroengines, and from their reports the Russian peasant was not yet a technician. Nevertheless, this new arm of propaganda being practised by the Russians seemed to bemuse some areas of Whitehall where it was taken seriously.

The boisterous Latins in their black fascist shirts were becoming easier to understand, and at least Italy, unlike Russia, was not cut off from the rest of Europe. It was, I think, from closely studying the dictatorial antics of Mussolini that one first learned to recognise the precepts of the dictator. Thus, if your régime begins to grind to a halt at home you must discover a foreign enemy or, even better, engage in a small foreign war. You must also have or invent an internal enemy so you can get rid of the people you don't like or who might criticise you. These people are called spies and saboteurs or even reactionaries. Mussolini decided to choose a foreign enemy, Ethiopia, but his little campaign was destined to become the subject of international politics. It produced the abortive Hoare-Laval Pact which in turn ousted Sir Samuel Hoare from the Foreign Office. But in those early days of my apprenticeship, apart from the effects of the Wall Street crash, the Russian propaganda, and the antics of Mussolini, the rest of the world seemed to be progressing fairly quietly.

I did, however, notice some political reports coming in from Germany which indicated considerable political unrest in the southern part of that country. According to my informant a party calling themselves the National Socialist German Workers' Party, largely backed by ex-Army officers, was beginning to revolt against the existing Weimar Republic, which seemed incapable of controlling the Communist elements in Germany. A man calling himself Adolf Hitler, who had been sent to gaol in 1923 for leading a march in Munich, was making inflammatory speeches.

Under the Treaty of Versailles the German Army of the Weimar Republic was very closely controlled and as it was not allowed to have an Air Force, the matter was really not in my immediate field of interest. Nevertheless, according to my agent, the speeches which had been made by Hitler were exceedingly belligerent, and when I recalled the officers at Schweidnitz they made me wonder whether these were the first signs of a resurgence of militarism in Germany. It was shortly after this that reports started to come through from other agents in Germany—which were also reported in some sections of the press—that the Germans were training military pilots secretly in Russia. There was a suggestion too that they had some Army officers at the training camp. This of course brought an immediate request from the Air Ministry for further information. I therefore asked whether the agent who had been reporting on the Hitler antics could be brought to London so that I might have a talk with him.

I looked him up in our records and found that he was a man of about forty years of age, a Baltic Baron who had been dispossessed of his lands by the Bolsheviks. He was now resident in Berlin and was acting as a political correspondent of *The Times* newspaper as well as being one of our agents reporting on politics in Germany. But now came the more interesting part of his history: he had a British passport, he was married to a British wife, had served in the Wiltshire Regiment in World War I and during that war had transferred to the Royal Flying Corps. He had alas been found unfit to fly but operated in the balloon section, and was listed as being entirely pro-British. Apart from speaking perfect English he also spoke fluent German, Russian and French. I was elated, and felt that somehow here might be the man that I had been looking for. His name was Baron William de Ropp.

I arranged to meet Bill de Ropp at the end of 1931 in the lounge of an hotel not far from our office where we normally entertained agents from overseas, as it was obviously undesirable to have them at head office. I must say I was a little surprised to find a perfectly normal Englishman about 5 foot 10, with fair hair, a slightly reddish moustache and blue eyes, dressed in a good English suit. As he got up to shake hands he greeted me in perfect English without any trace of an accent. I don't believe anybody could have taken him for anything other than English born and bred. I introduced myself by name as a member of the Air Staff as I did not at this stage wish him to know what my real job was. We went to a quiet corner table in the restaurant and conversation automatically turned to the old days in the Royal Flying Corps. He told me of his experiences in the Wiltshire Regiment and of his disappointment at not being able to become a pilot; however, he said there was quite enough excitement amongst the balloons. He also told me about his life in Berlin as a journalist and as a keen observer of the German political scene. He and his English wife had a small flat in the Kurfürstendamm which was a cross between Piccadilly and Fifth Avenue, New York. In the 1930s it was the liveliest place in Berlin and one was apt to be accosted on the pavements by boys and girls alike.

As our luncheon progressed it was clear to me that de Ropp was highly intelligent and had a spontaneous, neat sense of humour; there was nothing cumbersome about his talk or his thinking. He would obviously be able to make decisions quickly and he seemed, from his conversation, to be a good judge of character. I was now following the same procedure that had been practised on me by Archie Boyle before I got my job; halfway through lunch I was convinced that this man was genuine, but it was not until the end of the meal that I began to broach the subject of my difficulty in obtaining information about what the Germans were intending to do about rearmament in the air.

Bill had kept his ear very close to the ground and knew one of the original Nazis, Alfred Rosenberg, who had been the leader of this new National Socialist Party when Hitler was thrown into gaol back in 1923 for attempting his *Putsch* in Munich. Bill told me about Rosenberg's antecedents in Lithuania and how, since both of them came from the Baltic provinces, they had an automatic tie-up. Bill had been introduced to Rosenberg by a fellow-journalist in Berlin, and from that moment Rosenberg had seemed to seek out Bill not only for the pleasure of talking to him but also with the motive of using him in some way to help the Nazi cause. In addition to being the author of the Nazi ideology that combined the myth of Aryan supermen and racial purity to form the basis of the new Nazi type of pagan religion, Rosenberg was also the editor of the principal and only Nazi newspaper, the *Völkischer Beobachter,* which was to become their primary instrument of propaganda before Herr Goebbels got on the air. Rosenberg

was very close to Hitler and to Hess, and although he never
mentioned rearmament to Bill, he had talked a great deal about
the Nazis' aims when they got to power. Apparently there
was no doubt in the mind of Rosenberg, at the end of 1931,
that the Nazis would be in power within a few years. It was,
said Bill, an exciting programme and from the odd bits that
Rosenberg let fall, a dangerous one to boot. Nevertheless for
the time being he was playing Rosenberg along, helping him
to understand the articles in *The Times* newspaper criticising
the National Socialists and generally acting as a sort of English
contact whom the Nazis in due course sought desperately to
enlist. Rosenberg had explained to Bill that the Party had absolutely no contact with the British Embassy, which seemed to
have been warned off this new National Socialist movement.
It was therefore vital to try to get English contacts who might
be persuaded to understand the Nazi aims.

Bill felt sure that something could be done to get the information that I required, but he asked for time to think it over
and promised to communicate with me shortly through his
contact in Berlin who normally forwarded his political reports
to our head office. It had been a long and very interesting
lunch and somehow I had come away with confidence in this
man who, I believed, was not only a British subject by passport,
but also a British subject at heart. Although Bill had been very
calm and matter of fact when he was telling me about Rosenberg and the apparent aims of the Nazis, I scented an underlying excitement which I myself felt at the prospect of the upsurge of this new Party; if it came off, and there seemed every
reason to believe that it would, it would be a political time-
bomb.

It was several weeks before I received a report from Bill,
who had evidently thought the whole matter out very carefully.
First, he confirmed that the information about the Germans
training pilots and other officers in Russia had been leaked
by the Russians as a slap in the face to this new National Socialist
anti-Communist Party, which seemed to be gaining ground
in Germany, and he felt that there was no doubt that it was
true. I don't know what action was taken by the Government

over this, but probably a small protest was lodged through the Embassy in Berlin.

Bill went on to tell me that he had talked to Rosenberg since he returned and that there was every prospect that he, Bill, might be put on the Nazi payroll as their English contact, a fully-paid agent whose job would be to interpret the articles in *The Times* to Rosenberg; to try to influence Dawson, the editor of *The Times* in London, to be sympathetic towards the Nazis; and to do everything possible to make important British contacts for the Nazis in England. Then came the most interesting suggestion of all and one which altered the whole course of my life during the thirties. Bill's proposal was that he should bring Rosenberg to London on a visit, and that while in London he would introduce him to the editor of *The Times*, together with one or two members of Parliament or others in the public eye, and give me the opportunity of meeting him myself. Bill felt that if I was reasonably convincing I might impress Rosenberg enough to be asked back to Berlin, which would then give me the opportunity to open up the contacts I needed to get the information required. He again stressed the fact that the Nazis were desperate to get British connections in high places and that if he could bring off this visit it would cement his job as Rosenberg's English agent.

Some of the archives which have been recently dug up in Berlin state that de Ropp was definitely called Rosenberg's English agent, which has led a number of people to brand him as a double agent working for the Nazis. He never was a true double agent, although admittedly he took money from both the Nazis and ourselves. He did from time to time inform Rosenberg of people who had been either talking or writing in favour of the Nazi Party in England; the German Embassy would then get in touch with these people and invite them to Berlin. Several important admirals and generals who were interested in the political revival did indeed go to Germany in this way. Later, de Ropp was ordered to go to England to explain to the Duke of Kent the aims and objectives of the Nazis. The request had originally come from King Edward VIII, but it was thought advisable to make the contact through his brother. However, at no time did Bill bend his loyalty to Britain throughout all the time between 1931 when I first knew him and the end of the Second World War.

I was very excited at Rosenberg's proposal to come to Britain and talked it over at once with my Chief. I pointed out, as Bill had done, that Rosenberg was totally unknown in this country; that he would come over as an ordinary civilian at my own invitation; and that de Ropp would look after him the whole time he was in London. Provided that his contact with the press was limited to a talk with Dawson there was little risk of the press in general making anything out of the visit, nor in fact would they ever know that he'd been here. I also pointed out to my Chief that this might be my breakthrough to get the information the Air Ministry wanted and that I should be more than grateful if he would approve the scheme. He was extremely sympathetic but he told me that he would have to discuss the matter with Robert Vansittart at the Foreign Office and would let me know in a day or so what my reply to Berlin should be.

Permission was granted a few days later but I was warned by my Chief that the invitation must come from me, purely as a private person and ex-Royal Flying Corps friend of de Ropp, and that I must be extremely careful to whom I introduced Rosenberg, with the understanding that if I made a mess of it my job would be in serious danger. I was ready to take all these risks and duly sent a personal invitation to Rosenberg, through de Ropp, written in my own hand on the notepaper of the Royal Air Force Club. Bill was obviously delighted and stressed the fact that Rosenberg was also very pleased at the idea of coming to London. A visit was arranged for April 1932.

I tried to polish up some of the rusty German which I had learned in the prison camp, but I knew that Bill was an expert interpreter and I thought it might allay suspicions if my German was not too good. I felt quite sure that some contact of the Nazis in London would probably try to check up on me, to see who I was and what importance my position indicated. They would find me as large as life in the Air Force list, with a one-room office in the Air Ministry in Kingsway—admittedly full of other people's filing cabinets—where I could be seen and was seen occasionally. I made a point of making my number with the doorman as I came and went between the Air Ministry and my offices somewhere in Whitehall.

Had I enough contacts to make myself seem sufficiently important to impress Rosenberg? As soon as I had started work in London I took good care to look up a number of my old friends who had been at Oxford with me and were now in important positions, either in politics or in business. I had made a point of accepting invitations to the House of Commons, where in turn I was introduced to MPs, especially those concerned with aviation, who now knew that I was doing some job at the Air Ministry itself. I was often called in by members of the Air Council to report on one or other aspect of any information that I had been able to obtain. It was little, I agree, but maybe it would prove enough. I had been introduced by Archie Boyle to the head people in the Society of British Aircraft Manufacturers so that I had open invitations to visit any of the aircraft factories, and during the first year of my work in London I had managed to establish a very wide field of informative contacts.

These contacts worked both ways. I could name-drop to Rosenberg and prove to him that I knew my way around the establishment. Equally these contacts were useful to me, for through them I learned what was going on in British aviation and politics. They helped me to understand the latest inventions in my own technical fields, enabled me to see how much further ahead or behind German aircraft development was, and allowed me to get the feel of how people in positions of power in England were thinking. You cannot convince people that your foreign information is useful unless you understand how it slots into the knowledge they already have. An Intelligence agent must always remember to keep his finger on the pulse of his own country.

There was one aspect of my work which did not satisfy me, however. In my own office I kept in the very closest touch with my military, naval and Foreign Office colleagues. I discussed everything with them which might have a bearing on their work and they did the same. But once the information had passed out of our office to the various service ministries it appeared that there was very little contact indeed, and I myself took to going to the War Office or the Admiralty to meet and talk with the Intelligence branches where I considered their work complemented my own. It was considered a new departure, and, I think, frowned on by some of the pundits, but all those of us who worked together in Intelligence in M16 felt that there should be a joint Service Intelligence Department which received and assessed all the information we obtained; this was not to come until after World War II, but now I imagine, in the Ministry of Defence, it is much easier for everybody to keep close liaison.

However, Rosenberg's visit was one thing I was going to keep entirely to myself until I saw how it worked out; and as de Ropp was a loner in Germany and had no contact with any other of our agents in that country, I felt certain that news of his visit would not be leaked back to this country through any other source.

Meantime, by the beginning of 1932, I was getting to know my job; where and what I had to look for; what was useful and what was a waste of time and money. RAF Intelligence had only begun in earnest in 1928 so I was right in at the beginning. Before this date it had mainly been concerned with keeping the peace in the Middle East, but now its role was world-wide. One of my first jobs was to interpret information coming in from newly acquired agents in the field and to check their value as a source. Often these reports were from untrained observers and so appeared nonsense at first glance. It made me realise that if I was to obtain worthwhile material, I would have to recruit men who knew what they were looking for and why. For example, a man in Holland sent in an observation report saying that he had seen a new type of aeroplane actually flying backwards; it was then up to me to find out what the man was talking about. In this case, on further enquiry I discovered that the aeroplane was a new type being tried out by the Fokker Company which was experimenting afresh with the old system of putting the elevators out in front of the aeroplane. This had made it look to our agent as though it were going backwards. This system had originated with the French Farman brothers in 1912 but had been abandoned as unsuitable around 1915. Had I sent in the report in its original form I should have been subjected to the ridicule of the department; but once I had found out the explanation, the information became relevant.

I learned that the Russians were starting to build aeroplanes which were precise duplicates of those being built in Britain and America. Obviously they had, through their Communist organisations, stolen the plans from our aircraft factories, giving them the name of a Russian designer to try to camouflage the fact. One has only to look at the Russian aeroplanes today to realise that the same process is going on, especially in the case of Concorde.

But snippets of information did not get me very far. What I wanted was the grand framework of any new Air Force that was going to be built in Germany, and for such details only the top would do. Rosenberg looked like being my great chance.

April came and went but no Rosenberg. Apparently he was too busy to come until autumn. Well, at least that gave me the chance to check up on his past so that I did not put my foot in it when he finally arrived. Bill was to fill in all the details. Was Rosenberg Jewish in any way, I wanted to know, for that was what the name suggested? However, Bill explained that this was not an uncommon name amongst those Germans who had settled in Latvia a number of generations ago. He was most certainly not Jewish or he would not have been accepted into the Nazi Party. Bill went on to tell me that Rosenberg, having grown up in the Baltic province, went to the USSR as a student and was there during the Revolution in 1917. It was in Russia that he first became aware of the close association between the Jewish people in Russia and Communism. Trotsky was of course himself a Jew and somehow the impression that all Jewish people were Communists must have stuck in Rosenberg's mind. It is, I think, true to say that the

Jewish people in Russia regarded Trotsky as their saviour and that many Communist ideas, including those of the collective farms and community living, had spread to the Jewish settlements in Palestine when I was there in 1933.

From Russia Rosenberg came to Munich and joined up with the Hitler movement in 1920. There is a story to the effect that he brought with him some spurious document showing that at a Jewish Convention in Geneva plans had been made to take over the finances of Germany and the rest of Europe. This proved to be his passport into the Nazi Party. Apparently they took no trouble to find out whether or not it was true; it suited their arguments at the time. He was well read and appeared to have based the philosophy of the new Party on various writings, such as those of Le Garde, who wrote in 1829, and more especially on the works of Houston Stewart Chamberlain, the renegade Englishman who took German nationality and wrote so convincingly about the Germans being the master race that he is said to have encouraged the Kaiser to attempt the hegemony of Europe before the First World War. Rosenberg was also influenced by the works of Nietzsche.

By 1930 Rosenberg had become the political philosopher of the NSDAP, as the National Socialists called themselves before they became known as the Nazi Party; but Bill was quite firm in his belief—and I agreed with him—that Rosenberg was still somewhat muddled as to the precise formula which the ideology of the new state should adopt when the Nazis came fully into power. Rosenberg himself claimed that in the early days Hitler was but the mouthpiece of Rosenberg's own writing. This may have been true for a short while but it didn't seem to take Hitler long to make up his own mind as to what he wanted to say and how to say it. Nevertheless, Rosenberg remained very close to Hitler and as the editor of the Party newspaper was in a very powerful position. However, it was Bill's opinion that Rosenberg was much too quiet and scholarly to cope with the swashbuckling extroverts who had joined the Party during the 1920s and were now pushing themselves towards the top. It was also Bill's opinion that he was not a blood-and-thunder militarist and that if and when the Party came to power and started on a more militant course of action, Rosenberg's influence would fade somewhat. But meantime he had plenty to keep himself occupied, trying to establish the new religion of Nazi ideology. The Party had of course suffered an unpleasant setback when General Ludendorff, who was one of its original sponsors, retired from the scene. Although he had openly supported the Party he retired when Hindenburg became President.

Rosenberg had married a boyhood sweetheart when he was still a student but this had come to an end. He had remarried in 1925. However, neither Bill nor I ever met his second wife or his little daughter because there was evidently some sort of understanding in the Party that the members did not bring their wives and families into politics in public, and even Bill, who knew Rosenberg very well during the thirties, was never invited to his house.

By 1930 also, the National Socialist Party had won a sufficient number of seats in the Reichstag to overthrow the Communist elements and ensure the collapse of democracy as soon as Hitler could claim the Chancellorship. This then was the background of the man whom I was going to meet and through whom I eventually established my 'Nazi connection'.

It was a glorious autumn day when I met Bill and Rosenberg off the Harwich boat train at Liverpool Street Station. In Rosenberg I saw a reasonably well-built man of about my own age, some 5 foot 11, with dark hair, hard, somewhat roundish face and a blob of a nose. He was entirely unlike the photographs I had seen of him, the somewhat emaciated figure of the early days having obviously put on weight. He had a pleasant smile and a firm handshake and was dressed in a perfectly reasonable suit which, for some reason I never understood, still managed to proclaim he had come from the continent, even though Bill had probably vetted his outfit. He seemed at that first meeting intelligent and cheerful. I don't know whether the English had a reputation amongst the Nazis for lightheartedness, but somehow Rosenberg was determined to be jolly. He cracked one or two well-prepared jokes and it was not until the following day, tutored I suspect by Bill, that he settled down into an easier relationship. It was obvious that he was anxious, perhaps a little over-anxious, to make a good impression and above all to talk to me, and anybody else whom I could introduce to him, about his beloved National Socialist movement. This delighted me as it was just what I wanted to hear. I had no intention of approaching the subject of rearmament on Rosenberg's first visit; I had decided to sit, listen and encourage him as much as possible.

Bill and Rosenberg were installed in an hotel noted for its excellence, and that evening I arranged that we should all dine together at the same quiet little restaurant where I had first taken Bill to lunch. Here Rosenberg soon lost his false jocularity.

Firstly, I wanted to make quite sure that Rosenberg was sincere in his desire to make contacts in Britain and that this was not just Bill's suggestion in order to feather his nest in Berlin. But I need not have worried, for Rosenberg started out on this theme. He complained in the first place about the attitude towards the National Socialists shown by the British press, and then he bewailed his inability to get any contact with the British Embassy in Berlin. It seemed to him that the Embassy had been told to avoid the National Socialists, which made it difficult for them to get any of their ideas across to the British, and he felt sure that these ideas would be acceptable if only we knew of them. After all, were we not the people who had at one time conquered most of the world? I took him up on the word 'conquered' and reminded him that our Empire was primarily a system for installing law and order amongst underdeveloped nations where previously corruption and local wars had decided the issues. However, he went on to point out that what the National Socialists were trying to do would be much on the lines that we had followed, in that they were themselves determined to try to establish the rule of the Aryan races in the world and copy the British in bringing law and order not only in Germany, where the Communists had been attempting to disrupt the nation, but also in wider fields as well. The only way in which they could interest the British in their objectives was to make influential contacts in

Britain who would, perhaps, themselves come to Germany, see what was going on, and tell the British public through the press.

Was Rosenberg willing to expound the Nazis' policies, if they became the power in Germany? He said he would much rather that his Führer should do this if ever I visited him.

This was a step in the right direction as far as I was concerned, but I did suggest that he at least expound to me his own work in Germany, and this started him off on the entire new ideology of which he was the high priest. He had just written a book called *The Myth of the Twentieth Century* in which he attacked the 'turn the other cheek' attitude of the Christian religion; it advocated instead a return to the ancient gods of the Nordic people in which the worship of the sun, of power and authority seemed to be basic essentials, but above all the worship of themselves, the supermen, the Aryans of this world, the true inheritors of the earth.

This was big stuff and frankly, looking at Bill, I had a job not to smile too much. Nevertheless, as I listened to this young revolutionary and realised the scope of the new ideology he was proclaiming, I became not only fascinated but also extremely alarmed. After all, it had only been fifteen years since the Russian Revolution and the Communist ideology had been imposed on the Russian peasantry; the farmers had been killed in their thousands and everybody had been brought down to one level. Were we now going to see another revolution, and were the ambitions of a future Germany going to be to impose their ideology on the Western world just as the Russians were now proclaiming that they were going to impose Communism throughout the world? Surely, I thought, after the First World War we had dispensed with the ambitions of world conquerors. Were we going to see it all starting up again?

The Germans were marvellous organisers and as I listened to Rosenberg he gave me some idea of how they were going to organise the German people. They were not, he said, going to make the same mistake as the Communists and try to eliminate all private enterprise, but they were going to impose government authority. They would do away with trade unions and people would be directed to their jobs. Only this way, he said, could they overcome the appalling conditions of unemployment and the inflation of their currency, which was ruining not only the spirit but the health of their people and leaving them wide open to Communist doctrines. The youth of the country especially was going to be organised and it would be part of Rosenberg's job to train them in the new Aryan ideology. He was already preparing plans for great colleges in which to train youth leaders.

He rambled on through a fairly long dinner while I kept him well supplied with a pleasant hock. Rosenberg was obviously enjoying himself. He seemed to have borrowed most of his ideas from earlier German writers and I felt that there was a great deal of mythology and ancient German folklore in his grand conception. However, I made up my mind to try to dig a little bit deeper into the subject of Rosenberg's new religion because by now, near the end of 1932, it looked as if the Nazis would be sweeping the board. I was beginning to understand why Bill had been so anxious for me to meet Rosenberg. I could understand too how difficult it was for Bill himself to put over in his report to our office what was really happening in Germany. Our own Government seemed very happy to sit back and take absolutely no notice—a maddening attitude which I myself was to run up against during the next few years.

The Foreign Office seemed to have told the British Embassy to be extremely careful in their dealings with the Nazis. I never knew whether this was by order of the Foreign Secretary of the day or a matter of general policy. Rosenberg never knew either why he could make no contact and it worried him. Yet Vansittart was all for making contact. It just didn't tie up and always had me baffled. I always understood that it was Vansittart's insistence in the Foreign Office that Germany was rearming which made Eden force him to resign, but I never knew for sure.

The next day Bill had arranged a lunch for Rosenberg with Dawson, the editor of *The Times*. This was important from both their points of view; for Bill it gave him the prestige necessary to make him useful to Rosenberg, and for Rosenberg it was an insight into the freedom of the press in Britain. He learned direct from Dawson that British newspapers were not in any way controlled, at least in peacetime, by the Government. Hitler had never believed this and in consequence had blamed Rosenberg for his lack of ability to control criticism of Hitler in *The Times*. Rosenberg at least seemed to understand that there was no question of muzzling *The Times*. He was probably one of the few Nazis who ever understood this, as a result of this early meeting with Dawson, but he never seemed able to convince Hitler.

Dawson also found the meeting of interest and proved an attentive listener: Rosenberg felt that he had made a good impression in this area and was positively jubilant when I met him later in the afternoon. De Ropp too was pleased, for it was to be the beginning of a much closer association between them.

That evening I invited round a few people who I thought would be discreet and yet at the same time prove impressive. Nigel Norman, who was at that time principal organiser of private flying clubs in England, came, together with a couple of MPs, namely, Alan, Lord Apsley, who had been in the Gloucester Yeomanry and at Oxford with me, and another MP who was interested in aviation matters. I warned them all to be careful of what they said, to keep the conversation in a low key and not to start Rosenberg off on a long description of National Socialism but merely to make his acquaintance for future use. It all went off quite well as Rosenberg was suitably impressed, although he seemed almost more enthusiastic about the RAF Club where we met than with the people, as he had never encountered such an institution before. It never ceases to amaze me how our London clubs and our country pubs enchant foreigners.

The following day I had made arrangements for a lunch with Oliver Locker-Lampson, who was the organiser of a right-wing group calling themselves the Blue Shirts. These should in no way be confused with Oswald Mosley's Black Shirts but, as I suspected, any coloured-shirt organisation delighted Rosenberg, and when he heard that their objective was to counter Communist propaganda he was even more enthusiastic. Here surely was a brother revolutionary; what would they not do together when the time came?

Locker-Lampson rose nobly to the occasion and met us at the Savoy. He was a bit overwhelmed by Rosenberg's exuberance but rallied valiantly. The luncheon he gave us was so good I got the distinct impression that Rosenberg's volubility came a bad second to the excellent lobster. However, here was something for Rosenberg to tell his fellow anti-Communists back in Berlin, and it reinforced his belief that I was an obvious admirer of colour-shirted chaps, a part I would have to play if I was to mix with the Nazis. Unfortunately, Rosenberg later showed his gratitude by sending Locker-Lampson a gold cigarette case from Berlin as a token of his esteem. Not wishing to be associated with the Nazi Party, Locker-Lampson refused the gift and I had the difficult and delicate task of returning it.

Entertaining one of the possible potential leaders of a foreign political party is hard work. I wished to ingratiate myself but not too strongly; I wanted him to see something of England but not to get a false impression. I hired a car, drove him round the Surrey countryside, took him to see my old school, Charterhouse, showed him a typical English pub, and generally treated him as an important visiting dignitary. It seemed to be a success. Rosenberg appeared convinced that I was the sort of contact he needed; he also accepted Bill as a valuable German agent. We now both hoped to get right to the heart of the Nazi Party.

It is recognised in Intelligence circles that after a while one develops a 'nose', whether it be the ability to spot the real thing from the fake, or a feeling that such and such a person knows more than he is telling and is likely to be useful to one. I also possessed the ability to tuck away bits of information in the back of my mind, ready to bring out when they fitted some new part of the puzzle. Now these useful attributes gave me the strong feeling that I must get to know this man Rosenberg and dig deeper into the whole German set-up, and that it was going to be important. The British Embassy and all their attachés, counsellors, secretaries and advisors might think nothing was going to come of German National Socialism but there were a few, a very few of us, who thought otherwise. Just how important it was to be and how quickly it was to develop I did not then guess. Nor could I have foreseen that a series of otherwise sane British politicians could in a few years bury their heads so securely in the sands of domestic party politics as to land England into a second world war unready and unarmed. "Considerable absence of clear thinking", as my Chief would say.

As I saw Bill and Rosenberg off in the murk of Liverpool Street Station on a foggy day, Rosenberg promised that as soon as his Party was firmly in the saddle I should be one of the first Englishmen to come to Berlin to meet and talk with Hitler and see the set-up of the National Socialist movement for myself. With one of his few smiles, he promised that the station would be nice and clean for me.

My own feelings on first meeting Rosenberg were, as a Christian, disgust; as one who had served in the First World War, alarm; but as an Intelligence officer I was excited. Bill and I formed a strange relationship with this man. He seemed genuinely to like his fellow Balt, Bill, and I had been the first person to ask him to London. Although nearly all the ideas of National Socialism were repugnant to an ordinary Englishman, there was, over the next five years, a strange fascination in seeing them put into practice with such little delay, a state of affairs which would have been impossible in a parliamentary democracy. It was like watching a nightmare come true. Part of me hoped that the British Government would be right in ignoring what was happening and pretending the Nazis would never come to power, while another part of me was fascinated to see my worst hunches realised with the speed and efficiency only a dictatorship can accomplish.

3
Berlin 1934

In February 1934 Rosenberg, true to his word, invited me to visit Berlin and see for myself what National Socialism was all about. Now at last I felt my opportunity to penetrate the Nazi Party had come. During 1933 I had not been idle and had done some homework.

Many people at the time wondered how it was that a nation which had been vanquished in the First World War and had been reduced to a rather hopeless republic could, in so short a time, have trampled on the growing seeds of Communism and turned to the glowing promise of a new resurgent Germany given by the strange little corporal whose oratory was not only compelling but, of course, told his listeners exactly what they wanted to hear. Throughout the ages youth has let off steam by fighting; wars have thrown up their heroes and then, for a time, youth licks its wounds until another generation grows restive. This, I think, is particularly true of the Germans. How well the little Austrian corporal gauged the aspirations of the youth of Germany in the early thirties. They desperately wanted a cause and a hero. It was the boredom and disillusionment of the youth of Germany which created the climate for the National Socialists to flourish in, but for the sake of those whose memories may be getting a little dim I believe it would be helpful to delve rather deeper into the history of the rise of Adolf Hitler and even go as far back as that incident in Schweidnitz when I had seen the soldiers of the German Army return from the wars determined to have their revenge. I believe it was this latent resentment which was partly responsible for firing Hitler's imagination to make Germany once more a great nation, for while he was still in the Army in Munich, just after the First World War, he joined one of the many small political groups which sprang up during that chaotic period. It was a time when Communist violence was rife and the Communists were themselves working for a red take-over in Germany. Hitler finally left the Army in 1920 and took over the leadership of the National Socialist German Workers' Party, the NSDAP. This small political group had the backing of his former Commanding Officer, Ernst Röhm. He and his friends started to recruit their own band of thugs called the SA, or the Brown Shirts, who began to give the Communists as good as they got. Later, Röhm himself was to take over command of the SA.

It was three years after he had taken over this small political outfit that Hitler felt he had enough support with the aid of his Brown Shirts, now about three thousand strong, to seize power in Munich. He also counted on the support of no lesser a person than General Erich Ludendorff, at one time Chief of Staff to Hindenburg himself, and one of the most powerful men in Germany. The coup was a fiasco, and it was during the march of the Nazis through the streets of Munich that they lost sixteen of their members, shot down by the police. Rosenberg had been in the march himself and had narrowly missed being shot, or so he told me. Even Ludendorff's support had proved ineffectual and Hitler was sent to prison, but not before his name had become known outside the borders of Germany. The outcome of the failure of this *'Putsch'* was that the German officers, including Ludendorff himself, withdrew their support from Hitler. I think it was this action which sowed the first seeds of mistrust between Hitler and the Army, a mistrust which was to emerge from time to time throughout the next twenty years, sometimes in suppressed anger, at other times in open revolt and attempts on Hitler's life.

Not very much was heard of the NSDAP again until about 1928 when, having decided to go all out for power, this time in a more constitutional way through the ballot box, Hitler barnstormed up and down the country. That he was a dynamic speaker there is no doubt, but I have never understood the psychology of the extraordinary crowd euphoria which he generated. He undoubtedly had a message which appealed to the German mentality and at the election of 1928 his Party got nearly a million votes and twelve seats in the Reichstag. Rosenberg held one of these and he used to tell me about these turbulent times.

In 1930 Germany was overwhelmed by the disastrous inflation and misery which stemmed from the economic chaos following the American slump and, according to Rosenberg, the withdrawal of credits by some of the Jewish banks. Whatever the cause, a depression which had so seriously affected America itself eventually spread right across Europe, and the German people were only too ready to listen to the promises of a better land from Hitler.

In the elections of 1930 the Party got six and a half million votes and 172 deputies in the Reichstag, while the Communists only took 77 seats. Now the Weimar Republic was tottering, but Hitler needed money badly and it was at this point that some sections of German industry and also some of the banks, believing that Hitler was the better bet, let him have it. The year 1932 was yet another of political chaos in Germany. In England we got used to reading in our papers about another general election in the Reich, but in July of that year the Nazi Party, as they were now becoming known, won nearly 230 seats in the Reichstag with fourteen million votes. Hitler now saw the Chancellorship within his grasp and too late the Army realised that their traditional role as the power behind the throne was in danger.

Before the First World War the German Army, or rather the great General Staff, were more than just soldiers, they were an integral part of the social and political life of the country. To be an officer in the Army was the ambition of most young men; all doors were open to them. Their officer corps was conducted with very strict social rules of marriage and behaviour; they were the élite of the land, and the generals had as much say in the affairs of state as the civil Government. The defeat of the Army in the First World War was a bitter blow to their old prestige; nevertheless the old spirit remained, and gradually, in the late 1920s, the generals began to prepare for a revival of their old power. There was a secret agreement with the Communists under which German officers and NCOs and airmen were trained in Russia contrary to the Versailles Treaty. It was not surprising therefore that with Field Marshal Hindenburg as their President the Army was opposed to Hitler as Chancellor. But the Nazis took little notice, and with their large majority they proceeded to dissolve the Reichstag; by 1933 the Army could no longer hold out against Hitler. He became Chancellor in January of that year. The new ruler of Germany had got there constitutionally and very largely through his own amazing oratory; then to cap it all the Reichstag was burned down. It did not take Hitler long to outlaw the Communists altogether, murder their leaders, and with complete power in his hands embark on a totalitarian régime. Now his only rival was the Army, and by 1934 the generals didn't like the way things were going at all. In their view if anybody was going to rule Germany as dictator, then it should be one of them, and to add to their fears many Communists were now transferring to the winning side and joining the Brown Shirts.

There was much speculation in England as to whether or not the Nazis had burned the Reichstag down in order to give themselves the opportunity to take complete control of government. They certainly seized the opportunity. Rosenberg's version, however, which he gave to me, was that they did not plan the fire and that it was in fact a Dutch Communist who started it. Nevertheless, it was too good an opportunity to miss. Rosenberg himself had been a member of the Reichstag before the fire. I felt he took great delight in showing me the black-

ened ruin. Apparently he had once been ejected from his seat
personally by the then Jewish Chief of Police. He never forgot
or forgave. At the time Bill thought it was possible that the
Russians, who took the Nazi movement much more seriously
than we did, got one of their sympathisers to do the burning
in the hope that the reaction of the German people would
be to turn on this Nazi menace and destroy it. Whatever the
truth, the fire worked for Hitler. The Nazis took over 'total'
administration of the country, and the Communists were
brought to trial and found guilty of burning the Reichstag.

There was no excuse for the mild surprise of His Majesty's
Government. The writing was on all the walls, illuminated by
the swastika. It was not in diplomatic language and it was apparently deemed prudent not to read it.

Hitler had written his book *Mein Kampf* while he had been
in prison as a result of his early revolutionary activities in Munich. It was a militant book setting out the beliefs and principles
of the Nazi dictatorship, and with its promises of military conquest it was designed to get the support of the Army, a very
necessary ally in any political coup. I was therefore able to
brief myself about the aims of the new movement before going
to see the author.

After he had been in power for a few years Hitler is reputed
to have written a 'revised version' which, if it ever existed,
was never published. Rosenberg referred to it once; I never
saw it but I can guess at some of the changes he made to
the original. It would, I feel sure, have emphasised more
strongly his hatred of the Communists and probably pinpointed
the necessity for recasting the military priorities with a greater
bias to the East than the West. It would also have emphasised
the proper place of the Army in a National Socialist state.

In preparation for my trip to Berlin in 1934 to see Bill de
Ropp, I had suggested that he let Rosenberg know that my
job included writing reports to the Foreign Office on the information sent back to the Air Ministry by the air attachés
and any senior officers who had been travelling abroad. This
would prove that I had definite access to the top people in

the Foreign Office, and would also be in line with my duties as liaison officer on the Air Staff.

I don't know whether it was as a result of this information but Rosenberg, now at the peak of his power in Germany, evidently persuaded Hitler that it would be a good thing if I came to Berlin as the Air Attaché. Not only would I be a point of contact with the British Embassy but he no doubt thought that my conversation would be less diplomatically reserved than that of the other Embassy staff. The outcome of this request is also interesting as it shows the jealousies which existed within the Nazi Party. Hitler himself must have instructed Goering to ask for me as Air Attaché, a line of action which Goering probably resented. However, according to Rosenberg's diaries published after the war, the German Air Ministry made a very 'blunt demand' to our Embassy in Berlin for me to take up the appointment. It was of course refused by London and Archie Boyle rang me up to let me know what had happened, but Rosenberg took the refusal to be on account of the way in which the request had been made and decided to get his own back on Goering. He somehow found out that Goering had made private arrangements with a member of one of the foreign embassies in London to keep him supplied with information about the Royal Air Force. This form of espionage against Britain was completely opposite to Rosenberg's brief from Hitler and evidently he got pretty mad, because he informed de Ropp of what Goering had done. It didn't take our security services very long to winkle out the person concerned. Thus, in fact, Rosenberg had done us a very good turn and I asked Bill to thank him quietly. I give here the extract from Rosenberg's diaries, which were published after the war.* (This one is from a report from Rosenberg to Hitler, dated 18 December 1933.)

I was told that the German Air Ministry had made demands in such a blunt manner from the British Air Attaché in Berlin, that he felt obliged by his office to report these demands to London. Thus a plan

* The excerpts from Rosenberg's diaries that appear in this book were first published in *Das Politische Tagebuch, Alfred Rosenberg*, Musterschmidt-Verlag, 1956.

of Germanophile circles has been baffled: the plan was to ask for our special friend from the English Air Staff, Major Winterbotham, as an Air Attaché. Nevertheless, without the knowledge of the German Embassy in London, they succeeded in getting a confidential person into the Embassy of another mission, who was able now to give all the information. I let Baron de Ropp know, who passed it on directly to the Air Staff in London.

It is amusing to see how Rosenberg got his own back by informing us through de Ropp that the German Air Ministry had planted an agent in another Embassy. It enabled us to plug the leak and, as no doubt Rosenberg calculated, sowed some seeds of mistrust regarding the sincerity of a supposedly friendly nation.

A matter which I wanted to resolve with Bill before I visited Berlin was my rusty German. I had learned a certain amount in the prison camp but if I was going to join in any conversations, especially with high-ranking Nazis, my mediocre understanding of rapid conversation might slow up important interviews and jettison their significance. I therefore suggested to Bill that I should come over knowing no German at all and on every occasion use him as my interpreter. In fact, I would know enough to be quite sure that he was giving me a correct version; moreover, it would make it seem less likely that I was a spy, for any agent sent to Germany would be bound to speak the language perfectly. Instead I would concentrate on the person who was talking, to try to judge their character, their veracity and their confidence in what they were saying, while Bill would take in every word and translate the main theme to me as we went along, and later back at his flat we could write out almost verbatim what had been said. Bill had also asked me, before I went to Berlin, to make up my mind on the subject of giving the Nazi salute. From his own experience he advised me never to do so unless we happened to be in a crowd where I might get roughed up if I didn't comply. Far better, he advised, to behave in a completely British manner, for the Nazis respected this attitude which was most unlike that of some of their other hangers-on who would give the 'Heil Hitler' salute whenever possible.

My activities between 1933 and 1938 were closely connected with the rise of Nazi Germany and the rebirth of her mighty armed forces. Although I may sometimes tell it in a light vein, consistent with the character I assumed for my association with the younger people to match their new-found exuberance, the underlying theme was always in deadly earnest. When the invitation from Rosenberg finally came, I once again discussed the whole matter of this strange adventure with my Chief, who in turn discussed it with Sir Robert Vansittart at the Foreign Office. Both these men throughout the thirties believed in the German menace and permission was therefore granted for me to undertake this somewhat unusual mission. I had explained to my Chief precisely how I proposed to conduct myself, and he in turn had reiterated the warning that if I put a foot wrong both the Air Ministry and the Foreign Office would disown me. I was advised, however, as a member of the Air Staff on leave in Germany, to make my number with the British Embassy. This would be a natural step and provided I did not put my foot in it too seriously they would probably help me. In the event it was a member of the British Embassy who put both feet in it during my first visit to Berlin.

There was in February 1934 no scheduled air service between London and Berlin, so I had no option but to use the sea and rail route. This was, however, the only time I had to use the slower method; afterwards I had a free seat on one of the Lufthansa JU 52s, those aircraft that looked as if they were made of corrugated iron; sturdy horses which could and did become war-horses overnight during the Spanish Civil War.

On the train from Holland to Berlin I had been given a compartment to myself and no doubt the guard had been instructed to see I was not disturbed. My mind went back to the last time I had been in a German train, to an unpleasant night in the bitter cold of January in 1919 when, as prisoners of war, we were huddled in our train at Frankfurt-on-Oder on our way home. Someone who didn't like us had connected up the coaches to the gas used for lighting the carriages and in the dark turned on the taps. There was no light but one of our number broke a window in time and just saved our lives.

Now in 1934 an elderly Jewish woman came into my compartment. She talked a little while to try to find out what I
was doing as an evident VIP on my way to Berlin. She shrewdly
summed up my inquisitive nature and with, I imagine, considerable risk to herself warned me of the evil intentions of Hitler
and his men. I gathered she was the wife of a publisher in
Berlin and had been to England to make arrangements for
her family to leave Germany without delay. She was lucky
and wise.

I became sadder and more puzzled as I went back and forth
to Germany in the following years as to why the Jewish people
in Germany with all their intelligence and ingenuity appeared
incapable of foreseeing what was in store for them. There
seemed to be a paralysis of mind and a feeling that it could
never really happen. Perhaps they hoped for some strong foreign intervention, or some reaction from the Army. Perhaps
they and others overseas underestimated the number of adher-
ents to this new Nazi movement. I, as a newcomer to the scene,
was soon to see for myself the swing to National Socialism as
the Brown Shirts came out like ants from a nest—tall ones,
short ones, fat ones, thin ones, bearded ones, middle-aged and
young ones. Perhaps it was because this odd collection in uniform was so unlike the popular conception of an army that
its political strength was at first underestimated.

As the overnight train from Holland drew into Berlin I was
totally unprepared for my reception. Evidently all the other
passengers had been warned to remain in their compartments
and while the train moved slowly along an almost empty platform my coach came to a halt with all the precision of a VIP
train at Victoria Station in London, right opposite a real red
carpet. Two black-uniformed SS men came to my compartment, carefully took my hand luggage and helped me down
on to the platform. It was the first and only time I have had
a red carpet for my exclusive use. As I stepped down from
the train, a little bewildered, I saw Rosenberg in an immaculate
new Nazi uniform some ten yards away looking rather self-
conscious and evidently wondering what my reaction would
be. Behind him, arranged in a semi-circle, were a number of
tall, black-uniformed, white-gloved SS guards with their hands

on the two pistols in their belts. On either side of the red
carpet were the railway officials. To them and to Rosenberg
and bodyguard the whole thing was deadly serious, but I noticed that Bill was doing his best to keep his face straight and
it was as much as I could do to look duly impressed. There
was a 'Heil Hitler' salute from Rosenberg and then a welcoming
handshake, a few words of greeting, a click of many heels and
then the Nazi Movement Drill Number One went into immediate action.

This was the first time that I had encountered it, but I was
to do so many times in those early days of the 'revolution'.
You turned sharply in the direction of your car or your hotel,
or wherever you were making for, and you did a half-walk,
half-run for it. You jumped into your car, the engine of which
was already running, and clutched whatever you could to pre-
vent yourself making an undignified backwards somersault as
the car jumped away. I just caught sight of the bodyguard
jumping into the second black Mercedes, when we were off,
speeding along the broad street in two minutes flat from the
time I stepped from the train! My first thought was: "What a
waste of my one and only red carpet." I had hardly had time
to savour the situation before we were gone.

Travelling in a top Nazi's Mercedes motorcade had its points.
You got there quickly. The white buses, together with other
traffic, pulled in dutifully to the kerb, the brown-shirted supporters on the pavement, and indeed many of the ordinary
civilians, halted, faced the road and shot out their arms in a
'Heil Hitler' salute, and the beswastika-ed policemen swelled
with new-found importance as they waved you across the inter-
sections. The reason, of course, for the rapid movement drill
was that ever since the Munich marchers had been shot up
by the police, the top boys of the movement had taken care
not to be easily picked off. So the drill was established. At
least it made you pick up your feet when running up hotel
steps. I even saw Goering doing it surprising lightly for a man
of his size. These tactics, like the interminable 'Heil Hitler'
salutes, eased off gradually as the régime became stabilized,
but the habit died hard even up to 1936.

In 1934 the 'Heil Hitler' was one of the most extraordinary manifestations I have ever seen. It was, of course, based on the old Roman greeting, but out in the streets of Berlin to see the whole population greeting each other with this unlikely gesture made them look rather like a chorus in a Hollywood musical, and from the looks on their faces many of the more elderly citizens treated it as such. But it served its purpose: it bolstered the pride of those who bulged a bit in their uniforms, was good visible propaganda, a sign of togetherness, and it gave reassurance to those who needed it. To me both the Nazi salute and the clenched fists of the Communists showed the ability of power-hungry demagogues to impose their wills on the mixed-up mentality of the masses. The uniform of the 'Brown Shirts', who were thick on the ground, not only ensured obedience to the 'Heil Hitler' salute, but also kept me dipping my hand into my pocket to satisfy a never-ending assault by the more menacing brown-shirted males shaking swastika-decorated collecting tins under my nose. I took to filling my pockets up with small change before venturing out on the street as, I imagine, did everyone else. The Nazi exchequer was evidently a bit bare in early 1934, despite what they were collecting from the unfortunate Jewish shopkeepers.

I stayed with Bill and his wife in their flat on the Kurfürstendamm. They put me up on a divan in the sitting room. The flat was fairly high and looked out over the back, which was lucky because the Kurfürstendamm was the most fashionable street in Berlin, a bit noisy both by day and by night. How different were the square roofs in Berlin from the old crazy ones of Paris.

Bill's flat was both central and comfortable, and after the experience of my VIP arrival I was glad to be able to rest a while and try to take in the whole bizarre situation. The only satisfaction was that as revolutions and dictatorships go I was in at the top. I wanted Bill to brief me thoroughly on my visit; whom should I meet? Where should I be going? What must be avoided in conversation? Bill told me of the profound effect the knowledge that I had direct access to the head of the Foreign Office had had on Rosenberg and I decided to cement this point on my return to London. Nevertheless it was going to be vitally necessary to do one's homework thoroughly, and quite apart from my Nazi connection, I wanted time to see something of Berlin while I was there. Although Bill's wife, 'Jimmy', was an excellent cook, we usually only had breakfast in the flat and then took our other meals when and where we could. The weather helped; it was fine and crisp and dry. Rosenberg had told Bill I should meet his Führer the following morning.

Several people have told of their first meeting with Hitler. To some, no doubt, it was just an amusing experience and made a good story. But after all I had heard from Bill and had seen for myself in the streets, I now felt that this man was going to affect deeply not just me but all that I cared for. I felt that I must try to get to know him, how he thought and what gave him such an extraordinary hold over the Germans. I had learned from Bill something of Hitler's early history, of the strange driving force in this rather obscure corporal, of his extraordinary oratory and of his unquestioned leadership of the Party. I was to see for myself over the next few years how this little man seemed to be able to change his whole personality at will, especially when he got in front of a microphone, and the effect his oratory had on the vast masses that he addressed. It seemed to invest him with a Messiah-like quality for the youth of Germany who flocked to his banner. In his speeches the utter ruthlessness and the sheer efficiency of the Nazi plans seemed to unleash a latent spirit of bloody aggression. It spelled Danger with a capital 'D'.

This was the man I was now going to meet. Could I, I wondered, make a success of our meeting? If so, it would mean that I would be able to come back to Germany from time to time and keep my eyes and ears open, so long as I kept my mouth shut.

Unlike some of Hitler's other visitors I was fortunate in that I had no official or parliamentary status to maintain. I had no false dignity to preserve or oversized self-importance to be wounded. In the event I had considerable difficulty to keep a straight face, not from any nervousness, but merely from the apparent absurdity of the whole set-up. It was just too fantastic and somehow unreal.

It was the morning after my VIP arrival. I had travelled light, just a grey flannel suit over a pale blue shirt, and packing only the proverbial toothbrush; Bill put on a new bow-tie, a blue one to match his eyes and "accentuate the Aryan", as he put it. We got a taxi direct to Rosenberg's office. Berlin was looking quite gay, in the proper sense of the word. The cafés in the Tiergarten were getting set for their morning customers, and the profusion of the bright red Nazi banners gave more than a touch of colour. By contrast Rosenberg's office was rather drab; there was no posse of black-uniformed guards outside, no vast rooms with polished floors, but it was nevertheless workmanlike and he obviously employed a fairly large staff. He was still the editor of *Völkischer Beobachter,* the Party newspaper, as well as doing all the other odd jobs I have already explained. However, we didn't wait long here and this time, instead of the great black Mercedes motorcade, we just went in Rosenberg's own car to the old Chancellory where the new Chancellor, Hitler, presided. True to form we got out of the car, cantered up the steps through the great archway, straight into the looking-glass land of Alice.

Here in the great hall with its vast floor of large black and white marble squares were neatly arranged a score of tall figures in faultless black uniforms, their white-gloved hands resting on the guns on either side of their belts. Each was standing stiffly to attention on his allotted white marble square. The illusion was startling and as a black pawn stepped smartly forward to inspect the party I fully expected the black queen to come skipping down the great stairway. The black pawns also extended up the stairs, one on either side every three steps, and as I followed up behind Rosenberg I had the new experience of being visually, if not physically, frisked. I got used to it after a while.

By the time I reached the head of the stairs I had a feeling, so tense were these gentlemen in black, that had I not been 6 foot tall with blue eyes and fair hair, I should have been bundled off to some distant dungeon; not even the prisoner-of-war camps of the First World War had the same sinister aura of such ruthlessly efficient security. Of course the whole set-up was also meant to impress visitors, especially German ones. We had to wait a little while in the red plush anteroom. Rosenberg was silent and, I think, a little nervous as to what sort of impression I should make on his Führer and also because we were being kept waiting.

Apparently the gentleman responsible for producing the plans for the whole new network of motorways across Germany was in with Hitler at the time. As he emerged from the guarded double doors his grin was the measure of his success. He had got the go-ahead and was almost incoherent with excitement that his plans had got his beloved Führer's blessing. Dr Fritz Todt was efficient. Within four years I was to see some of the results of this interview in the shape of completed motorways, each straight as a die for five miles, then a slight turn in order, as Todt put it, to keep the drivers awake.

Suddenly the great double doors swung open and I entered between two tall black-uniformed guards. The fact that I topped them by an inch or so no doubt gave me some confidence as I watched them once more visually but expertly 'frisking' me. Bill and Rosenberg followed somewhere behind but I was too intent to notice how far away they were.

It was a long, well-proportioned room; through the tall windows with their fan-shaped tops and blue brocade curtains the pale February sun cast a glow on some twenty yards of polished, honey-coloured wood floor. Tapestries hung on the opposite wall and right at the other end behind a large desk, I think it was of French design, sat the man I had come to see, forelock, mini-moustache and all. He was dressed in a simple brown shirt and black tie with nothing on his uniform to proclaim him the new prophet. Perhaps the whole set-up was intended to symbolise the simple austerity of the new Chancellor and for a fleeting moment I could envisage the vast room filled with opulent Victoriana, while Bismarck, that other dictator, his Prussian blue uniform fully bemedalled, greeted his ambassadorial visitors with pomp and circumstance. Now as I approached him, Hitler's amazing likeness to the comic cartoons one had seen of him made this simple scene even more fantastic and I remember feeling how absurd it was that I should be doing the long walk alone.

By the time I arrived at the other end I had to remind myself of Lord Chesterfield's advice to his son on the impropriety of public laughter and I managed to confine my sense of the ridiculous to a wide smile. Maybe Hitler wasn't used to people smiling broadly at him, but it seemed to work for he stood up, out shot a hand, not in the now familiar salute but to be shaken in the ordinary civilised way. He, too, was smiling and the first thing that struck me were his extraordinary protruding eyes. Many people have commented on their apparent hypnotic quality but to me they looked as if they stood out a bit too far from their sockets. Nevertheless, they were friendly. His complexion was far too pink and white because, I suppose, he was spending much of his time indoors in his office during the daylight hours. Later as he got out and about more he developed a tan. Neither of us spoke for a moment. I think I was too busy studying this man; he was certainly weighing me up. But then Rosenberg and Bill, who had remained slightly behind me, came up smiling and everybody started talking at once. It struck me again how nervous Rosenberg had been as to whether I should hit it off with his master, but I was to learn later that Hitler liked tall people and as I looked unmistakably Aryan and somewhat informal in grey flannels, I was evidently a success. It was immediately obvious to me that Hitler and Rosenberg were close friends although any cordiality was absent, whether by design or due to Rosenberg's evident reserve I could not judge. It was also evident that Bill was now right 'in the party' too. Formality was discarded and hair was definitely down; Hitler suggested that we move to the small round table some yards away. It was the only other piece of furniture in the room barring a few straight-backed chairs.

We sat down and Hitler started to talk. He seemed to have a soft spot for airmen; I suppose, having been an infantry corporal in the First World War, there was still some glamour attached to the *Fliegers,* those men who were, as he now described it, the last to experience the individual chivalry of war. Anyway, we talked about the First World War, and the fact that I had been shot down by Goering's bunch but was in no way bitter about my eighteen months as a prisoner of war pleased him. His voice was quietly normal, the harshness of Berlinese gently rounded by his Austrian origin. We talked as people who had shared a war talk in clubs and bars the world over. He was a perfectly ordinary, relaxed human being chatting about old times and being skillfully led on by Bill to talk of the present. "Yes", he too "believed in the strange comradeship of the air", and he hoped I would find the lads of his new Air Force as good as the old ones. I must meet some of them. Oh yes, the German Air Force was coming along nicely. The young men could now abandon their gliding exercises and get down to real flying training. He went on to tell me the latest figures of aircraft, which no doubt included those both in the flying training schools and in the squadrons. He was well briefed and proud of it and obviously enjoyed talking quite freely. I wondered why.

The Germans, under that ill-conceived document, the Versailles Treaty, were not allowed an Air Force, and up to the time that the Nazis took over they had to confine their open activities to gliding. As I had already found out, their General Staff had managed to train a few pilots secretly in Russia, but the completely open defiance of the Treaty was a new line and a pointer to what was to come. I wondered what His Majesty's Government would do about it and why Hitler had been so frank with me. The answers to these two questions, which appear from time to time in these pages, show clearly the policy of the Nazis towards Britain and of the British Government towards its own people during those fateful years 1935–39. For the moment I hadn't worked the thing out, but I was glad to get confirmation from the number one Nazi of information I was receiving from friends in other countries about his intentions to start building a new German Air Force and also some idea of his future plans. It would, I hoped, help me to convince the Air Staff that they should take the matter seriously. Convincing the British Government was something else.

But now Hitler turned towards me, looked me straight in the eye and informed me that his Luftwaffe would have some five hundred operational aircraft by the end of 1934 or early 1935, and I felt that I was going to find out why I had been asked to come to Berlin and what it was he wanted me to tell people in London when I got back. Speaking quietly and with natural conviction, he told me how he and his colleagues believed that unless something drastic was done some time in the not too distant future, some dozens of small black, white and brown states and countries would be pursuing an entirely nationalistic policy, and everybody would be trying to order the world to their own particular advantage with the resultant chaos and risk of wars. "This," he said, "would be intolerable."

I realised that multiplicity of authority was anathema to a dictator and was therefore not surprised when Hitler continued: "There should be only three major powers in the world, the British Empire [as it then was], the Americas and the German Empire of the future." He stressed the fact that the British Empire had brought a wonderful civilisation to a large part of the world and he had no wish to disrupt it at all. As regards the future German Empire, this would include the rest of Europe and the lands to the East. In this way no single power would be able to dominate the others. England, with one or two exceptions, would continue her role in Africa and India, while Germany would take care of Russia and together we could decide the policy for China and the Far East. All questions of economic, material and cultural improvement could be much more easily and quickly resolved between three great powers. It was to be as simple as that.

I didn't think he had brought me all the way to Berlin just to hear his ideas on the future world; his next sentence was the really important one and was the basis of the theme which was to be pumped at me every time I went to Germany. "All we ask," Hitler said, "is that Britain should be content to look after her Empire and not interfere with Germany's plans of expansion." In other words, that we should keep our noses out of it. He went on to say that it would do us no good to get involved in another war, that the Germans themselves would look after the 'crushing of Communism' in Russia; they didn't ask for our help at all. I remarked that this seemed a very big undertaking and perhaps he would be good enough to tell me more about it some other time. He smiled a bit wryly.

It was then that I made a remark which seemed to trigger him off. I said that I gathered that he heartily disliked the Communists. Up to this point the four of us had been sitting quietly round the table listening and talking, but a sudden change now came over this little man. Colour suffused his face; the back of his neck, I could see, went red; his eyes started to bulge even further; he stood up and, as if he was an entirely different personality, he started to yell in his high-pitched staccato voice, which now echoed round the walls of the great room; he addressed not three people but an imaginary three thousand. He ranted and raved against the Communists; it was the most extraordinary exhibition. So this was the sort of thing which was supposed to mesmerise the German people. To me it was absurd and rather funny, though this was before Charlie Chaplin had made such a shattering comedy of the whole business. I couldn't help smiling just as Hitler was delivering one of those twenty-words-all-joined-together pieces of Teutonic vituperation. He looked down at me and in a flash he stopped, his bulging eyes returned to their sockets, his face became a normal colour and once again he became calm. He caught my eye and actually smiled himself as he sat down. "That," he said, "is what I think of the Communists." I felt that somewhere carefully tucked away this little Austrian had got a sense of humour. Would that he had retained it. He must have been the only one in the outfit with the ability to laugh at himself.

I had already arranged with Bill that he should concentrate on each item about which Hitler would talk while I myself would try to assess the sincerity of the man, whether he was telling the truth or not, what the motives were behind what he had to say and generally what made him tick so loud and surely.

His strange outburst had, I think, startled Bill as much as it had myself, though Rosenberg, who must have been used to this sort of thing, just smiled blandly at his Führer's astonishing performance. Nevertheless, I think that all that he had told us before his strange outburst on Communism had been genuinely what he believed in and hoped for. His language about the Communists was too vivid to be anything else but a reflection of his absolute obsession with the destruction of a force which otherwise threatened to destroy him.

I was still puzzled at the extraordinary change in Hitler's personality when he stood up and harangued us about Russia. I remember telling Bill when we got back to his flat and were discussing the interview that I felt the little man possessed some sort of dual personality that he could switch on at will. Was he a schizophrenic?

Our interview, supposed to be twenty minutes, had lasted nearly an hour. Now Hitler got up and as we stood talking he told me that Anthony Eden and Sir John Simon, the then Foreign Secretary, had been over to see him. He had hoped for some support from Britain but as a result of getting none, he had left them in no doubt as to his decision to rebuild his Air Force and had told them that as far as he was concerned, the Versailles Treaty was dead. He added that he had been unable to get on with Eden and Simon and that he didn't like the too-obvious crease in Anthony Eden's trousers or his pointed shoes. To Hitler, "They merely added to the pomposity of the immaculate diplomat." It was then that, as if throwing in an afterthought, Hitler told us that he had informed Eden that he did not propose to build an Air Force larger than the combined air fleets of Britain and France for the defence of the Reich. Whether this assurance had given any comfort to the politicians I do not know, but from an airman's point of view it was a piece of nonsense. The French Air Force at the time consisted of a large number of ropey old kites which were unfit to take the air against any modern aircraft, while Britain's light bombers and fighters, primarily used to keep order in the Middle East, were also out of date. This declaration of intent was an obvious bit of Nazi duplicity. Numbers of aircraft may mean something to a politician, but from my experience it was quality that counted, and if Germany was now to start from scratch, in a very short time one hundred completely modern aircraft would be worth three hundred of our out-of-date ones. This then was the crux of what I should have to find out. What would their Air Force consist of? What would be the proportion of bombers to fighters? The different types they would build would show the sort of war they intended to wage. It looked as if the Air Staff would have a job to educate the politicians on this subject since the build-up of a vast modern German Air Force would pose an unacceptable threat to ourselves and the French unless we did something about it quickly.

Hitler then went on to make another interesting remark. He said that, "in view of the lack of any support from Britain", he had now had to sell half his birthright to the Army, this despite the fact that he was in effect the constitutional ruler of Germany. I did not immediately grasp the significance of what he said, but later it seemed to indicate that the Army was now to have a large say in the sequence of events. We took our leave, and as I shook hands with Hitler he remarked that I must come back and see everything which the Nazi Party was doing for the German nation. This, of course, was the invitation I had badly wanted and which I hoped would enable me to come and find out more as the years went by. But how many years had I got?

As we came downstairs there was again the sharp click of the heels of the black pawns on the white squares in the hall; Rosenberg was now swelling with importance since the interview had gone beyond his wildest dreams and there was little doubt that he himself had been deeply impressed by the candid conversation of his Führer. He dropped us off at Bill's flat where we hurriedly sat down with pencil and paper to remember every word that had been spoken and to add our own impressions on this extraordinary interview.

The first thing that had struck both of us was the utter frankness of Hitler's long talk. He had talked rapidly, never searching for words, and was obviously saying what he meant to say and what he meant to do as he outlined to us the programme for his Thousand-Year Reich. Here was the dictator of Germany telling me what he was going to do in the not far distant future. I kept asking myself why? He had evidently been told by Rosenberg of my connection at the Foreign Office and my job in the Air Staff. Did he think, I wondered, that the British Air Staff was as powerful politically as Goering was in Germany? Bill agreed that there might be something in this, but he pointed out that this was only one reason. The main reason must be that the Nazi plans necessitated a neutral Britain. A neutral America was much more within their grasp, with its large German population and an already established Nazi *Bund* in America; but they needed to turn British opinion in their favour and they had not had the same opportunity as in America. It was Rosenberg's belief that he might be able to build up such a connection in Britain by using people like myself. "That", said Bill, "is why you have been invited to Germany", and the more I could find ways of convincing the Germans that I was passing on their message, the closer Bill would be able to get to Hitler.

However, to get down to the interview in more detail, a main point which had struck us was the complete denunciation by Hitler of the Versailles Treaty; it was, he said, "dead". Then he had included the rest of Europe, barring Britain, in his sphere of influence, as he called it, which we judged to mean that he would probably try to have a quick war against France and that the invasion of Russia was already being planned. The next major point was his intention to build up a vast Air Force, and if all the old British and French aircraft were included in the deal, it looked as if Hitler had in mind a first-line Air Force of some two thousand modern aircraft. If this was to be an offensive weapon, as it obviously must be if he carried out his plans, then presumably at least a third would have to be bombers of one sort or another. Both Bill and I thought that they had probably already decided on such a figure and had then put across the idea of a defensive Air Force equal to the British and French together in order to sweeten the pill for the politicians.

It was extraordinary how quiet the visit of Eden and Simon to Hitler had been kept in England, but it fitted in with the

British attitude of ignoring the Nazis which was to be only too evident during the next few years. Hitler's point about selling half his birthright to the Army was interesting but we couldn't make out exactly what had happened. No doubt he had been having trouble with the Army. What had he given them in exchange for their loyalty? Had he agreed to a war of revenge against France before they would tackle Russia? Had he given them the right to decide the timing for the offensives? Obviously he must have given them the right to build the Army on their own lines. But that he didn't altogether trust them was evident from the way he was building up his own private army, the SS black-uniformed guards. Were they also a warning to the Army to keep in step or else?

Between us Bill and I drew up a report on the whole interview. Looking back, never before or since have I spent such an important hour. Here was our horoscope being laid bare before us by the man who was able to make it all come true, if he could keep a neutral Britain . . . if . . . if. Here too was the key to my job, the *quid pro quo* for the way in which I could get them to let me see how they were rearming in the air. My Chief had told me before I left London that Sir Robert Vansittart had his own Nazi connections. Later he and his wife went to Germany to visit Hitler. Other British politicians also had German contacts. A member of Parliament, I knew, was a friend of Baron Werner von Fritsch, the Chief of Staff of the German Army. Von Fritsch was against war, for he believed that a powerful Germany with a very powerful Army could achieve all she needed without fighting in Europe. No doubt he kept my parliamentary friend informed about the build-up of the German Army. But as far as I knew, I was the only Englishman with high-powered Nazi contacts who could verify what I was told. Neither Hitler nor Rosenberg knew this but I was in a much stronger position than anyone else, for I had now been given the bare framework of the new Luftwaffe and as soon as I returned to London I would be able to start work. Through my Intelligence contacts in Holland, Warsaw and Prague I hoped to be able to get details of flying schools, training programmes, aerodromes and aeroplane factories, for data about these would show how quickly their Air Force was building up.

I was to meet Hitler several times and see him on innumerable occasions before the end of 1938, but only once again did I see a faint glimmer of humour on his face. It was when he was the undisputed Führer of the rearmed Reich. Ribbentrop, who disliked both Rosenberg and de Ropp—the dislike was mutual—was back in Berlin as Foreign Secretary after his disastrous term as Ambassador in London. The old informality was 'out' and Bill and I had been invited by Ribbentrop to a very official reception. It was just before the 1938 Nuremberg Rally. Berlin was full of foreign princes and politicians who, even if they did not intend to jump on the Nazi band wagon, were preparing to play it both ways. The American diplomats and press were being given the soft treatment and there were the usual adoring hangers-on, including starry-eyed Unity Mitford. Now all the guests were formed into a great circle ready to receive the imperial handshake.

I must say Hitler did it very well. There was none of the strutting, heel-clicking, bending-in-the-middle nonsense so beloved by the military. He came quietly along, a rather cheesy smile beneath the absurd little moustache. Bill and I were standing together, and as he shook hands the fixed smile broadened into a grin and for a fleeting moment the sparkle of fun came into his eyes as he murmured: "See how far I've come now."

Ribbentrop had not heard what was said, nor had he been meant to; this he obviously considered an insult. He glared at both of us. We had no doubt been invited to see Ribbentrop in all his glory to remind us that he was now in charge of foreign affairs to the discredit of Rosenberg. Bill began to chuckle and I thought it was time to make ourselves scarce. So full of intrigue was the whole atmosphere at that time, you could not help seeing and hearing little groups of people looking you over and discussing who you could be.

Rosenberg had not been present; in fact, Ribbentrop had allowed nobody to spoil his triumphant presentation of his master and himself. But we found Rosenberg having a beer at his favourite café not far from Bill's flat. He even raised a smile when we told him about the "twitching wine waiter", as Ribbentrop was dispassionately called—he had a twitch of the face which was uncontrollable and had been a wine merchant in civil life. Jealousy between Ribbentrop and Rosenberg had been evident as far back as 1933 when Ribbentrop first started to push his way into Rosenberg's amateurish efforts at foreign relations. It was but one more example of the in-fighting and duplication of responsibilities which were so marked in high Nazi circles.

During the time in which I observed Hitler, I saw how each year took toll of his health and sapped his joy in life: his features grew sallow and puffy and his expression increasingly troubled. I always found it impossible to assess his character, for his two personalities, a quiet, interesting talker and a staccato-voiced rabble-rousing tub-thumper, could seemingly be switched on and off at will. Not even his small sense of humour could account for his absurd quiff and moustache. How did it come about that this little Austrian corporal could achieve the authority and stature to lead a nation and finally the madness to alter the history of the world?

Rosenberg told me that when the movement started in Munich, Hitler was the 'talker' of this strange band of rebels. At first they had little clear idea of what they wanted to do except change the existing order. One got the impression that if there had been a Hyde Park Corner in Germany, Hitler would have been there on his soap-box. One can visualise the rather undecisive authorities of the day saying, "That little troublemaker again." I gathered that it was only after this band of rebels had worked for some months on the ideas of Hess and Rosenberg that the basis of the new ideology began to emerge. "The Blueprint for Change", as Rosenberg called it, began to get around. Even the rebels were surprised at the number of supporters. As I have said, the climate was ripe; Germany wanted a new hero.

In the early days, according to Rosenberg, Hitler had leaned to some extent on his close friends, Hess and Rosenberg. His ability to hold an audience was one of his principal assets to this small group. Rosenberg described it as hypnotic; it may have been, though it did not hypnotise me. But I have seen a crowd of many thousands whipped up to a state bordering on mass hysteria by this extraordinary man.

Adversity is always supposed to bring out the best in genius. There is little doubt that Hitler's imprisonment by the German Government gave this small band of political rebels time to sort out their ideas and clarify them in book form—Hitler's *Mein Kampf* and Rosenberg's *The Myth of the Twentieth Century.*

There was some speculation abroad at first as to whether Hitler was just a puppet of his Party. Personally, I don't think this was ever the case. Certainly he was probably their spokesman at the beginning owing to his gift of the gab, but there is no doubt in my own mind that he became their leader as of right.

Gradually he found stronger men to support him, more used to action than dreaming up new philosophies; with them he grew in power and authority, if not in wisdom. Alas, the stronger men who had jumped on the band wagon began to pursue their own pet hates and theories. Streicher and Himmler got busy with the Jews; Hess got cracking on the trade unions, which he dissolved, though maybe this saved post-war Germany from some of the crippling effects of antiquated prejudices in this field. Rosenberg was given a free hand to go ahead with his plans for an Aryan Pagan Europe; Goering built himself an Air Force; von Schirach trained the youth of Germany to be fit to fight and to be fertile; but Hitler was certainly in full command.

Alas, with power came not so much corruption as megalomania. How very few mortals can handle power. Generations of authority coupled with responsibility often bring justice and compassion, but this was hardly likely to happen to Hitler and his henchmen. Eventually the gods had their way. To anyone listening to Hitler during those final days in his bunker in Berlin ordering his long-since-disintegrated armies to new positions of defence on the Eastern front, his madness and destruction appeared complete; and yet if one sets aside for a moment all the more bestial activities of the Nazis, Hitler was the sole outspoken challenger at that time of the Communists. Somehow he foresaw the troublemaking, the intrigue, the subversion, the mistrust and the misery that Communism would bring throughout the world, while apparently unaware that he himself was setting out on an equally disastrous course.

4
Nazi Leaders

Rosenberg was evidently determined that I should meet Hess
as well as Hitler. All three had been very close friends over
the years and I myself was anxious to meet the very top Nazis,
not because they would tell me much themselves, but to be
seen talking to them gave me the green light for conversation
with other less important yet more informative members of
the Party. I fancy that Rosenberg was also quite pleased to
show off his English contact. I was anxious, too, to give these
people the impression that I was on a serious mission, and I
didn't want to get mixed up with any of the British hangers-
on whom Bill told me were beginning to filter into Berlin.
There would then be too many awkward questions to be answered, and the possibility of inquisitive people making enquiries back in London. Bill had already explained to Rosenberg
that I was a reasonably important person, not to be compared
with the whimsical Unity Mitford or any of the glamour-seeking
youths.

There was one top Nazi whom I was not anxious to meet,
however, and that was Goering. Still, it wasn't likely to happen
as he and Rosenberg had scarcely spoken since the débâcle

over the London Air Attaché incident. Rosenberg wished I
had got the job and Goering felt robbed of his secret source
of English information, so it would be best to maintain a low
profile in that direction. Nor did I wish to meet anyone I had
known in the old days if I could possibly avoid so doing. At
the reception described in the last chapter, I'd nearly run into
Prince Paul of Yugoslavia, who had been a good friend of mine
at Oxford. In those days he had been a cheerful young man
who played equally well on the polo field or in the boudoir.
As a younger brother to the King he could look forward to a
life of leisure, sport and pleasure. But when his brother was
killed, he had to take on the responsibilities of the regency,
and he then became subject to the pressures of the Nazis. Being
a good friend of England he tried to back the future of his
country both ways. Just as Bill and I were taking our places
in the circle of band-wagon hoppers for the reception I spotted
Paul across the room. I quickly moved behind a large Bulgarian
General and luckily was not recognised; at least I don't think
I was. Open recognition would have been highly embarrassing.
It was also fortunate for me that there were no members of
the British Embassy present.

Now that I was going to meet Hess, I didn't quite know
how I should handle him. With Hitler it had been compara-
tively simple to give him a lead and let him talk, and I had
sensed that he was pleased with the way our interview had
gone; but Hess might be more difficult. Bill had warned me
that he was a well-educated and highly intelligent man who,
as deputy to Hitler, always backed him up in a rather quiet,
self-effacing way. Hess was, when required to be, a forceful
speaker, but I too was to gain the impression that he was more
concerned with the well-being of his own country than the
conquest of others. I never saw him mixing with, or talking
to, any generals. I was therefore anxious that Hess should do
the talking rather than Bill, and I still felt that my apparent
inability to speak German was, at that moment, one of my
best insurances against being thought to be a British agent
or a professional Intelligence officer. I therefore decided to
choose a number of questions which a Britisher, supposedly

interested in Nazi methods, would ask and let Hess give me the answers. I knew it was vital at this first meeting to behave like an enthusiastic, albeit inquisitive, individual, to keep any questions on a broad basis and avoid any side questions dealing with the Luftwaffe. Details would come later, and I didn't at the moment want Hess discussing me with Goering. With some trepidation, which I hope I didn't show, Bill and I, this time without Rosenberg, were conducted to Hess's large basement office in the Chancellory by two SS guards. In some way the whole atmosphere of this basement was not nearly so friendly as that of the sun-lit Chancellory upstairs. One felt that people came here to be told what they were or were not to do, and the long rows of hard wooden benches could hardly have made them feel comfortable.

Hess, unlike his master, was ever content to be the shadow. He avoided the limelight and I think few people knew him intimately. His brown shirt also lacked any form of decoration but, like the rest of his clothes, was extremely well cut. His flared breeches could not have been improved upon by Savile Row; he was tall and slim, with a good leg for a boot; indeed, his boots were the envy of the Party. Not only were they real leather but they fitted him well, and the shine on the black leather would have done justice to a cavalry batman. I could not make up my mind at first whether he was shy of foreigners, not quite sure of himself, or just plain eccentric. He was certainly fastidious.

He had a very important job, that of Party organiser, and did it extremely efficiently. He and Rosenberg appeared to get on well and in the 1920s there had been, as Rosenberg told me, an inner circle—Hess, Rosenberg and Hitler, the originators of the ideas on which the Thousand-Year Reich was to be built. In due course Hess was nominated by Hitler as his deputy, while Rosenberg faded more into the background.

Hess sat behind a large plain wooden desk and as I came up to say "How-d'you-do" he struck a pose. He remained sitting, arms folded across his plain brown shirt, one beautifully shod leg thrust out beneath his desk, his thick black eyebrows drawn down to a scowl. Was it because he did not want me

to see his eyes that he stayed thus until I came right up to
him, or was it that I was an unknown Englishman and ought
therefore to be properly impressed?

There was something odd about the Nazi uniform which I
had never been able to pin down. Now, suddenly, I got it. In
England in the twenties or thirties we were quite unused to
anyone wearing just a soft shirt buttoned up to the neck and
down to the wrists and accompanied by a black tie; worn with
tie and jacket or open-necked, sleeves rolled up, yes. Perhaps
it was my preoccupation with this uniform rather than his scowl
which got him to his feet, or maybe it was my failure to click
my heels and give a 'Heil Hitler' salute or look in the least
impressed with his pose. Anyway, he got up, actually smiled,
and shook hands. I suppose they had to try on the big stuff
in case someone expected it.

We began talking and the first thing I asked him was whether
it was really necessary to dress up all their Party members in
uniform. Hess did not try to bluff at all. He had obviously made
a careful study of his fellow-countrymen and their psychology.
He pointed out that "in a bloodless revolution", such as they
had carried out, it was necessary to have some visible solidarity.
Also the Germans liked a uniform; it gave them a sense of
"belonging to a group". He went on to explain that the Germans, perhaps because they had not been colonisers like the
British, were, as a people, not so self-reliant; a uniform gave
them a sense of togetherness.

I could of course have added that it gave some of them a
good handle with which to do a bit of bullying and persuade
others to join the movement; it also enabled them to strut.
And a uniform was useful when it came to collecting money
from the public. However, I forebore to comment; instead, I
asked him to explain his dislike of trade unions. This he put
down entirely to the Communist elements which had pene-
trated the movement in the 1920s. Now in the 1930s everybody
had to work for the Reich and the terrible hunger, inflation
and unemployment had made it necessary for him to be able
to direct labour to the proper factories and to ensure that the
factory workers neither demanded nor got a larger slice of

the cake than any other section of the community. I enquired whether the unions had accepted this. Hess smiled a little wryly and said that the people as a whole were fully behind the Nazi policy. I thought of the wooden benches behind me and of the hordes of SA Brown Shirts I had seen in the streets. Hess was right.

As Hess didn't volunteer any other information and began to rustle a pile of papers on his desk, I thought it was about time we terminated the interview. I nodded to Bill and he agreed. I had learned little that I didn't already know, but at least I'd made my number with this man and I found that on several future occasions he was much more friendly than he had been at our first meeting. I also found a certain depth of character and level of intelligence which was often missing in other Nazi leaders. There was a latent sensitivity in place of the ruthless efficiency of the Goerings and the Himmlers. His poise increased but always seemed tinged with diffidence: I doubt if he could ever have succeeded Hitler had things turned out differently. He was a good pilot and used to fly his own aeroplane about Germany; his flight to Scotland in the early part of the war was quite in character. Despite his lack of self-confidence he had ample courage. He must have realised that for all the endeavours of the Nazis to keep Britain out of World War II, she looked like fighting on, and that this would be a disaster for Germany. His flight was a last attempt to persuade the British to make peace. He faced only a 50-50 chance of survival and a 99-to-1 chance against success, yet he took the risk of this desperate gamble.

It was normal courtesy to call at the British Embassy. Anyway, the Air Attaché was an old colleague of mine in the Air Ministry who knew what my real job was and had, in all probability, been warned by Archie Boyle that I might turn up in Berlin. I wanted to advise him of just what I was doing in case of accidents and of the fact that I was travelling on leave but with the permission of my head office and the Air Ministry. I also thought it fair to give him a little information about my conversation with Hitler. He was excited at my news. It was quite obvious that the Embassy was pretty well in the dark as to what was going on, and he explained to me that the only information they appeared to get was the chat they had with other attachés at diplomatic cocktail parties. I presumed the same thing went for the Ambassador as well. Anyway, I told him the figures that Hitler had given me for his Air Force to date and that I should be going south personally with Rosenberg for a few days but would give him full details, if he wished, before I left Germany. I did not, however, wish him to incorporate this in a report to London because I myself would be making the report when I got back.

Rosenberg had informed us that he had a long-standing engagement to go down to Weimar for a Party get-together with the local area supporters. It was to be a three-day trip and he had a number of speeches to make. He thought that it might interest Bill and me to go with him. Not only was this a grand opportunity to see how the Nazi revolution was shaping up in the provinces, but it would also be a chance to talk quietly with Rosenberg alone, both on our way down and while we were there. It was arranged that we should set off in his car the following morning. I also think that Rosenberg was anxious to show his friends down at Weimar that he had an English 'friend' and, presumably, indicate that he was getting British support for the Party. However, I didn't approach this subject with him, thinking it better just to see what happened and play it by ear.

We set off next morning in Rosenberg's black Mercedes, without any bodyguards. The road to Weimar passed through some very attractive country but I was surprised to find how much of it was poor sandy soil, not rich agricultural land. However, it did grow good timber. Lunch of jugged hare and a bottle of hock in an old timbered inn at Wittenberg was served by a rather flustered landlord in traditional red waistcoat and white apron.

Rosenberg seemed more relaxed than in Berlin—the strain of life in the capital must have been very heavy in those early 1930s. He had already lost some of the freshness I had seen in London. He had become dull and preoccupied much of the time; his complexion was sallow and it was difficult to get him to smile. He was taking himself far too seriously and only became lively when carried away by his own enthusiasm for some project such as the sterilisation of the unfit. I was not so shocked at this policy as some people might have been, as I had often discussed the matter with a doctor friend who believed that voluntary sterilisation should be agreed to by parents who had produced more than one child with an incurable disease. However, compulsory sterilisation was another matter.

After lunch we strolled around the ancient town, and as we looked up at the old church, Rosenberg let me have a glimpse of one of the reasons for his atheism. "You know," he said, "if we in Germany hadn't spent thirty years fighting amongst ourselves as to how we were supposed to say our prayers, you British wouldn't have had the chance to annex half the world."

We passed through the green valley of the Elbe, lazy in the wintry sun, into the hills and forests. How wonderfully kept the forests were, every tree straight, in apparently endless rows of weedless precision. Forestry is a great art in Germany; the State Foresters are men of considerable importance in the community; they even have a uniform. Complimenting Rosenberg on the tidy rows and the apparent absence of ill-formed trees I inadvertently set him off again on one of his pet subjects. Not only were all the trees to be perfect in Germany; the people, too, were to be subject to a strict genetic code.

Even then, only a short time after they had come to power, the Nazis had started on a policy of sterilisation; anyone who had produced a Mongoloid or abnormal child would have to submit to sterilisation. After all, was not the Third Reich going to last for a thousand years, and we all knew that long before that there wouldn't be enough food to go round. "If the great Nordic races, and that includes the English," said Rosenberg, "are to survive, there will be no place for weaklings or fools. Is it not better to have a healthy, happy people by using such sciences as we have? Already, too, we are selecting true Nordic women for our breeding experiments."

Diabolical logic perhaps but I had no doubt whatever that it would be carried out, given the time; I had visions of blue-eyed, blond-haired studs! I have always believed that the difference between man and the other mammals was that the possession of a soul, or whatever you may wish to call it, gave man the right of freedom of choice, whether good or evil; but the Nordics were now to be treated like a vast herd of pedigreed cattle in order that they might survive. This was 1934 and it was happening already. In fact when Rosenberg turned to look straight at me, I wondered whether he was about to offer me a holiday at one of his Aryan farms. The idea of siring a squad of little Nazis was too much. I changed the subject. What he had told me was an alarming forecast, and when I remembered what I had seen in Berlin—the wrecked Jewish shops and what the Jewish woman had told me in the train—a massive Jewish exodus from Germany seemed inevitable. At that time I could not foresee the slaughter of the Jews which was to take place, but I was left in no doubt about the strength of anti-Semitic feeling.

I asked Rosenberg what they proposed to do about the elderly. Would they follow the example of the Bushmen of South Africa and abandon old parents so that lions and hyenas could finish them off? Rosenberg thought this was a tremendous joke but declined to be drawn into an answer. Would all this, I wondered, apply to us in Britain if we failed to survive another war against Germany? However, I didn't wish to pursue the subject at that time because, as I said, I was afraid I might be offered this free holiday, provided that I passed the test of being a pure Aryan.

Rosenberg had an excellent driver. Herr Schmidt was a tall, Scottish-looking man of about thirty-five, with reddish hair and neat ginger moustache. A racing driver before coming to Rosenberg, he was a thoroughly cheerful type who ate with us and smoked endless cigarettes, but despite his good driving we did not arrive in Weimar until after dark.

It was raining, but nothing dampened the ardour of the local Nazis, and as the car slid up to the hotel steps the Heil-ing became a roar. Here was a hero of the revolution come to

Weimar, the home of the dead republic, and Weimar was going to show him what it could do. The Party members, many as yet wearing only a scarlet swastika armband on their ordinary clothes, were full of enthusiasm. The floodlights caught the brilliant colour of the beswastika-ed banners which, though hanging limply in the drizzle, formed a solid canopy of crimson above the streets. It all seemed unreal and yet it was somehow exciting. I remember thinking that a band would have rounded off the scene, but looking back on my time in Germany, it seems to me that bands were specifically reserved for the military. I never remember hearing a band playing at the head of the SA or the SS, for instance. Maybe it was thought that such music might detract from the personalities of the leaders. Certainly, as regards noise, Hitler's voice was quite enough.

There was no galloping into the hotel here. As I stood on the steps with Rosenberg my hand was shaken a hundred times by Party members of every conceivable shape and age, some crying with emotion. It is just no good suggesting that National Socialism was thrust upon the German people; the great majority swallowed it hook, line and sinker.

We were already a little late but we managed to get a cold snack before going along the street to an enormous hall where the rally was about to take place. I had no idea what to expect but the tension and excitement were building up and I found it contagious. After all, this was my very first revolution as seen from the top at close quarters, and quite irrespective of their sinister programmes explained to me by Hitler, Hess and Rosenberg, the wild enthusiasm of these masses of ordinary citizens celebrating the so-far bloodless revolution and overthrow of an established form of democratic government was so alien to my own way of life as to make me feel I was taking part in the revival of some great medieval pageant. As we entered the vast building—Rosenberg, Bill, myself and two of the local bigwigs—the heads of about five thousand people turned and watched in silence as we made our way up the long aisle to the front row of the hard wooden chairs. In front of us was a large amphitheatre, with tier upon tier of choristers, several hundred strong. They were men of all ages, from the young and eager to the old, moustached, bespectacled Teuton so familiar in our fairy stories. On a small platform between the choir and the body of the hall was a lectern from which Rosenberg would make his speech, but somehow the eagle's wings had been straightened out to resemble the Nazi badge.

The whole audience and choir had risen as we came in. Now, as we reached our seats, like a well-drilled battalion of sergeant majors, they gave the 'Heil Hitler' salute; arms shot out beside and behind us, one just missing the top of my head from the row behind. Three times they shouted *'Heil!'* as one man, down went the arms in silence and everyone sat. Despite the hardness of the chairs, there was still an odd feeling of unreality about it all. I did not wish to embarrass Rosenberg so I compromised by giving the Nazi salute this time; I feared I might have been lynched otherwise. I never recognised what the choir was singing as the din was terrific, but I caught odd bits of Wagner at his loudest.

I think the story that Hitler had a collapsible spring support up his sleeve must really have been correct. I have seldom seen a more pathetic sight than when at the end of a rousing Nordic speech by Rosenberg, the whole choir sang *'Deutschland über Alles'*, right arms outstretched, starting just higher than the shoulder, but, alas, gradually sinking as the verses wore on. A sharp tap of the conductor's baton and up they all came again, only to subside slowly once more. Have you ever tried to sing with your arm outstretched level with your eyes for about ten minutes on end?

When the rally broke up, Rosenberg, who had to talk to a great many people, handed me over to a bunch of young Nazis—cheery lads, proud of their ability to speak some English—and we all went off to the traditional beer-cellar. About a hundred young men were there, in infectious high spirits. We talked no politics, the beer was good and flowing freely when suddenly a waiter, with his eyes standing out on stalks, told me an Englishman wanted me on the telephone from Berlin.

I have found by experience that members of British Embassies abroad, by virtue of their complete diplomatic immunity, attain a shattering sense of personal security. This state of affairs in no way extends to an ordinary United Kingdom citizen visiting countries with somewhat nervous governments. Perhaps that is why the Air Attaché on the other end of the phone, which I knew would be tapped, had no idea of the cold wave which went down my spine.

My friend in Berlin was as cheerful as ever but I am afraid I was icy. Apparently he had mentioned the first of my talks to the Ambassador, Sir Phipps, as the Germans called Sir Eric Phipps, who had demanded to see me at once. I presumed either that my friend had failed to tell him I was out of town for a few days, or that information direct from Hitler was so rare that he wanted to take the credit before I could return to London; hence the summons back to Berlin. I pointed out that I was not subject to the whims of the Ambassador but would get back as soon as I reasonably could.

I expect I must have looked a shade too thoughtful as I returned to my drinking friends but I had to make up my mind quickly. I was wondering just how the Air Attaché had managed to get through to me in that beer-cellar. He must have been in contact with Rosenberg's office, probably for the first time, and then through all the various connections down to Weimar until he finally found me in the beer-cellar. This would, of course, have given the Germans plenty of time to put on their recording machinery, and I had little doubt that everything that the Air Attaché and I had said would be faithfully recorded. However, I felt that I had been sufficiently curt on the telephone to show my displeasure and had cut short any indication of the real reason for my summons to Berlin. Neither I nor Bill had any idea at that time how much use the Nazis thought we might be to them as unofficial links with London. Politically they could not take too long a shot.

I spotted Rosenberg coming over to my table. Bill was wisely staying away. I took a quick decision and explained to Rosenberg that, as he knew, my Government was a little edgy about individuals, especially ones with some important official connections like myself, coming to Germany at that time and I feared I was in trouble with my political superiors. How soon could he get me back to Berlin? I could not tell whether he swallowed my excuse, though my companions certainly did. More beer all round and not to worry! Anyway, I bluffed it out until midnight, then went across to the hotel with Bill.

Rosenberg, Bill and I each had a large room to ourselves next door to each other on the main floor; soon after I had gone to bed, dead tired but fitfully awake, I heard a sound that took me back fifteen years—the measured tread of a sentry going up and down the passage outside my room. So this was it. Well, maybe I had better make the best of a comfortable bed while I could. Eventually I must have gone to sleep. I awoke to a knock on my door. It was Rosenberg; he was already dressed and as he came over and sat by my bed he managed a fleeting smile.

I do not know how long he had been preparing his little speech, but as he sat there and quietly sympathised with me in my troubles with authority, he told me of the glories of defiance of the old order, of the splendid thing I was doing in standing up for the new. He personally would ask Hitler to see that no harm came to me for coming over to see him and his colleagues. He had rearranged his whole programme so that we could return to Berlin a day sooner. Ah well! Now for breakfast. The sentry had been stationed for his own protection, he said.

As Rosenberg was busy with the Party organisers I spent most of that day looking around the old town of Weimar, which is, to the Germans, much the same as Stratford-on-Avon is to the English, with the added advantage of Goethe being accepted as the genuine author of his own works. His old house had been turned into a delightful museum. On the walls were original Dürer drawings and the rooms were full of exquisite period furniture. Why worry about the Corps Diplomatique? I only hoped that my friend would not be overcome by more diplomatic madness and ring me up again from Berlin.

Next day we set out early. We had several stops to make, the first at a Hitler Youth school for boys of about ten to fourteen years old. Owing to the change of time-table we arrived a day earlier than expected, and apparently no one had warned the headmaster. Disaster! Everyone running in all directions. Rosenberg, quite unconcerned, led us into a large classroom, bare but for an enormous table in the middle, its foot-high sides holding what seemed to be a large sand pit. I thought at first that this was rather elementary stuff for the slightly older children. However, the teacher took one look at me and went red; the kids, close-cropped, round-headed and brown-shirted, grinned at his discomfiture. One half of the school was learning how to attack a well-defended position held by the other side. The sand pit was in fact a battlefield made up into hills, trenches and strongpoints, and the battle was obviously at a critical stage.

There was only one thing for it; I volunteered to join in the game and brought a little aerial warfare into play for the attackers. They were a cheery bunch of kids, poor little devils. Normality was now re-established and amidst a chorus of 'Heil Hitlers' we went on our way. But not very far. Our next call was to be at the House of Nietzsche, and this, I now suspect, was one of the main reasons for Rosenberg's visit to Weimar.

I have already mentioned Nietzsche in connection with the Nazi philosophy, but I never expected to see what was going on here. It was a large house, steeply gabled, standing well back behind dark pine woods. Inside were massive carved pine-wood staircases, doors and cornices; the whole place had an overbearing rather than a pretentious air. A frail little old lady dressed in black, her pale blue eyes managing a proud smile, welcomed us in. She was introduced to me as Frau Nietzsche, the author's widow, though I learned later she was not entitled to the status. Beyond the hall in a vast, sombre, book-lined library were about twenty young men and women working like ferrets on the author's works. I concluded they were compiling some sort of anthology.

Rosenberg had first introduced himself to me as a Doctor of Philosophy; no mention as to when he had got his degree, but he had at some time read Nietzsche and added him to his hotchpotch of philosophies. In fact, I could not help but agree with Bill that in view of some of Rosenberg's rather disjointed utterances, he must have borrowed most of his 'philosophy' and strung it together to make up his Nazi religion of the great Aryan racial cult. Later, I gathered from a remark of Rosenberg's that there was some basic Nazi philosophical work in preparation here. I wonder if the study was ever finished. Anyway, over a cup of coffee served from delicate Sèvres china off an incongruously massive carved pinewood table the little old lady talked to us of the days when Mussolini studied at her husband's knee and Hitler himself had been a frequent visitor. Did Nietzsche hold the secrets of successful dictatorship?

I think it was probably the visit to Nietzsche House which started me searching a little deeper into the origins of this Aryan and anti-Semitic theory. But it was not until after the war that I was able to discover a little more about medieval German history. I learned that at one time there was a belief that the Aryans were one of the surviving tribes of Atlantis, supposed to have been supermen, credited with supernatural powers. As the legend grew, the theory of the master race grew with it. Purity of Aryan blood was of vital necessity to preserve these powers, even in the early Middle Ages, if, as they believed, the master race was to remain unimpaired. In those days the Turks and the Moslem Arabs to the East were considered the greatest danger to European Christendom, and Arab (Semitic) contamination had to be avoided at all costs. It is not difficult to see how this dividing line came to be applied to the Jewish population as well.

Throughout the Middle Ages there seems to have been the usual conflict between the 'goodies and baddies' in Europe, both seeking to gain or regain power through the help of the supernatural; the goodies by following their difficult path to the Holy Grail, the baddies by the black arts and association with the Devil. There were the Christians and the anti-Christians, the latter, of course, adding to their appeal the fact that Christ himself was a Jew. Somewhere buried in the Middle Ages were the origins of the crooked cross, the swastika, the symbol of the anti-Christ.

Down through the centuries the belief in the supernatural

powers of the Aryan master race persisted amongst the German tribes. Then in the twentieth century Kaiser William II fostered the ancient cult for his own ends. Urged on by the English author Houston Stewart Chamberlain, who wrote that Christ was not a Jew but an Aryan after all, the Kaiser proclaimed the Christian master race, which gave him the excuse to try to prove the ancient Aryan myth when he opened the flood-gates of the First World War.

It was not until well after the Second World War that the very early days of Hitler were examined in detail, and it became evident that he and his friends in Vienna had been closely concerned with the black arts and the quest for supernatural powers. By some it is believed that his initiation into the black rituals were responsible for his apparent sex perversion, which caused at least two of his women friends to commit suicide in despair. It is also suggested that Hitler believed in reincarnation and that both he and Himmler postured as the reincarnated spirits of certain unsavoury but powerful demagogues of the Middle Ages. It seems possible that this accounts for Hitler's passion for the Wagnerian version of the story of Parsifal.

All this was unknown to me in the 1930s. Did these odd ideas have something to do with the extraordinary way in which Hitler seemed to be able to change his personality at will, I wonder? How far was he, too, obsessed with the Aryan myth? Another story suggests that he believed deeply in the power which came with the possession of the ancient spearhead, supposedly that which pierced Christ's side at the Crucifixion. This spearhead had long rested in the museum at Vienna where, it is said, Hitler spent many hours gazing at it. Immediately after occupying Austria he is said to have seized the relic. It was later found by American troops in Nuremberg and returned to Vienna.

Whatever the answer may be, there is no doubt that Hitler developed an extraordinary authority within himself. Would that he had used it for good instead of evil.

We made very good time on the misty road back to Berlin

and I was thankful to get to Bill's flat and to the telephone. I still had to be careful. I managed to cool my friend's ardour at the Embassy and agreed to come round and see Sir Eric the next morning. Bill's wife had cooked a splendid meal so we spent that evening having a post mortem on our eventful trip.

5

Blitzkrieg

I was in no mood to be gentle when I went to the Embassy to ask the Air Attaché what the hell all the hurry was about. He explained that they never seemed able to get any information direct from the Nazis so my visit to Hitler had excited the Ambassador. All they ever obtained was gossip from other diplomats. I made a mental note not to disclose all I knew to the Ambassador but to stick to the question of the number of aircraft that Hitler had told me about as I knew he had divulged something of this to Eden and Simon.

The Ambassador himself was calm as I explained that I'd been Rosenberg's personal guest, so had not been able to return sooner. I forebore to mention the mess his Air Attaché had made with his telephone call, skated over most of Hitler's points so that he could not get enough of a story to put it on paper, and concentrated on the detail of the five hundred aircraft. The last thing I wanted was a garbled version of my meeting which could be misinterpreted by those in London who did not care for the contents. I did my best to explain to the Ambassador that as no existing type of aircraft had been classified in this number, it looked as if they had included training aircraft in their figures and also possibly their fleet of JU 52 transporters, which had been built in such a way that they could be easily converted to military use. Even this detail was too much for him. Then and there he drafted a telegram to London addressing it to "King and Cabinet Only." It began: "Squadron Leader Winterbotham states . . ."

My worst fears were being realised. Information in the wrong hands, out of context, without the backing of further facts, can be a two-edged weapon in politics and can all too often boomerang back on those who obtained it in the first place. I would have preferred to deliver all that Hitler had told me to my own boss first, check it against other known facts, and have time to evaluate it fully before letting it reach the politicians, but ambassadors are ambassadors and one simply cannot argue with them. I knew that his telegram would set the cat among the pigeons somewhere in Whitehall and make it doubly difficult for me and my own department later on, so I played everything down as much as I could.

I was most careful not to mention that I was going straight on to a special luncheon party given by Rosenberg for fear the Ambassador should send for me again later and catechise me further. Instead, I took quiet and careful leave of him and walked back to the flat. I was not certain who would be at the luncheon party but rather suspected it would be Goering; not an altogether pleasing prospect but possibly fruitful.

Horsher's was a magnificent restaurant with dark oak panelling and a resplendently Victorian red plush decor. In the great dining room stood a vast table with a snow-white cloth bearing up manfully beneath the heavy array of silver and shining glass. There was something, too, very splendid about the traditional German waiters in their black knee breeches, white stockings, red waistcoats and white aprons. The room, the decor and the waiters all conjured up an aura of sumptuous luxury. When I expressed my admiration to Rosenberg I was not surprised to learn that Cabinet ministers, generals and even royalty had been wont to feed and entertain their guests here in the past; now the Nazi hierarchy used it for the same purpose.

I was just wondering how the great swashbuckler himself

would react to our meeting when two men in their late thirties were ushered in. After a quiet exchange of greetings and messages with Rosenberg, the latter turned to me and said that it was a great disappointment to him that Goering was not able to come today but that he had sent two senior members of his staff to represent him. They were then introduced to me as Commodore Ralph Wenninger and Commodore Albert Kesselring. Both names struck a chord in my memory.

The German Army published every year a list of the officers filling the various appointments at their War Office. Our own service ministries did the same, and I had for some time studied the German book carefully because I had the idea that if a secret Air Staff was to be formed it would probably be based on a military pattern. By the end of 1933 I noticed that each department of the German War Office had an attached officer added to its staff. One of the names rang a bell from my First World War flying days, and after careful examination, it became evident that these attached officers were mostly ex-First World War Air Force pilots. There was little doubt in my own mind that this was an Air Staff in training, camouflaged in the German War Office until the day when Goering's new Air Ministry would be inaugurated and the new German Air Force launched on the world. At that time, of course, it was still officially non-existent. Wenninger and Kesselring were two of these officers. Wenninger was tall, fair and slim; he had pleasant manners, a wide smile and, from what I could judge, not too many brains. His short black coat and striped trousers fitted him and he looked comfortable. Kesselring was of a very different calibre. Square, swarthy, with thick black eyebrows and a taciturn, almost rude, manner, he made it quite obvious that his ill-fitting coat and trousers, which had very broad black and grey stripes and were evidently borrowed for the occasion, irked him. He was not happy out of uniform.

Next to arrive was Herr Loerzer. He was introduced to me as the man who ran all gliding and civil flying club operations for young pilots. Finally, the main guest appeared, General Walther von Reichenau. So Hitler had given the green light for me to meet some of his top Air Force and Army people.

After what Hitler had told me about the tension between the
Army and the Nazis, I was a little surprised to see the enthusiasm with which Rosenberg introduced the General. He must
obviously be a Hitler fan. Later I was to learn that General
Reichenau had carried out the subtle stroke of making every
Army officer and conscript take a personal oath of allegiance
to Hitler. Some of the older generals didn't care for this as it
undoubtedly weakened the authority of the General Staff *vis-à-*
vis the Nazi Party, but it had put Reichenau right at the top
of the Nazi favourites.

He was tall and good-looking, a monocled, slightly balding,
duel-scarred, square-headed General of the High Command.
There was only a small crease in his immaculate green uniform
where he habitually bent at the waist on introduction. The
seating arrangement at the table was that Rosenberg sat at
the head; on his right was the General; I came next to him
with Loerzer on my right, and opposite were the two air commodores on Rosenberg's left and then Bill de Ropp. From my
point of view this was a good arrangement because the General
would be turning towards me when he spoke and Bill would
be able to hear everything across the table. As we sat down
I glanced across at Bill and saw that his eyebrows were twitching a little bit, which suggested to me that he thought this
was going to be a very important meeting. I don't think Bill
ever knew about this habit of his when excited but it always
alerted me.

Rosenberg opened the proceedings by reminding me that
I had asked the Führer if I could learn more about the Russian
plans, so the Führer had then asked General Reichenau, who
was the principal planner for the operation against Russia, to
talk to me. Rosenberg's little speech was rather stiff as he tried
to indicate the importance of the occasion, but it certainly
made me sit up and take notice. Here was the top man going
to tell me all about it; it seemed incredible. I thanked both
Rosenberg and the General for sparing me their valuable time,
which seemed to break the rather formal atmosphere, and the
General started talking in almost perfect English. Anthony
Eden had suggested a ban on the building of all bomber aircraft,

he said; would I give my views? I thought that this was rather a fast one to bowl at me without any previous warning. However, it was not difficult to answer. I replied that undoubtedly the thought behind this suggestion by the politicians was an endeavour to stop the bombing of innocent civilians as a method of warfare, but unfortunately politicians are not technicians and the officers opposite me would undoubtedly be aware that if such a ban occurred it would put a stop to the building of civilian transport aircraft as well. To give only one example, the Germans' own JU 52 transport aircraft were so designed that the baggage compartments, which were at the centre of gravity, could become bomb bays overnight. I noticed that Kesselring's eyes were downcast and he was blushing slightly, but after all they'd asked for it. I then explained that although Eden's suggestion was desirable, I didn't see how it could possibly be carried out. The General had listened intently and he now nodded across to his two junior officers and said, "There, you have your answer. Now I want to tell the Major about my plans for the Communists."

The red-waistcoated waiters were busy with the soup and the drinks, but I for one hardly noticed what I was eating, nor I think did the General. I could hardly believe what he was telling me. Here, in 1934, in Berlin, I was being given the whole plan for the invasion of the USSR. Not only that, but the description as it went along left me in no doubt that the German Army had decided on an entirely new strategy of warfare. The conversation was so startling it has remained in my mind ever since; I will put it down in a form as close as possible to its original wording.

The General started off by telling me that in the coming invasion of Russia speed and surprise were to be the two great elements of victory. He explained that the invasion of a great country like Russia would have to be done between the melting of the snows in the spring and the arrival of the frosts in the autumn, and to accomplish this they would invade Russia by driving vast tank spearheads into Russia at a speed of approximately two hundred miles a day. As the conversation was entirely in English, Rosenberg didn't understand it and he sat stolidly at the head of the table. Wenninger, who did understand English, was looking more and more astonished, while Bill, whom I saw fleetingly out of the corner of my eye, was almost jumping up and down in his seat with his mouth half open. There was no question of this being a rehearsed bit of propaganda. I didn't want the General to stop here, so I began to look a bit puzzled and I suggested to him that such warfare might be difficult in Russia with its great areas of marsh and woodland. At this point he put his left hand on the tablecloth with the three middle fingers stretched fairly wide and pushed them across towards the silver candle sticks in the middle, saying that fortunately Russia was a very large place so the German tank spearheads would be able to go round the marshes and woodlands and not through them. However, the speed at which they advanced would be such that the Russians would either be cut off and surrounded or would have to make such a precipitate flight that they would be unable to take any equipment with them. I then said, "Well, how about your own equipment at that speed?" "Ah," said Reichenau, "this is just what we are planning; you see the vast tank spearheads will be rather like an arrow, broad at the base and fanning out. As they proceed, motorised infantry will come up and take over the flanks that they have opened up. Artillery, too, will help them defend these flanks while we push further and further ahead." "But do you not expect any sort of opposition?" I asked. "Surely the Russians have plenty of guns if nothing else?" Reichenau now looked across at the other two opposite him and said, "These gentlemen are going to take care of that; we are going to destroy all opposition from the air." I thought for a moment that this might be the basis of their question about bombers, but if they were going to destroy all opposition in the way of artillery and tanks from the air it would have to be fairly low-level stuff and large bombers are not the best and most manoeuvrable aeroplanes for this sort of thing. 'Perhaps,' I thought, 'they are going to build some sort of fighter bomber that is fast and easy to handle at low altitudes and can carry just one large bomb.'

Myriads of questions raced through my mind but I didn't

wish to halt his excited flow of information. I carefully picked on points to query which I hoped would stimulate rather than anger him.

Surely at a speed of two hundred miles a day it would be extremely difficult to keep the troops both fed and supplied, I enquired? The Russians, I knew, had a policy of always living off the land; could the Germans do likewise? Reichenau hedged, and to my horror nearly stopped, uncertain as to whether to answer. Then he picked up again. The motorised infantry, as they rushed forward, would not have to carry food or ammunition themselves; it would all be brought up separately, much of it by air, and of course the infantry defending these broad flanks would also have tanks and massed artillery. There would be special aerodrome units.

Here was yet another vital point. I wondered how they were going to keep their fighter bombers, or whatever was to be their aerial artillery, close enough up behind the tank spearheads? Were they going to build aerodromes as they went along? "Yes," replied the General, "if necessary, but one must remember that there are only going to be a certain number of these spearheads." He didn't say three, but I'd gathered that from the way he'd described it with his hand. And these would be going up the main routes of East-West communication so that there would be several aerodromes already available to them together with roads and railways. Fodder, too, for horse-drawn transport would be brought up, probably by air, as there might be some areas they wished to defend which would be hard to reach except by horse and the infantry. Nevertheless, the masses of motorised infantry being poured in behind the tank spearheads would ensure that they held the ground they had taken. And, according to his calculations, or rather mine, if they went forward at their scheduled two hundred miles a day, it wouldn't take them very long to reach their obvious objectives of Leningrad, Moscow and the Black Sea shore.

General Reichenau seemed absolutely certain that they would be able to pull all this off and he now turned to both de Ropp and myself and said, "You see, the whole war in Russia will be over in the early summer. No doubt it will take a good while to mop up the vast Russian forces which have been split up and surrounded." Again I didn't want him to stop, so I looked a little sceptical and said, "Well, we've always been taught in our history books that the Russian winter has proved the greatest Russian General." Reichenau put his fist quietly on the table and with great emphasis said, "There will be no Russian winter, it will be a German winter, all our troops will be comfortably and warmly housed in the great cities and towns of the Communists."

It was an astounding climax to a most extraordinary preview of what the great German Reich proposed to do in the not far distant future. As he paused for breath, the General's face was red, glistening with enthusiasm, glowing with euphoria for the heady excitements of an aggressive war. There were so many questions I longed to ask but knew I dare not. It was the first time I had ever heard the word *'Blitzkrieg'* but some idea of its potential was slowly forming in my mind. I had a blurred vision of an entirely new technique of warfare: the aeroplane allied to the tank moving forward together in a lightning advance to encircle the enemy forces and strike home into the heart of his country. Would they send similar tank spearheads into Europe, and if so would they come over the Maginot Line or to the north through Belgium? What sort of defence could anyone put up against such power?

I hoped such thoughts did not show on my face and that I'd looked suitably impressed by the General's amazing performance. A delectable charlotte russe had arrived in front of each of us but he was not eating. I on the other hand wasn't going to leave it; indeed, I thought a little hiatus in the conversation might encourage him to think of more data, so I turned to Loerzer on my right and asked him about his young pilots and their flying clubs, or whatever he liked to call his initial training centres.

Meanwhile the General had a few words with our host, clearly asking Rosenberg whether this was the sort of information I wanted to know. Rosenberg obviously hadn't understood a word, for he was nodding in a rather foolish manner. Kesselring looked worried, and quickly gave Rosenberg the gist of what had been said, whereupon Rosenberg turned to me and, speaking in German, said, "I'm sure it's not necessary to ask you not to pass any information on to the Communists." Bill translated this for me, so I looked suitably horrified and assured them that it was certainly quite unnecessary to ask me, which seemed to satisfy everybody.

While the conversation ebbed and flowed around me I concentrated on this hazy, indistinct picture I had in my head of hundreds and hundreds of tanks thundering across the Russian countryside with some sort of aerial artillery covering them, knocking out all opposition. Captain Basil Liddell Hart had been writing on the threat posed by tank warfare for some time. The tank, he believed, would determine the outcome of the next war. Although we had only a few in the British Army, as did the French, it seemed to me that the Germans would be unlikely to go into war without some new gun and shell which would pierce our own tanks' armour. Would this be mounted in their air support? What sort of gun would it be? What sort of aircraft would this *Blitzkrieg* demand?

Was all this information offered to me authentic and would anyone believe me when I returned to London? But above all, I kept wondering what sort of question I should be asking right now at this very moment, when I had such a talkative exponent of this new method of warfare in full flood. If the tanks were to have this close air support, I finally decided to ask General Reichenau, would they be able to carve out forward aerodromes as quickly as they required them?

Oh, yes, he replied. Of course they had made preparations for this. There would be special aerodrome units flown in behind the tank spearheads. These men would provide complete aerodromes, together with entire aerodrome service. Squadrons would not have their own particular workshops, these would be provided by the aerodrome service together with armourers, refuellers and aerodrome guards. All the pilots would have to worry about was coming back to their landing strips, where they would be refuelled, rearmed and have any light damage repaired for them. All rations and fresh equipment would be ferried in to these advance posts. It was obvious that this was going to be a big organisation on its own. In World War I every squadron had its own mechanics and repair shops which followed the squadron wherever it went; now it looked as if this organisation was to be entirely separate, and I wondered how it might work. However, Reichenau went on to say that as the war was going to last such a short time, it would hardly be worthwhile repairing any of the badly damaged aircraft; anyway there would be plenty of new aircraft to draw on. This pointed to a vast number of aeroplanes being made if they were to have at least a hundred percent reserves always on tap.

Reichenau explained that the tanks and infantry would also be supplied by air. No soldier would have to carry more than his rifle and combat kit; there would be no cumbersome trappings as in 1914. Ferry planes would transport everything the infantryman needed so that he could maintain his speed of advance. There would be no heavy lorries holding things up as they bogged down in shell-shot roads.

In the hour and a half which we had taken over lunch, during which Reichenau hardly ever stopped talking, I had learned enough to keep me thinking for weeks to come. Would I ever be able to put this story across in London, and if I did would anybody ever take any action on it? As we rose he said, with blithe confidence, that he hoped that what he had been able to tell me would convince my friends in London of the Nazis' intentions. He bowed discreetly from the waist, said a word to Rosenberg and departed. So Hitler was not only going to invade and occupy Russia, he was going to destroy the Russian Army; a primary essential for victory which Napoleon himself had failed to do.

The reader must realise that the Nazis, who were themselves daily gaining experience in the battle for men's minds, saw at much closer quarters than ourselves the tyranny of Communism, the massacre of farmers and intellectuals, the police state in which families were made to spy on each other and where murder was the reward for one word out of place. In those

early days the Nazis felt that they had saved their country
from Communism; they could not understand why we too were
not violently opposed to Stalin's régime. They felt that we
should welcome the destruction of the Bolsheviks. Some of
them even felt that we should help in this anti-Russian drive;
or, if we would not offer positive help, then the least that we
could do was to stay neutral and well out of the way while
the Nazis got on with the job.

Was Hitler's obsession to march against Russia the cause of
his disagreement with the German General Staff? Did his remark to me about having to sell them half his birthright refer
to their determination to eliminate any possible resistance in
Europe before going to Russia? Did they find the thought of
revenge for the defeats of the First World War preferable to
his Eastern dreams? I never found out exactly what the reasons
for the irritations between them were, but something always
seemed to cause friction between Hitler and his generals. The
generals' refusal to fight on two fronts was presumably the
reason why Hitler and the Nazis were so anxious to keep Britain
out of a next war. With Britain out of the way, they could
finish off the rest of Europe in a few weeks. Having heard
Reichenau's lecture, such a proposition seemed all too likely.

But how would they produce the vast armaments and Air
Force necessary to carry out the sort of operations he'd been
talking about? The difficulties of achieving such a prodigious
effort must be obvious for all to see. Now that I knew what
to look for, it should be easy to garner sufficient information
to assess whether he'd been discussing a Nazi pipedream or
a reality that must already be beginning to take concrete shape.

I must find out exactly how the Germans were beginning
to prepare for war. Would one of their new aeroplanes being
built be able to "destroy all opposition from the air", and if
so, how would it be able to fly so low? Was it feasible to use
aircraft as advance artillery? I must discover what sort of armament this aeroplane possessed and what kind of bombs it would
use. In England at this time we were only using thirty- to
fifty-pound anti-personnel bombs, but it sounded as if the Nazis
had something much heavier in mind.

As far back as the turn of the century the French had produced their famous 75-millimetre gun; this had formed the bulk of their artillery up to the middle of the First World War. Were the Germans now going to produce a weapon which could be used not only on tanks themselves but as a field gun and also an anti-aircraft gun? It would need to have amazing versatility and immense armour-piercing power.

I never met Reichenau again but was able to follow his career during the war when he commanded the Sixth German Army in Belgium. After the fall of Europe he led it in the invasion of Russia. His *Blitzkrieg* methods, expounded to me with such typical German thoroughness, were successful in Poland, in France and in the initial stages of the attack upon Russia. But the Russians retreated so fast that they escaped the German pincer movement, leaving a scorched earth behind them. Winter beat the Germans to their objectives; in a very cold railway carriage, surrounded by snow, General Reichenau finally shot himself, knowing that the conquest of Russia was impossible.

6
Progress

The lunch party was now over. Wenninger and Kesselring bowed themselves out, but Rosenberg suggested we sit down with him and Loerzer and have a talk. I was more than astounded when he turned to me and asked which of the two German officers I considered would make the best Air Attaché in London. He hastened to add that, of course, "he would be accredited at first as a civilian attaché", but he didn't think "that would fool anybody". In any case it would not be for very long.

It was not a difficult choice to make. Wenninger with the clothes that fitted him, and some form of grace, his ready smile and the fact that he spoke English reasonably well seemed the obvious one, nor did I think he would be likely to learn very much that we did not want him to know. I later discovered, when he got to London, that it was his wife, a cousin of Ribbentrop's, who wore the trousers.

Had Kesselring's surly silence during lunch been assumed in order that I should not choose him for the Air Attaché's post? Or had the Germans brought him along in order that it would seem that I should have a choice although they had no intention of sending Kesselring? I could not tell, but he was certainly never surly in later encounters.

I didn't see Kesselring again until the 1936 rally in Nuremberg when he had blossomed into a General. He was then courteous and smiling as Rosenberg introduced him to me as the Chief of the Luftwaffe Staff. No wonder he hadn't wanted the job of Air Attaché. Rosenberg explained that Kesselring had had a considerable part in the build-up of the Luftwaffe and was entirely a Hitler man (rather I imagine on the lines of Reichenau). His promotion had been quick, but despite his welcoming manner I was to find him hard to draw out. He did tell me that he expected to take command of an air fleet, but when I asked him what that would entail, he replied that it was a mixed command of bombers, fighter bombers and fighter aircraft, and he refrained from giving me any numbers. Kesselring then offered me a lift back to Berlin in his own aircraft which he piloted himself. I accepted, and as we parted company in Berlin he left me in no doubt that he intended to get right to the top of the ladder before the coming "expansions" were over. The last time I met him was in 1938. He had duly got command of his air fleet, the one which was to be primarily and fully ranged against us in the Battle of Britain.

But back to the luncheon in 1934. I had had little chance of talking to Loerzer during lunch, but I now found him quite willing to tell me how he would be able to train his young pilots on powered aircraft after years of frustration when they were only allowed to use gliders. He hastened to explain that at the moment they were only small, civil aircraft, but after I had told him what Hitler himself had told me, he admitted that proper military training aircraft were now beginning to be used. I didn't push the question as to precisely what sort of aircraft they were, but I assumed that Loerzer, although he too was dressed in ordinary civilian clothes, was really helping to organise the initial flying training schools for the new pilots.

Ever since I had learned from Hitler that he was going to form a new Air Force, I knew that I must talk to some of the pilots. However much information I obtained from the officers higher up, it was the pilots who would really tell me what was happening; what were the snags and advantages of their various aircraft. While I was talking to Loerzer I thought of a way to meet them. Would he like to bring five or six of his young pilots over to England in their light aeroplanes later that summer? I assured him that we would entertain them at a civil aerodrome, putting them up at the Royal Air Force Club in London for a couple of nights. Loerzer jumped at the chance and said that he would get permission from the Führer as soon as possible.

Looking back it was rather a bold invitation to offer on the spur of the moment but I felt pretty sure that I'd get the necessary permission and backing in England. I had several good friends in the civil flying club business whom I could put fully in the picture, knowing that they wouldn't let me down.

Loerzer took his leave and Rosenberg dropped us back at the flat. Bill and I would have liked a rest but we knew we must sit down there and then to make notes and assessments.

I felt that my interview with Hitler, together with this lunch, had given me an eagle's eye view of what the Nazis intended to do and how they meant to do it. How many others outside their own circle had been so entrusted? Hitler and his friends seemed to be determined not to fight Britain again; was this attitude to be believed? From a close study of Hitler while he was talking and a careful analysis with Bill of what he had said to me, I was certain that he had not been bluffing. He had said what he really believed and had specified exactly what he intended to do about a new Air Force. As for Reichenau, his behaviour over lunch had been too spontaneous and enthusiastic to be anything but the truth. Clever as he was, he could not have kept up the continuity of his story had it been nonsense.

Bill remarked on Rosenberg's gaucheness as a host and wondered what sort of future he could expect in the rough and tumble of the Nazi hierarchy. We both thought that he had overplayed his hand by inviting Goering *and* Reichenau, probably to impress us with his own importance, and that it had been lucky for us that Goering had failed to turn up. His presence might have subdued Reichenau and would certainly have spoiled my lunch.

Together we planned how to handle Wenninger when he became Air Attaché. Archie Boyle would quickly understand the position and would undoubtedly see he received an appropriate welcome. Kesselring might well be of use to us in Germany if we could maintain contact, although his initial surliness had been disconcerting.

Bill agreed with me that Reichenau had certainly not been putting on an act, his zealous ardour went far beyond prepared propaganda. He had given us the truth and a tremendously valuable basis on which to build our own plans; now we must find out more about the strength of their armed forces and the dates they had in mind for their operations. We would need to widen our contacts right across Germany.

If the Nazis were going to trust me at such a high level, I would have to cement this loyalty with some positive actions of my own. The invitation to the young pilots was my first move, but there would have to be others. I would also like to meet more high-powered Nazis. Bill laughed at this, pointing out that the Nazis were paying him to bring British people into their circle, so he supposed he might just as well bring Nazi leaders into ours.

We then settled down to complete notes of everything that had been said, with impressions and comments, for as memories are not infallible, records are essential. I particularly wanted to get down on paper exactly what I felt about the National Socialist régime as a whole. Despite the ridiculous saluting, an enormous number of people were now marching in step; the leaders were full of high spirits; there was urgency and purpose behind all their ideas; they were heady with power; they knew where they wanted to go. This combination of exuberance, dictatorship and intention made them formidable.

They had been defeated in 1918 but now they were going to be victorious. Not for them the old failed methods of warfare which had proved so unreliable. They were going to fight their next war with new tactics. Just as we had produced the tank in 1914, so the Germans were now going to produce aerial artillery. They were going to use a unique blend of the plane and the tank. Had we been defeated in 1918 we too might have thought up different strategies for the future instead of resting on our victory.

As I thought about all Reichenau had said about his *Blitzkrieg*, much fell into place. The Germans, I realised, had the intelligence to see the potential of the aeroplane. In World War I it had been used for reconnaissance only, helpful in obtaining information from the air of what the enemy ground forces were up to; but they were going to turn it into a fighting force superior to both their Navy and their Army. No doubt this was why Goering and his new Air Staff had pride of place in the hierarchy. Hitler too clearly believed in the enormous potential of the Air Force as a strategic weapon. They were going to use aeroplanes as artillery, in defence of their destructive bombers, *and* as transporters.

The information I had been given related to a Russian campaign, but with the overwhelming tank force which the Nazis were preparing, such a continental type of open warfare was, I could see, equally applicable to France or the Low Countries. It did not at first seem likely to be used against England because the transport of large numbers of tanks across the Channel would be a prodigious undertaking, which could only be done if the Germans had first destroyed our Navy and our Air Force. Moreover, I knew that the planes the Germans were building at that time were not suitable for starving Britain out, nor for total war against Britain, as they did not have the range to blockade the western approaches from the Atlantic nor to make anti-shipping patrols far out to sea. But they could always develop new types of aircraft.

As I mulled over in my mind all that Reichenau had said I came back again and again to the speed factor, two hundred miles a day. How on earth, for instance, was the front line going to keep in touch with the back-up forces? Normal telecommunications by landline would be impossible to lay at that speed; aerial communication would be essential. If they used radio links, would they be in code? What system and method would they employ? Equally, I realised that my normal Intelligence channels would be useless in obtaining information about any advance at that speed. Neither spies, nor pigeons, nor aerial photography would help us, for we would never be able to obtain the information quickly enough for it to be of use. It was not going to be a war in the least like 1915 with its static trench line, but a sweeping campaign of tremendous movement with troops driving forward behind a spearhead of tanks.

The next day I took my leave of Rosenberg and thanked him for his hospitality. He reminded me of what Hitler had said, stressing the necessity for Britain to mind her own business—in rather more polite language—and enlarging on Hitler's remark about the building up of the Air Force; that they had no intention of creating one larger than the combined forces of France and Great Britain. This no longer rang true after what Reichenau had told me, for it hardly fitted in with the vast forces necessary for Nazi expansionist plans. Still, no doubt it would be swallowed as a useful sop by the governments of our two countries whether or not they believed it. Rosenberg evidently felt that my visit had been a success, for he asked me back later in the year for the Nuremberg Rally.

Back in London, that March of 1934, I was glad to see that at long last the press was taking notice of Hitler and had reported a speech of his foreshadowing the demise of the Versailles Treaty. I felt a twinge of smug satisfaction to know that he had already told me it was dead.

My Chief was impressed by all my activity and asked for a full report as soon as possible, with one copy for Vansittart at the Foreign Office and three more for the service ministries. Having done that, I wrote out a most effusive account of the wonders of the National Socialist movement, what it was doing for Germany and what it hoped to accomplish. In it I incorporated the principal points that Hitler had made, stressing the need for Britain to keep out of future wars and mentioning that I had met Reichenau. I had this particular report copied on Air Ministry paper with 'Copy to the Foreign Office' typed along the bottom. I then arranged for this report to be leaked back to the Nazis through one of the embassies in London which we knew had contact with them.

The following extract from Rosenberg's diaries shows that this report did indeed reach Nazi ears. (This one appeared on pages 28 and 29 of the diary and was dated 14 May 1934.)

Major Winterbotham was here 'on vacation' from the 27th February up to the 6th March. Then I arranged for him to meet Reichenau, Loerzer, Hess, two Commodores, and finally Hitler. Major Winterbotham conveyed the greetings of the British airmen. The Fuhrer said that the Air Force had been the truly knightly weapon of the World War. As for the rest, the English have been a dangerous enemy because Germany was forced to keep two-thirds of her aeroplanes on the English frontline. Moving to present times, the Fuhrer gave expression to his conviction that no doubt the French were superior in numbers of aircraft but he considered the English stronger in value. As for the rest, he might be in favour of considerable reinforcement of the English Air Force, primarily for the following reason: that he was to demand for the defence of Germany a certain percentage in relation to the fleets of our neighbouring states. Now this necessary percentage was approaching the British numerical strength, a fact he did mind very much because various inferences would be drawn from it; England could have twice as many aircraft and even more, this would be only welcome.

The conversation took a satisfactory course and Winterbotham made a brilliant report in London. I went to Weimar with Winterbotham and de Ropp, to show him the style of our meetings. I showed him the Goethe-Haus, the Nietzsche-Archives; then coffee with the eighty-year-old Frau Foerster-Nietzsche, who had an astonishingly vivid mind; then we visited our school in Eggendorf, where the burgomasters of Thuringen, together with jurists, etc., have courses. There was a short address on the duty of ideological training. All these things, especially the frame of mind in Germany, deeply impressed Winterbotham; everything was so far from any propaganda.

My true and rather more frightening reports produced immediate reactions. Lord Londonderry, the Secretary of State for Air, and his Under Secretary, Philip Sassoon, wished to see me. Lord Londonderry was jubilant for here at last was something concrete. He was having the greatest difficulty in making the Cabinet take notice of the Nazi upsurge but at least I had produced some facts.

Archie Boyle was also delighted to get hold of such detailed information, though his remarks about the Air Attaché's behaviour are unprintable; a change was made in that appointment shortly afterwards. He promised to keep up my credibility with Wenninger and to give any help, should it be needed, when my German pilots arrived. Sir Robert Vansittart's reaction was also favourable to my report and my Chief asked me to his flat a few evenings later. Here, over a bottle of port, I gave him some sidelights on the Germans I had met. His chuckle was most infectious and those private visits to him became a ritual each time I returned from my German visits.

However, at the Foreign Office I had created a maelstrom. My report coming on top of the Ambassador's telegram had upset Cabinet circles. Sir Samuel Hoare, who had been a previous Minister for Air, was not at all pleased and he made his displeasure known extremely clearly. Both my Chief and I were puzzled by this but feared that it had something to do with Eden and Simon's visit to Hitler; they hadn't got much information and had not yet dared to admit that the Versailles Treaty was dead. It was difficult to understand why my more detailed knowledge was now unacceptable, especially all I had obtained on the subject of *Blitzkrieg*. Was it perhaps because the visits of Eden and Simon had so far been kept secret, at least from the public, and that my report circulated to the service ministries had brought the whole matter to the attention of many more people? If Sir Robert Vansittart appreciated the information, why didn't Sir Samuel Hoare? This ostrich attitude of a senior Cabinet minister was the first indication I had of the way in which the British Government were apparently determined to ignore the whole problem of German rearmament; a policy which was to put us in mortal danger when we found ourselves unprepared for a second world war.

My Chief told me that in view of the displeasure of a senior member of the Cabinet, I should be wise not to return to Germany for a while. He added that ministers come and go, so I probably wouldn't have to wait too long. Meanwhile I should try to fill in the pieces of the German rearmament picture in other ways.

Now that I felt I had got a definite framework into which to fit information about the new Luftwaffe, I produced a questionnaire which I sent round to 'our men' in the various capitals of Europe. I told them that it was based on solid data about the revival of the Luftwaffe, for I knew quite well that the Intelligence services of our friends in France, Holland, Finland, Poland and Czechoslovakia would themselves be very keen to act on the guidelines I'd given them. The countries to the east of Germany might even be able to infiltrate trained engineers into Germany, for there were many pockets of German-speaking people in Poland and Czechoslovakia and both these countries were anxious to know everything they could about future German rearmament.

My questionnaire asked where new aerodromes were being constructed; what aerodromes had actual flying aircraft stationed on them; how many aircraft, for instance, could be counted in the air at the same time. Was there any sign of an advanced military training aircraft which would obviously be noticeable for its speed and sound? A keen lookout was to be kept for men in the new blue Air Force uniform. They would probably have badges on their arms explaining their trade, and the badges would show if they were training to be pilots, air crew, mechanics, fitters or other auxiliary personnel. A few drinks in a beer-cellar might elicit further information from such people. I was also interested in any extensions being made to the big aircraft factories, such as Messerschmitt down south in Munich, Junkers and Heinkel. An increase in aeroplane construction would mean a tremendous recruiting drive for labour in the area, so it should be obvious to a well-trained agent.

While waiting for answers to come in, I looked around for further lines to explore without leaving England. I went down to the Bristol aero-engine factory to have lunch with Ken Bartlett. I'd known him for some time and had found him most useful in briefing me on the output, construction and performance of the Bristol engines which powered so many of our aircraft in the early thirties. I fed Ken a few scraps of what I had learned about the rebirth of the Luftwaffe, which was enough to make him think he might be able to do a bit of business with them. It would be a sprat to catch a mackerel, but if we could get Ken Bartlett in amongst the German aero-engine engineers some useful information might be obtained. I felt that the Germans could scarcely ignore such an offer; even if they never intended to buy any Bristol engines, they would at least like to know what we were doing, and Ken Bartlett was an old enough hand to know how much he could tell them.

I had a letter sent to Rosenberg on Air Ministry paper suggesting that the Bristol Aero-engine Company might be able to assist them in powering some of their new aeroplanes. The bait was swallowed and Bartlett was allowed to take to the Germans all the details of one of the Bristol engines still on the secret list, but which was not our latest model. By 1934 we had learned from our successes with sea-planes in the Schneider Trophy races against the Italians that as speeds of aircraft were increased so was the necessity to streamline the aeroplane itself, and the great areas of the air-cooled Bristol radial engine caused far too much resistance at these increased speeds to make them a suitable proposition for future fighters. Bartlett's mission was therefore hardly expected to succeed since the Germans had always preferred 'in-line' engines, even in the 1914–18 war. Nevertheless, if the Germans showed no interest at all in the Bristol engines, it would prove that they were building all their engines for their new air fleet themselves. We might also learn where these aero-engines were being built and whether they were being standardised or individually constructed for different aircraft.

Ken's mission was an evident success. Rosenberg himself took it as a symbol of Anglo-German co-operation; I suspect it made him feel that he was one up on Goering for having engineered Bartlett's introduction. As we had suspected, the Germans did not require a radial engine but Bartlett's report, which he made direct to the Air Ministry, gave us a very good line on German thinking for aero-engine construction in the immediate future, especially at the Junkers and Daimler Benz factories.

* * *

It was now time for me to organise Loerzer's visit with the
young pilots. Nigel Norman was a close neighbour of mine in
Gloucestershire and the owner of a first-class pheasant shoot
where I'd spent many a good day in the 1920s; he was a dedi-
cated airman and one of the foremost pioneers of civil flying
in the country. He owned and operated the small aerodrome
at Heston in the west of London which was the home of several
of the light aeroplane flying clubs in the London area. Amongst
these was the flying club of the Brigade of Guards.

Nigel was also an RAF Reserve Officer who had close ties
with the Air Ministry itself, since in those days all aviation
came under the Ministry. I knew him well as a personal friend
and knew that I could trust him. A number of people have
sneered at what they call the old-school-tie network amongst
Intelligence people, but the fact remains that far the best security is amongst people who know each other well, have probably been at school together or have worked closely in some
field so that they have had time to assess the other's character.
Security generally breaks down where people take something
for granted. Nigel was intrigued with the idea of the young
German pilots coming to Heston, and I had no difficulty in
persuading him to co-operate over the proposed visit. I advised
him that they would be young pilots recently recruited to the
new German Air Force, but that they would be in the guise
of civil pilots and would be shepherded by a so-called civilian
called Herr Loerzer, who was quite obviously in charge of
initial flying instruction in Germany. Nigel asked me if he could
put the secretary of the Guards Flying Club into the picture
as he knew him very well, and I agreed to this. Thus both of
them knew the real purpose behind the visit; in addition, the
scheme had the personal backing of Archie Boyle at the Air
Ministry. I was also able to co-opt the services of a cousin of
mine, Lindsay Everard, who was not only a member of Parliament but was the chairman of the Flying Clubs Association
in Britain. We now had the perfect set-up for this visit. I neither
knew nor cared whether the Foreign Office had been approached on this subject. It was purely a matter of civil aviation
for the Air Ministry to decide. Nevertheless, it was kept as

quiet as possible. All concerned were advised to say nothing to the newspapers, but if they were directly tackled by a member of the press they could say that it was a purely friendly visit by a few German civil pilots.

Not surprisingly, I was distinctly nervous when the time came for the visit, for there were people in Britain who might have objected had they got to hear about it. I impressed upon Nigel and the Guards Club not to question these young pilots on .any military subject. I knew that they would have been warned to watch their tongues, but I wanted the visit to seem a purely social one. I aimed to cash in on it later, as I hoped they'd ask me back to their headquarters in Germany.

The visitors were given a cocktail party reception on arrival at Heston by the Guards Club before coming up to the RAF Club in Piccadilly for dinner and to stay the night. I have seldom seen such an exuberant bunch of youngsters; they were tired from their flight, but happy. Above all they seemed to be tremendously impressed with the RAF Club, for nothing like it existed in Germany. The food, the comfort and the service were all remarked upon and a demand was then and there made to Herr Loerzer to start a similar institution in Berlin.

Next day we arranged a small coach to take the pilots round London, followed by an official lunch at the Club with Lindsay Everard presiding and as many German-speaking young English civil pilots as he could muster. It was a splendid affair, but I only managed just in time to stop one of the English enthusiasts proposing a toast to the new Luftwaffe. In the afternoon the young pilots went down to get their aircraft ready for take-off the following morning. Loerzer had been considerably impressed with the welcome given to his young lads and told me that he would certainly report direct to the Führer when he got back to Berlin.

They were a good lot of youngsters, these young Luftwaffe pilots. I believe on Hitler's orders the tradition of the chivalry of the First World War was to be revived amongst the fighter pilots at least; I imagine the bomber pilots and their crews had little time for such niceties.

One of the most important outcomes of this visit and one most useful to me was the founding of the Luftwaffe Club in Berlin in 1935. When I went over in 1936 I was made an honorary member. Not only could I take Bill de Ropp there, but I was able to sit and talk to the young German pilots. The Club itself was much more austere then the RAF one in London. The question of rank was far too obvious for the comfort of junior officers. There were few comfortable chairs, and the quiet, efficient service of the RAF Club was missing. But it served its purpose and the young Luftwaffe members were very proud to show it off to me.

It was while sitting in the Luftwaffe Club one day in, 1936 that I first heard of the dangers and difficulties of training with the Stukas: how the enormous speed generated in an almost vertical dive with a large bomb on board tended to pull the wings off the aeroplane; then, when the bomb was gone and the pilot pulled the aircraft out of his dive, he was almost pushed through his seat with the 'G' force. I learned that there had already been quite a number of casualties and that there was a great deal more to be done before the technique became operational. This was vital information for it was now evident that this form of aerial artillery was to be the second principal component of *Blitzkrieg*. Unless they could get it right, they would not be able to carry out the aerial destruction of all opposition for their tank spearheads.

RAF officers in England whom I consulted about dive bombing were extremely sceptical. They thought that it was so dangerous, killed so many people and was so wasteful in trained men and materials that it would never be used, and that the Germans would soon give up their experiments and realise that it was a waste of time and energy trying to perfect such an unlikely method of attack. The RAF people certainly had no intention of testing it out in England.

I found this inability of the English to understand the potential of the dive-bomber most worrying, for I felt sure that the Nazis would persevere with the development of this new concept in aerial artillery, which included the added factor of a built-in screeching terror for those being bombed. It would obviously be immensely effective at clearing a path for tanks as it could spot its target without additional air reconnaissance aid. It would also be extremely difficult to counter-attack either by air or by anti-aircraft methods. The chances of an anti-aircraft shell hitting a dive-bomber travelling at such high speed seemed remote to me. But I could get no one to take an interest in such counter-measures since the people at the Air Ministry technical branch thought the Germans would never use them.

Part of this opposition sprang from the Englishman's inability to see the Air Force as a primary offensive weapon. Since World War I we had used aeroplanes to keep the peace in the Middle East and on the north-west frontier of India, but no one saw them as having primarily an aggressive potential. Their development was seen as a logical extension of their uses in the 1914–18 war for reconnaissance, aerial photography, observation and defence. The RAF was the junior arm of the fighting services in Britain. It did not have such a prominent position in the life of the nation as the Luftwaffe had in Germany, and the British seemed unable to visualise it in a new role. So often I found it difficult to explain what I knew because it just did not fit in with the *thinking* in Britain at the time.

Another outcome of my visits to the Luftwaffe Club was that since I now went backwards and forwards to Germany in one of Lufthansa's JU 52s and there were invariably two extra pilot trainees on board, they used to come back from the cockpit to talk to me. They openly admitted that this flight to London was part of their training. Curiously enough, they seldom asked questions about the Royal Air Force; they already seemed to take it for granted that we were not going to fight them in a second world war. I suppose they'd been told so by their wishful-thinking leaders. That Rosenberg was hopeful of success in this field was shown by his report to Hitler on 12 May 1934:

England's air-fleet, being smaller than the French one in numbers, presents some difficulty as regards parity. I have been working on this aspect for eighteen months, and I had already discussed these questions with a young British officer in England in December 1931. This personal contact in London has turned out to be very productive.

During the past eighteen months we have continually given London reports of the political situation. All British Staffs were kept informed about our political opinions which unlike the British official news service, turned out to be true. This connection became more and more close. Therefore Major Winterbotham decided to undertake a short *Urlaubsreise* to Berlin, during which I could introduce him to you.

The result of this conversation was that the British Secretary of State for Air was well pleased, and Baldwin, who was informed at once, justified the German desire for security in the British Parliament by explaining that the Germans in Berlin and the Ruhr might have the same fear of an air-attack as the English in London. After that Major Winterbotham sent a letter on an official sheet of notepaper from the British Air Ministry saying that he would send to Germany an English officer as a representative of a big British aircraft company. This officer came here with an official letter of introduction and has been in touch with the persons in question, and his single-minded work justifies hopes that, first of all the Air Ministry, and then the staffs of the other British service ministries, will bring increasing pressure on British foreign policy.

As I first met Rosenberg in 1932 and he gives the date as December 1931, I don't think he can be referring to me when he talks about "a young British officer." But the whole report shows the tremendous effort Rosenberg was making to build up his success in the Anglo-German friendship field. It also shows how little the Nazis understood our system of government. They never seemed to grasp that our all-powerful Foreign Office took precedence over the service chiefs: they always presumed that it worked like their own set-up, imagining that our Chief of Air Staff had the same authority as Goering had in the Nazi hierarchy.

When Ralph Wenninger and his wife arrived in London, they were welcomed by Archie Boyle and there was a suitable sprinkling of RAF officers at the first cocktail party that the Wenningers gave in their flat in Kensington. Wenninger brought me two bottles of wild raspberry liqueur. I have little doubt he did this at the suggestion of Rosenberg, for I had told him that this was the only sort of liqueur I found drinkable in Germany. I just couldn't stand the sickly, sweet green potions which Rosenberg himself seemed to enjoy. Wenninger was given the usual careful conducted tours arranged by the Air Ministry. He was shown our Staff College and our training facilities, but there were three things which he was never allowed to learn anything about: our progress in radar; our brilliant system of control of the whole of our fighter air force from Fighter Command, which included our system of enabling our fighters to home in on approaching enemy formations; and our production of the Spitfire. This aircraft was later to catch the Germans completely by surprise.

Wenninger, like all the foreign attachés, used to visit Archie Boyle from time to time. On these occasions Archie would let me know so that I would be in the Ministry when Wenninger was there and would be summoned by Archie to meet him in his office. In this way I continued to establish the fact that I was a member of the Air Staff and nothing more. Rosenberg himself seemed satisfied according to the following extract from his diaries for 11 July 1934:

The Air Ministry emphasises that it will help us honestly but one should not try making them believe things, because they are receiving exact information anyway. The next Air Attaché for Berlin, who is closely connected with Winterbotham, will be a good man as opposed to the present one, who is a rather simple-minded man. Corresponding to that the German Attaché will be shown round in England.

By the end of 1934 I had a new ally. Desmond Morton was the member of our office team who sniffed out intrigues in foreign politics, but now he was given the special task of obtaining and collating all possible information on German armaments and on their war factories. He was told that his first priority was to be aircraft and aero-engine production. This took a great load off my shoulders and it meant that I could concentrate more on the role of the Luftwaffe, its training and strategy. Together, Desmond and I would be able to arrive at a much more accurate forecast of growth and performance. Morton obtained a complete list of existing German factories from Control Commission Records, together with their capacities. This made it easier to observe any extensions to existing factories or the construction of new ones.

The whole of Europe outside Germany had now been alerted, both by their own contacts and by my widely spread questionnaire, so by the beginning of 1935 estimates of German intentions and many other bits of the jigsaw were arriving in London. Estimates of Hitler's target varied from three thousand to five thousand first-line aircraft. At that time it was difficult to forecast which was correct, but we took a conservative view of four thousand, which proved to be right in 1939 but had been whittled down to three thousand by July of 1940.

It so happened that Desmond lived next door to Chartwell, the home of Winston Churchill, where he was often a guest at Sunday lunch. I was at first unaware of this and wondered why it was always on Friday nights that he would come to my office to help me work out estimates of progress of the build-up of the Luftwaffe, but I soon found out that on Sundays Desmond would give these figures to Winston Churchill. The following week there would inevitably be a parliamentary question by Churchill in the House of Commons to ask the Prime Minister whether it was a fact that such and such figures for the strength of the Luftwaffe were now correct. I was never certain whether the Prime Minister knew precisely, or even suspected, how Winston Churchill had obtained his figures, but Baldwin was always quite bland in his reply that he did not have any information on this subject. Such a reply was in line with Government policy at the time which ignored the Nazis and all their works, but it infuriated me, my Chief and now also Desmond. Our only compensation was that the airing of the whole subject in Parliament acted as a constant reminder to the Government that the figures were now becoming public knowledge.

Morton was a vital partner in our joint efforts to get to the truth of the Luftwaffe expansion, but early in 1935 a piece of rare Intelligence good fortune came my way which made our mutual search much easier. The new British Air Attaché in Berlin had been a prisoner of war with me in 1918 and was an old friend, so I had given him some idea of my connections with Rosenberg and the Nazis; enough at least for him to know what I was trying to do. I had, however, been careful not to compromise him, for there was a very strict rule in foreign embassies before the war that no member of the Embassy staff was allowed to take part in espionage. It was a wise rule because in delicate situations such as Berlin or Moscow, the planting of secret Intelligence on one of the attachés might easily have been a provocative attempt to discredit him. Anyway, my friend was sufficiently well briefed to know that when an envelope addressed to me dropped through the Embassy letter box it ought to be sent on to me in London as fast as possible through the diplomatic bag.

The envelope contained a sheet of paper about ten inches by eight and was obviously a photo of a single page from a book. At the top, above a black line, were letters and figures denoting that it was part of Volume D, Chapter 3, and in the centre the word GEHEIM, meaning secret; and on the right-hand side was the page number thirty-two, at least as nearly as I can remember. Beneath the black line came the heading: "The Establishment of Flying Schools," under which was a column which ran right down the page listing the names and locations of the flying schools of the Luftwaffe. There were some twenty-five in all. I shook out the envelope but there was nothing else in it. At first I thought it might be a hoax, but when I studied the list carefully quite a few of the names coincided with those that I had already received from other sources. Who, I thought, would have tried to fake the information above the black line? Obviously, if the symbols at the top were true, this was just one page out of a book. However, I wasn't going to risk sending it straight over to the Air Ministry without checking more of the details myself, nor of course was I willing to compromise the source, if he were genuine, by sending the list to agents overseas; so I picked out a number of the flying schools listed and sent their names to separate capitals in Europe for ratification. A few weeks later when I was beginning to get confirmation of the existence, or preparation for the existence, of these flying schools, a second envelope arrived from Berlin. This time it was from the same volume but the chapters and pages were different and below the line was given the complete establishment of a new German fighter squadron. It was almost too good to be true. It is in fact hard

to describe my reaction to these photographs. Here was I fishing in every European pond for any scrap of information which
would help me fill in the framework of the new Luftwaffe
and here on my desk was what evidently purported to be a
leaf out of a secret volume on the organisation of that new
German Air Force. With the second envelope had come a type-
written note; it simply gave the name and an obvious accommodation address in one of the suburbs of Berlin, but underlined
was a request that under no circumstances was the information
to be passed to the French.

My liaison over Intelligence with my opposite number of
the French Deuxième Bureau, Colonel Georges Ronin, was
extremely close. We knew each other's thoughts and exchanged
every bit of information we could about Germany. But now
I had to play my new source close to the chest. The source
must be someone well informed. I toyed with the idea that
it had come from Rosenberg himself. I don't think he would
have thought there was anything wrong in sending me information since he seemed so certain that Britain was going to stay
out of the war. However, it seemed much more likely that it
came from somebody on Goering's staff who was either violently anti-Nazi or extremely greedy. The extracts from Goering's 'bible', as I called it, kept on coming throughout 1936,
1937 and 1938. I suppose I must have had thirty or more of
these photos from all aspects of the Luftwaffe build-up. They
were of course always invaluable, but they were of the greatest
use now, at the beginning of 1935, when I'd not yet been
able to convince either the Government or the Air Ministry
that my conclusions were correct. There was no demand for
money enclosed in these photostat reports until five or six of
them had been received towards the end of 1935. When the
demand came it was a big one. My Chief called me in and
asked me for a very careful analysis of the value of these reports.

Money had never been readily available since I had joined
the Secret Service at the beginning of 1930, so I told my Chief
that if it was a question of saving money elsewhere, I would
rather give up a great many small sources to concentrate on
this one, so vital was the information. I showed him some of

the reports and the conclusions which they had confirmed and he seemed quite satisfied.

In due course a moustached and bespectacled passenger arrived at a Berlin station off the Hamburg train and deposited two small suitcases at the left luggage office. The ticket for the deposit was duly sent to the address in Berlin, and a day or two later another moustached and bespectacled gentleman collected the suitcases. It was the perfectly straightforward copybook method of transferring payment. The envelopes continued to arrive.

I would have liked to have arranged a meeting between this source and myself outside Germany so that I could pinpoint precisely which pages from the 'bible' I wanted, but at first I was hesitant to do so in case I compromised him. From 1935 to 1938 I remained patient and took what was given me. Then with the threat of war imminent in 1939, I thought it essential that we should meet in case he could be persuaded to defect and bring with him the whole order of battle of the Luftwaffe. An invitation was sent to him to meet me in Switzerland. A rendezvous was actually fixed for Zurich, where I waited for three fruitless days, but nobody turned up. I was not altogether surprised; if the source was in fact in a fairly high position in Goering's Air Force, he might well have been moved out of Berlin when things began to hot up. This surmise of mine was probably correct, for after coming back from Zurich I received no more letters.

It is difficult now for me to recall what each of the valuable photos contained but I do remember that one of them mentioned the Stuka dive-bomber and referred to special training for these squadrons, which confirmed what I had learned from the young pilots in the Luftwaffe Club.

7
Distractions

In February 1935 I received a command from Charles Medhurst, the Director of Intelligence at the Air Ministry, to accompany him on a tour of the Middle East, where the RAF was responsible for maintaining law and order. I had the strange idea that some Cabinet ministers thought I was being a little too vigorous in pursuing the German rearmament question when it was clearly against government policy to admit what was happening. The Air Staff were presumably persuaded that a month or two out of Europe would cool me down.

Charles was a charming travelling companion; on our leisurely journey out to Jerusalem he filled me in on the intrigues of the Middle East. We certainly had plenty of time to talk because Mussolini did not like British aeroplanes flying over Italy. Consequently, we went by slow civil aircraft from Croydon to Paris, then by train to Milan, on again by train to Brindisi and then by Imperial Airways four-engined flying boat to Alexandria. From Alexandria we took a train to Cairo, thence by car to the RAF station on the Suez Canal at Ismailia, and from there we travelled in two separate two-seater service aeroplanes to Jerusalem. These last were old open-cockpit aircraft, which meant dressing up in full flying kit with helmet, goggles and parachutes. By the time Hitler was ready with his brand-new Air Force, would we still be lumbering about in these slow old 'kites'?

Charles and I were to use these open-cockpit planes all over the Middle East. Mostly we arrived in one piece, but on my return trip from Amman the aircraft started to shed bits of hardware, including the exhaust pipe, so the pilot signalled to me to get ready to jump. I'd never parachuted before and didn't care for the idea one bit. Fortunately I saw one of the landing grounds used by the oil pipeline people not too far ahead, so I pointed to it and suggested he land there. He radioed his position and asked for a relief aircraft to come to pick me up. On another occasion we nearly had trouble when using a very large Vickers Vimy transport plane which took a party of us from Baghdad to northern Iraq.

I was put up by 'our man in Jerusalem' at his house. The lovely warm weather and pure fresh orange juice for breakfast were a welcome change from the cold February of London. I was briefed very thoroughly on the various sources of information which he had, the worries which were just beginning to crop up with the Jewish nationalists in Palestine and the ever-present intrigue between the various Arab states themselves. The one strong man seemed to be Abdulla of Trans-Jordan, the grandfather of the present King Hussein, but everybody had oil in mind, including the Egyptians. My host explained to me that the indigenous homosexuality of many of the leaders in the Arab world made it possible to contact their lover boys and so find out from them who was concocting what intrigue against which protector, financed by whom. On the whole the RAF seemed to keep a pretty tight rein on the area, although the ancient aeroplanes we had out there were unable to carry more than a few light bombs. Still, there was no opposition except the stray rifle bullet. The stray rifle bullet was, however, more of a menace on the ground in northern Palestine, and driving through Nablus by car it was best to go fast. The people to look out for were the infiltrators from the north who, even in 1935, were doing their best to undermine British influence in the Middle East.

Baghdad, Amman, Jerusalem and the Holy Land were names that had always fascinated me. Now I was able to visit them by air, albeit flying low over the hot desert in an old open-cockpit aircraft, which proved to be an extremely bumpy process. So clear was the pattern of the old irrigation canals which once carried the life-giving water between the Tigris and Euphrates that one could not help wondering whether it would not one day be possible for the cradle of Western civilisation to blossom again in abundance. Mesopotamia looked from the air like an endless crossword puzzle, with here and there a square blocked out by a crumbled ancient city. It must have been one of the greatest acts of destruction in world history when Genghis Khan and his Mongol hordes destroyed the irrigation system, causing the collapse of this vast Arabian food store.

While we were in Baghdad, that city of many streets, each with its own ancient craft—the copper beater, the carpet maker, and so on—we learned that the Ambassador was about to fly up with his wife, Lady Humphries, and his daughter to visit one of the big sheiks in northern Iraq. He invited Charles and me to go along.

The Sheik had prepared an air strip close to his camp where we were greeted by this large bearded man who wore a flowing black cloak over his spotless white robe; his Arab headdress and carved golden dagger denoted his sheikdom. Large, friendly brown eyes under heavy black eyebrows twinkled a welcome, and as we stepped from the aircraft there was a guard of honour of some hundred young men ranging in age down from about twenty-five to the youngest at ten years old. All were dressed in spotless white and at a sign from their father, they sang a very creditable version of 'God Save the King'. Sheik Ajil was proud of his sons, though he explained that these were not all of them. He led the way to his large goat-hair tent, where there were seven-foot-tall Nubian slaves as black as polished ebony to serve the traditional bitter coffee. More slaves attended with silver bowls of rose water and little hand towels made in Lancashire. The Sheik had been advised that Lady Humphries was not keen on sheep's eyes for lunch, so this choice morsel, traditionally kept for the principal guest, was tactfully absent, but a whole roast sheep on its bathtubful of rice was delicious. My only complaint was the sand: it was hard to sit on and it inevitably got into your mouth, owing to the fact that you had to eat with your already sandy fingers.

A Western-style marquee had been erected to accommodate the whole of the Sheik's family, except the women, for the 'talk' with the Ambassador. Rich carpets were spread over the floor of the conference tent, which with the colourful hangings on the camels and the giggles of the considerable harem seeing but unseen, were indications of the Sheik's wealth. Here, surely, was Abraham coming out of the north with his sons and his camels and his sheep and all his wives.

I was able to have a word with the Sheik's eldest son, who confirmed my information that German railway engineers had been in the area. There had been a German dream before the First World War of a Berlin-to-Baghdad railway. The dream was presumably still alive, with the added advantage of oil at the end of it. It was just another straw in the wind blowing eastwards from Nazi Germany.

The Holy Land, I think, fascinates everyone. If only down the ages Christendom had refrained from building great churches over all the most Holy Places, and then squabbling amongst themselves as to who should occupy them! Alas, the pilgrim business has ever been lucrative, whether to Mecca or Jerusalem; but there was one place in Jerusalem where I, at least, felt the compelling force of timeless belief. I still remember today the feeling I had then, that if only I could have got Rosenberg to stand with me before the Rock in the cool serenity of the Temple at Jerusalem, he might have paused in his pursuit of racial paganism and experienced the feasibility of a less extreme, less violent Thousand-Year Reich.

After this interlude I went to Cairo, where the perpetually ineffective Pan-Arab conference was going on. It seemed the Arab states had been talking about acting in unity for many years and no doubt would talk about it for many more, but Palestine looked like being a serious problem in the not far distant future.

* * *

Back in London I found that no more information about Goering's 'bible' had come in, but a considerable amount of fill-in material from other sources around Europe had appeared. The jigsaw was beginning to build up well; but I was now overdue to go to Paris to contact my opposite number there, for we had a great deal to talk about. Germany would of course be priority number one, but there were other countries which were becoming interesting. As both Czechoslovakia and Holland were going ahead with development of new aircraft and aero-engines, it seemed quite probable that at some time the Germans would make use of these sources of supply. Italy was increasing her air fleet but the vast Russian five-year plans were not proving very effective. It was difficult to get information out of Russia, but most of their aircraft were precise copies of either American, British or French types, so it seemed unlikely that they would suddenly produce anything which would surprise us.

Flights to France from that old grass aerodrome at Croydon in the large Handley-Page "box-kites" were luxurious. The take-off was at noon, followed by a large, leisurely lunch on a wide table in a spacious cabin. True the aircraft heaved about in the air a bit if the weather was bumpy, but you could get up and walk about if you wanted to. Arrival was a gentle touchdown at Le Bourget aerodrome, then a bus ride to the Place de l'Opéra. In the spring the Champs Élysées flaunted its sweet-smelling chestnuts in full bloom, albeit somewhat overpowered by the pungent perfumes of the Parisiennes.

Paris was alive and happy in the middle thirties. I used to stay with 'our man in Paris' and his delightful American wife. At that time they had a flat just opposite the Guitry house near the Champs de Mars. Both my host and hostess and my French colleagues saw to it that after working hours we enjoyed something of the traditional gaiety of the French capital. The great restaurants in the Bois de Boulogne were full; couture in Paris was at its height and the beautiful women were showing off their latest creations. But I must say that the Guitrys were far better entertainment off the stage than on. At least once during each of my visits there was a splendid scene. Yvonne Printemps, superbly befurred and carrying only her jewel case, would come out of the house and while standing on the steps alternately call for a taxi and hurl vituperation over her shoulder. Sacha would give as good as he got, his famous melodious voice cracking in an ever-rising crescendo of abuse. Yvonne usually returned the next day—I suspect it was her way of having a night off.

Fortunately, the headquarters of the Deuxième Bureau were not very far from where I used to stay, and I could walk round there in the morning to the green door in the large high wall not far from the École Militaire. An ancient concierge would open the door and invite me in to a little wooden hut just inside the gate to sign my name. There was a bare table and the usual ancient French pen with a crossed nib which one dipped into a bottle of ink recently refilled with water. Somehow you got the impression that the French Government did not spend much money on its Secret Service. The office of my opposite number, Colonel Georges Ronin, was furnished with a bare trestle table and some hard wooden chairs, a few filing cabinets and a map on the wall. In comparison my own office in London was positively luxurious.

Georges Ronin was about the same age as myself and had also been a pilot in the First World War. He spoke no English, was about 5 foot 11, clean-shaven, with a very keen sense of humour. We got on well together from the very first time we met. During the thirties, when I saw him often, we became very close friends. We would compare all the information on the German Air Force that both of us had collected during the previous three months, and it was interesting to note that although they lived next door to the Germans and had apparently easier access to that country, the French were unable to get any more information from agents than I was.

Unlike the British, the French Secret Service used to employ a number of women on espionage work. It suited the Latin temperament and they considered, probably rightly, that a good deal of useful information could be obtained in bed by a clever operator. There was, they admitted, always the possibility of the girl getting too emotionally involved, when the game might work both ways; but they insisted that on balance it paid off. I never heard of the process going to the lengths employed by the Communists, whose use of sex and homosexual blackmail for recruiting their agents under the threat of exposure was well known. The French were very delicate in their handling of the matter, but the whole set-up operated by the Security as well as the Information Departments of the French Secret Service was given much wider authority than our own, which was well circumscribed in London by correct police procedure. If I had to deal with any foreign agents in Paris the French were told about it, but they let me know that I could get away with anything except murder. I never had occasion to take any drastic action, but it gave me an extra sense of security to know that the police would turn a blind eye if I had to do so.

Talking to Georges before 1935 I always got the impression that the construction of the vast Maginot Line had given the French a sense of false security. If the Germans were rearming, so what? They would never get past the Maginot Line. But gradually my friend Ronin began to get a little uneasy. Would the Germans become so strong that they could ignore this grand line of fortification? France, like Britain, suffered tremendous losses during the First World War and it seemed unlikely that the French nation would be able to whip up sufficient enthusiasm to try to stop the Germans a second time in open warfare. Pacifism in France was probably even stronger than in Britain, and the Maginot Line mentality was comforting, if dangerous. I had of course told Georges all about my conversations in Berlin with Hitler and Reichenau, and we both agreed that if the Germans were intent on re-invading Europe, they would come with all the might of their new war machine round the north of the Maginot Line. Georges and I were not supposed to be military strategists. Looking back at the knowledge which we had, however, and tying it in with those remarkable but unheeded warnings of Basil Liddell Hart, one cannot but be amazed at the 1914–18 War mentality of the General Staffs of Britain and France, and the way in which the French General Staff, under General Gamelin, deployed their forces to meet the German attack of 1940 with but twelve divisions of troops holding the vital sector just north of the Maginot Line opposite the Ardennes front and their tank divisions scattered throughout the whole front. In many countries, the Government and generals responsible for thus blindly sending out a poorly armed, ill-equipped expeditionary force, out-numbered, out-gunned, out-tanked, out-flown and ultimately outflanked and outwitted, after they had been receiving information about *Blitzkrieg* for five solid years, would have suffered a fate much worse than being gently removed from office or promoted.

I wanted to find out as delicately as I could why I had been asked not to pass the Goering 'bible' information to the French. I had brought over some of the extracts of the flying school report, and I intimated to Georges that these were from a highly delicate source which I would not want him to pass on verbatim even to his French Air Ministry. Instead of taking me up on this, Georges just looked mildly puzzled, asking me if there was any particular reason why he should not do so. I smiled at him and said, "Well, that's what I'm trying to find out." And then for the first time since I'd known him he admitted that he himself was not sure of his own General Staff. There was some question, too, of a friendship between Goering and the French Air Attaché in Berlin. Georges said he didn't know how far it went, but he agreed that it would be wise not to say precisely where my new information was coming from. Provided I gave him the outline of the information so that he too could fill in his own picture, he promised that it would be so mixed up with all his other data as to be untraceable. I knew Georges well enough then to tell him that in fact it came from the German Air Ministry itself. He smiled broadly and said, "Now we're getting somewhere, aren't we?" So whenever I received the photo copies during the next few years I would pass them to Georges minus any of the page or chapter references at the top, and he in turn never allowed them to leave his own office except in a disguised form.

We then got down to details of what we knew. He was anxious

to find out more about the coming strength of the new Luft-waffe bomber force. I had very little on this subject then, but was to get a photo page dealing with the training of large numbers of air crews soon after I returned to London. Air crews are not used in fighter or dive-bomber aircraft, which are operated by single pilots. Air crews must denote bombers, and thousands of air crews meant hundreds of bombers, so I asked Desmond Morton to intensify his search for signs of larger aircraft being built. By autumn 1935 we knew that Heinkel, Dornier and Junkers were creating two-engined bombers, each one of which was capable of carrying one ton of bombs, but we did not know at that time what size the individual bomb would be.

The role of the bomber in coming wars was still uncertain in 1935; the concept of a heavy type of bomb was quite new to our thinking, for the RAF only had a few thirty- to fifty-pounders, which had been used defensively amongst rebellious villagers on the Indian north-west frontier. We had no large plane capable of carrying bigger bombs, nor had the French. If Hitler was going to build up a large bombing force carrying five-hundred- to thousand-pound bombs, then it could only mean that he was going in for total war. Nobody knew what the effect of heavy bombing was likely to be in 1935, but it was clear that such large bombs were not just for controlling rebellious tribesmen; their use would be bound to cause de-struction over a wide area. Nor had my experience of Nazis given me hope that civilians would be left out of this holocaust. In the end it proved to be the shock waves and not the blast effect from heavy bombs which did so much damage to build-ings and factories; they acted like a mini-earthquake shattering the buildings. But even if I did not understand as yet how the bomb would function, I could see that such huge ones would do incredible damage.

German participation in the Spanish Civil War did not hap-pen until 1937, but when it occurred it was an obvious practice exercise and a warning of what was to come. By then Georges and I were already concentrating on the subject, yet despite all the evidence and all the reports we both wrote about the numbers, types and performance of the German bombers, the outbreak of war still found Britain without a heavy bomber. The ignorant general public were stunned by the devastation caused by the block-busting five-hundred- and thousand-pounders dropped on London by the Luftwaffe. Again, as in the case of the tanks, there had been a lone voice crying in the wilderness, not Liddell Hart this time, but Air Marshal Victor Goddard, who had incessantly clamoured for four-engined bombers for the RAF in the thirties.

As the months built up through 1936 and 1937 the morale of France seemed to me to be gradually sinking, and even Georges, without actually giving me details, became afraid of a sell-out to Germany by the French politicians. In the middle of 1936 I myself saw some evidence of this. Bill and I were in Rosenberg's office in Berlin and Rosenberg was expounding his usual theme of why Britain should keep out of a second world war. He was telling me what I had already begun to fear, that the morale of the French Army and the French nation was bad, and that we were pinning our hopes on an alliance with a country that would be a broken reed. Why did we not take the bold path, break our alliance with France and give our support to a Germany that would destroy Communism for us? I don't know whether he had intended to needle me but I was certainly very annoyed at the suggestion that Britain would just tear up her treaties, and I said so. Rosenberg went red in the face and then he strode over to a filing cabinet at the other end of the room. He looked for and pulled out a file which he slapped on the table. "If you will take a look at that," he said, "you will see what I mean. For your information it is a list of prominent Frenchmen who are already in our pay." Something clicked very quickly in my brain. This was a highly dangerous moment. I closed the file and handed it back to him, but not before I had seen one or two names at the top of the list. I never gave this information to a soul except my Chief. To report it back to a Francophile Cabinet in London would have put a time bomb under me, but it was certainly a warning to be extremely careful in my dealings with Paris. I never even hinted to Georges of what I had seen. I was quite certain that all the officers whom I dealt with were absolutely loyal, but I suspected that they were uncertain of some of their own people at the top. It wasn't until after the signing of the tragic Hoare-Laval Pact condoning Mussolini's conquest of Abyssinia that it struck me that perhaps Sir Samuel Hoare had already had some idea of Laval's association with the Nazis and might have been afraid that I would find it out. If I had done so and reported it back to London, it might have upset his own association with that notorious French politician.

It didn't seem to matter how gloomy the situation became, Georges and his French colleagues were always determined to brighten up my visits. My arrival in Paris was the signal for an official lunch to be given by my friends of the Deuxième Bureau. The service pay in France was never over-bountiful, so a slap-up lunch on the Republic was very welcome. Seven or eight of Georges's colleagues would foregather at a well-known restaurant on the point of the Île de la Cité, not far from Notre Dame. There, in a private room looking out over the gardens with their shady trees, to the accompaniment of the occasional chuff of a barge going up river, we would eat food and drink wine fit for the gods. I suppose one can still obtain such meals if one is a millionaire.

We did not talk 'shop', and conversation inevitably turned to the best shows to see; the latest night spots where the most exquisite girls were to be found. Did I know that the principal dancer at the Bar Nudiste who, quite obviously, had the most perfect figure in Paris, was married to a wealthy industrialist who collected her in his Rolls Royce every night after the show? Did I know that the most beautiful nudes at the Bal Tabarin were English? How lucky we must be in England! As the lunch ended the younger members of the French party would begin looking at their watches and would be excused by their Colonel. The bare wooden tables in their offices would see them no more that day, but entry to the doors of the 'Houses of Pleasure, Officers for the use of' closed at three in the afternoon. The rest of us would sit on a while discussing whether there was anything more we could do to prod the politicians into practical preparation for what we felt sure was inevitable.

We would stroll back to the offices of the French Deuxième Bureau. The stout green gate in the high wall would be opened by the aged concierge, and as we entered we would secretively look left and right along the street to see that we were not being followed. On one occasion this solemn, cautious procedure was interrupted by the arrival of an ancient, rickety old lorry whose blue-bloused driver got out of his cab, took two mail bags from the top of the open lorry, threw them on the pavement and shouted: *"Voilà, pour les espions."* I was reminded of the true story of my Chief arriving at the offices of the Secret Service, which were at that time in a quiet road in Kensington. Milk for the office cups of tea was also being delivered to this apparently private house. The Chief casually asked the milkman who lived there and got the prompt reply, "The Secret Service." At least it gave my Chief a good excuse to move to more central quarters somewhere in Whitehall, though no doubt the local milkman there was equally well informed.

My host in Paris had lived in Russia for a good many years before coming to take the job of 'our man in Paris'. It was natural therefore that he should mix a good deal with the large contingent of White Russian émigrés in the city. They were a strange, unpredictable, delightful, courageous collection of people. Those that had been able to smuggle out jewels or cash had set themselves up in small shops. Some of the ex-Guards officers had bought taxis which they drove with Cossack cavalry élan. Many of the womenfolk—delicate, black-eyed china dolls, often princesses or grand duchesses—formed small groups and sang Russian songs to the accompaniment of balalaikas in the restaurants where borscht, blinis and vodka flowed.

A rather wizened ex-Air Force General, who never stopped smoking Russian cigarettes, painstakingly and skilfully compiled for me a list of the new Russian Air Force squadrons being formed in the USSR. Just how he got the hundreds of bits of information which formed the basis of his calculations as to the strength and disposition of the new Russian Air Force I do not propose to disclose, but at a time when Moscow had put an iron security net around the country, his methods were extremely ingenious. I used to sit through hours of smoke-laden arguments carried on between this old General and a Russian-speaking colleague in Paris and I gradually learned enough Russian to check for myself the carefully guarded secrets he had acquired. On paper it all looked formidable, but when studied in detail it did not as yet pose any real menace.

8

Politics

The British have always looked to their Navy for protection and have usually presumed that in times of war they can produce a powerful volunteer Army at remarkably short notice. Even by the 1930s the Air Force played no part in their thinking; it was merely considered to be a useful adjunct to Army reconnaissance. Herein lay my problem, for I was working at Air Intelligence and so I could not help but see that a radical change had taken place in German military strategic thinking which the British Government had neither recognised nor understood.

The Germans were giving their Air Force pride of place, for they were making it their most powerful aggressive weapon; it would ultimately be capable of striking not only at any country's Navy and Army but also at its transport, aerodromes, factories and civilian installations. The Nazis believed it was capable of being totally destructive. For this reason my figures on the build-up of Nazi air power were much more important than they seemed at first sight. Listening to the German leaders collating the facts and figures of their rearmament programme, I could not help but see that there was a logical consequence to it all. Their talk of 'expansion' might not include Britain, but their belief in an entirely different concept of warfare deserved notice.

The British still thought in terms of battleships and destroyers, of artillery and divisions of soldiers. Their generals were not even over-enthusiastic about the tank except as support for infantry regiments, even though the primary exponent, Liddell Hart, was an English Army officer. The idea of divisions of tanks on the German scale backed by massive air support never entered their minds. It was not that the military did not understand the words I used but rather that the ideas I was trying to put across did not fit in with their thinking. Our Army training was primarily of a defensive or administrative nature. Officers who had served in the First World War, either in command of infantry or artillery or even of a few tanks, found it difficult to switch their minds to a war of swift aggression.

But it was not only the military mind in England that failed to see the potential of air power. Neither the Navy nor the politicians saw it either. Indeed, the Navy failed to grasp its significance after the war had begun until the sinking of the *Prince of Wales* and the *Repulse*.

I suppose it was inevitable that I should feel frustrated that the information I was obtaining about the aggressive intentions of the Nazis did not seem to me to be receiving sufficient attention except by the Air Force Staff. I think too that it was difficult to convince people of the huge difference between the quiet, rather self-satisfied capital of London and the aggressive, ebullient atmosphere of a new revolutionary dictatorship. I began to feel that there must be something wrong with my own ability to convey the menacing new atmosphere of Germany to those in London. I soon realised that it could only be absorbed if one went to Germany itself as I did, moving around the country in the highest Nazi circles. Banners, rallies and revolutionary fervour were one thing, but I had been given the opportunity to see behind all this the ruthless efficiency which I felt would one day catch us unawares. It did so in France in 1940.

I thought it might help if one of our politicians came over

to Germany with me to see what life there was like. I chose first to approach Frank Fletcher (later to become Lord Winster), a member of the opposition Shadow Cabinet. I thought a member of the Labour Party with pacifist views would be more receptive to my suggestions, and as he had only recently ceased working in our office he would be more amenable.

I went to see him at the House of Commons. I don't know whether he was frightened at the proposition and was therefore making an excuse not to visit Germany or whether he was genuinely disinterested, but the gist of his reply to my request was, "My dear chap, I couldn't possibly do that. Do you realise that if a working family today has a cracked teacup, they can't even afford to buy a new one? I have really got to try to do something about that. That's politics, my boy." This extraordinary reply made me realise how impossible it was to drive home the Nazi menace to a Labour Shadow Cabinet minister.

Looking back I suppose it was not surprising that I found it difficult to follow the devious path of British politics during the middle thirties; the apparently deliberate failure of either party to accept or believe any information concerning Nazi rearmament and aggressive intentions frustrated all those who were trying to collect it and puzzled those people in the services whose job it was to ensure the safety of their country. One could not help assuming that if the Government decided to accept the information I was providing, they would eventually be forced to take some action, but that for political expediency they determined to procrastinate for as long as possible. I wondered why the Labour element of the Coalition, and later the Labour opposition, did not call for action to stop the Nazis. It seemed that neither the Conservatives nor the Labour Party were willing to risk the loss of votes by advocating a programme of even limited rearmament. It was true that after the holocaust of World War I, which was supposed to end all wars, the people of Britain were not anxious to fight again; and we now know that in 1935 Baldwin thought that whoever told the British public the truth and suggested rearmament would lose the vital votes needed to be returned to power in the coming General Election. It was probably also true that

if the Conservatives themselves seemed anti rearmament, Labour MPs were downright pacifist, and I was forced to the conclusion at the time that Baldwin and his colleagues must have
argued that if Labour came to power the state of affairs would
be immeasurably worse. I personally think that, in the light
of events which followed, Baldwin was wrong not to bring
all available information into the open in time to do something
about it. Winston Churchill, well briefed by Desmond Morton,
was continually asking questions in the House of Commons
on German air rearmament and yet I know that on at least
one occasion Baldwin rose to answer a question, with the latest
estimates which I had been asked to send to him at his urgent
request that morning in his pocket, only to reply that he had
no information on the subject.

Knowledge with the benefit of hindsight is always easy, but
I believe that if Baldwin had stood up and unfolded a picture
of the Hitler menace to the people of Britain, he could have
won the election of 1935 on a programme of limited rearmament, and a harder attitude towards the Nazis would have
been accepted. As it was, the first public indication that he
was beginning to regret his studied refusal to acknowledge
the facts came in May of 1935 when in a speech to the House
of Commons, referring to estimates of German air strength,
he said, "I was completely wrong, we were completely misled
on that subject." The second half of his remark was of course
untrue but he was evidently determined that somebody else
should take the blame.

My Chief, the Admiral, was usually a reasonably calm person
but Baldwin's phrase made him see red. It was a deliberate
remark, so no doubt the hunt for a scapegoat would soon be
on, and my Chief was determined that neither he nor I would
be the quarry. I had always kept him very closely informed
about all the information I was getting from Germany. Now,
in late June 1935, he summoned me to his room with the request that I summarise all the evidence I had ever obtained
right from my first meeting with Hitler and bring him samples
of the latest data that I had received, for, as he put it, "We've
got a tough situation on our hands now." It wasn't difficult to

make out an impressive summary from the information from our men in the various capitals of Europe; but, in addition, I had the material from Goering's 'bible', especially the page showing the setting up of all the training schools; an unanswerable rebuttal to any suggestion that my facts had been moonshine. I took the summary along to his office together with the actual photograph. He looked it over, ordered his car, rang the buzzer for his secretary and told her to tell the Prime Minister's secretary that he would be round at 10 Downing Street shortly. Thereupon he put my pieces of paper in his pocket, took out his bowler hat from the top drawer of his filing cabinet, placed it firmly on his head, unhooked the umbrella from the hat stand and marched out of the office.

It was the privilege of the Chief of the Secret Service not only to see the Prime Minister whenever he wished, but also to see the monarch, and one of the badges of his office was the key to the side door of Buckingham Palace which was presented to him by the King himself, a custom which I understand originated with King Charles II.

With the Chief of the Secret Service's complaint before him, Baldwin now took the opportunity he had been waiting for to let somebody else 'carry the can'. He ordered an enquiry into the whole subject of German air rearmament at Cabinet Committee level, to be held in July. At last we were getting somewhere. My Chief warned me to prepare my case very carefully. This I did, and a few weeks later, as we drove in his car around to the meeting, he again warned me that if I failed to convince the Cabinet of my views I might very well lose my job. "There are plenty of people", he said, "who would be only too delighted to get it."

I was taken by surprise by the strength of the Committee, and I think my Chief was too. Not only were there three Cabinet ministers seated at the long table when we arrived—Cunliffe Lister, later Lord Swinton, and on either side of him Lord Runciman and Sir Kingsley Wood—but facing them was a top-level delegation from the Air Staff: Lord Londonderry himself, the Secretary of State for Air: his Chief of Staff, Sir Edward Ellington; and also Air Vice Marshal Chris Courtney, Archie

Boyle and finally the young officer in charge of the German Section of the Air Ministry. Besides this Air Ministry delegation were my Chief, Desmond Morton and myself. I wondered whether the Air Ministry were going to oppose or help; they certainly looked remarkably glum.

Lord Runciman, grimly proper in his stand-up starched collar, took very little part in the proceedings; but Sir Kingsley Wood, who had once been Air Minister himself, questioned most intelligently. I knew that Lord Londonderry was on my side from that earlier meeting that I had had with him when I first came back from Germany. Chris Courtney was a personal friend of mine, as was Archie Boyle, but I had my doubts about the young Air Force officer who was responsible for collating all German Intelligence in the Air Ministry. He hadn't been there long and he'd never struck me as efficient.

It had always seemed a mistake to me that these young officers were only drafted into Intelligence jobs for about two years at a time, for no sooner had they learned the ropes than they were moved on. They never became deeply involved in what they looked upon as boring desk work but tended to hanker after their flying, which did not encourage efficiency in Intelligence. Moreover, they seemed to think that my job was solely to supply them with bits of information which it was then their sole responsibility to collate with any material they received from other sources. They did not welcome any discussion or specialist knowledge and were seldom willing to co-operate closely with me. Together with my colleagues in the Secret Service I was continually pressing for a more permanent system for Intelligence officers at all the ministries. We advocated a combined unit which would ensure the same co-operation amongst the three services that we in the Secret Service gave each other; but this, alas, was not to come about until the 1950s when the three services were combined under the Ministry of Defence.

I got the impression from Lord Swinton's opening remarks that he'd read all my reports and that he too was on my side because he began by asking the Chief of the Air Staff to state the Air Ministry's case. This was to my advantage because I would then know what arguments to bring forward. I don't think the Chief of the Air Staff had been well briefed because he at once indicated that the young RAF officer would do the talking. He didn't talk very long, for the burden of his statement was that he just didn't believe what I'd been sending in to the Air Ministry. I saw Lord Londonderry's eyebrows go up a bit at this, and Lord Swinton asked him if there were any particular items of information that I'd supplied that he didn't believe. He replied that it would be impossible for the Germans to train the number of pilots and air crews I was suggesting and for them to build the number of aircraft necessary to produce first-line strength of from three to four thousand during the next three years; therefore, the whole project was exaggerated. Swinton looked to Sir Edward Ellington for confirmation of this view, but the Chief of the Air Staff remained stolidly silent. Archie Boyle clearly felt bound to back up his young officer in some way, so he said that he hoped I would produce some irrefutable information to enable them to accept my figures. Well, this was just what they were going to get.

Lord Swinton then asked me for my views. I turned to the young RAF officer and enquired if he had noticed the hidden Air Staff in the German War Office list? He looked baffled, and all the heads of the Air Staff went up in disbelief. I explained how I had found this hidden Air Staff and how I had talked to two of its members. Not only that, but that I had myself helped to choose one of them to be Air Attaché in England. I then started right at the beginning and told the Committee of my meetings with Hitler and General Reichenau; I quoted some of the reports from our agents in other areas of Europe and explained how it all dovetailed with what the leaders of the Nazi Party had told me of their intentions. The Chief of the Air Staff was so completely absorbed in my revelations that it was clearly the first time he had heard any of this. As for Lord Runciman, the one and only remark he made during the entire conference was: "Did you really talk to that man Hitler?"

In sending details over to the Air Ministry I had never been allowed to give the precise source of the information. That would have been far too dangerous. But I did mark it with my personal estimate of reliability, by grading my sources on a sliding scale from A1 downwards. It was extremely rare to have absolute reliability, which was my category A1, but this was how I had described the information from Goering's 'bible'. Now I felt that it was imperative that I break this source secrecy and drop a bomb on this meeting, so I produced the two photographs and explained precisely what I believed they were. I then detailed the check-up results which I was getting on these lists of flying training stations from other sources and forthrightly announced that I personally had no doubt whatsoever that the whole of this organisation would indeed be able to produce all the pilots and air crew necessary to fit Hitler's schedule.

Still my young friend on my right demurred. Would nothing convince him? Turning to Christopher Courtney I asked him if he could remember our own figures on pilot production during the worst years of the First World War for he, like myself, had been through that war and knew the phenomenal number of pilots we'd turned out under pressure. Luckily he agreed with me that the number of flying schools the Germans were setting up would enable them to reach the pilot target I'd mentioned without any difficulty in comparison to what we ourselves had been able to do over fifteen years before.

By now I was almost home and dry. I'd been speaking for about an hour, but my young friend was determined not to give in. Maybe they could get the pilots and the crews trained in time but they couldn't possibly design and build the aeroplanes. He was adamant.

At this Desmond Morton rose to his feet and gave chapter and verse of the vast extensions being built at all the German aircraft factories. He quoted the great areas of land now turned into factory floor space; the quantities of tools and machinery which were known to have been supplied to these factories; and he explained that although the figures of actual output were slow to reach him, he anticipated that over the next year he would be able to get an accurate picture of total aircraft production in Germany which would agree approximately with my figures. Desmond was splendid. He'd got all the data at his finger tips and reeled it off in the most forceful manner so that there was absolutely no way of arguing with it. The Air Staff were now convinced. Lord Swinton was smiling broadly. The meeting was concluded, the Chief, Desmond Morton and myself leaving first. As I bowed to the members of the Air Staff on my way out, Archie Boyle gave me a perceptible wink. On the way back in the car the Chief said, "I think you did very well," which coming from him was considerable praise. But it was Desmond Morton, I pointed out, who'd finally clinched the case in our favour.

A few days later Lord Swinton took over from Lord Londonderry as Secretary of State for Air. Poor Lord Londonderry had been Baldwin's scapegoat. A most delightful man, I'd always felt that he was far too sensitive to be in the hurly-burly of politics in the thirties: he was much more suited to his role of brilliant political host at Londonderry House. Here he and his wife gave glittering parties for diplomats, politicians, writers and artists; he performed to perfection the delicate job of intermingling the various sections of national life. When I was invited to one of these some time later, Lord Londonderry smilingly asked whether the new Secretary of State was giving me all the support I needed.

As soon as Lord Swinton was installed in his new position, he sent for me to find out how co-operation between the Air Ministry Intelligence and my department was progressing. I explained that I still had to work on my own in fitting the pieces of the puzzle together as the Air Ministry personnel preferred to keep their collating to themselves. Then and there he sent for Archie Boyle and told both of us that in future there must be much closer co-operation and co-ordination. He then suggested that I find a suitable person to help me as it looked as though I would be having plenty on my plate from now on.

At last some momentum was building up; progress was being made and people were taking notice. This was the way I liked to work. It didn't take me long to recruit John Perkins, who was the younger brother of Robert, my local MP in Gloucestershire. A great friend and a great aviation enthusiast, he was also Parliamentary Under Secretary to the Minister of Air and was one of the people I had had along to help entertain the young German pilots the year before. My Chief, somewhat impressed, I think, with my performance, provided all the extra secretarial staff that I needed. We were on our way.

I was told later that as a result of the Cabinet Committee meeting that I had attended, Baldwin had agreed to set preparations in motion for the building of shadow aircraft factories and for the re-equipment and expansion of the Royal Air Force. This could now be done, he felt, without raising too much comment and it undoubtedly helped when, after Munich, Chamberlain gave the go-ahead for full-scale modernisation of Fighter Command. But it was all too little, too late. When, in 1936, Hitler marched into the Rhineland, neither we nor the French had any teeth to back up our objection, nor was it until November 1936 that Baldwin finally admitted his mistake in not taking German rearmament seriously. I quote from Hansard:

I put before the whole House my views with an appalling frankness. Supposing I had gone to the country and said that Germany was re-arming and that we must be armed, does anyone think that our pacific democracy would have rallied to that cry at that moment? I cannot think of anything that would have made the loss of the election, from my point of view, more certain.

So here at last was the admission why they did not want to know what I had to tell them. But I believe that Baldwin was profoundly wrong; the stakes were too high, the risks too great and our eventual losses too appalling to have passed up the chance to try to stop Hitler in 1935.

9

Détente

By March 1936 Hitler evidently felt that he was strong enough to challenge France and Britain to see if he got any reaction from them. In defiance of the Versailles Treaty he marched into the Rhineland. Both London and Paris were taken by surprise. Hitler had also taken several Luftwaffe fighter squadrons into this demilitarised zone. After both London and Paris had decided that they could do nothing about them, it was revealed that these few fighter squadrons had been flying from one aerodrome to another, changing their insignia from time to time, to give the impression that Hitler had a vast concentration of fighter aircraft to meet anything that the British or the French could put up. So Hitler got away with it, which must have encouraged him to think that the British and the French Governments' lack of action meant they were funking the issue. I have little doubt that he now felt convinced that the more he thrust his vast rearmament programme down our throats, the more embarrassed our Government would be and the less likely to start interfering in any future plans for expansion. His bluff had come off.

When I finally revisited Germany in the summer of 1936 I

found a very different Rosenberg from the one I had got to know in 1934—more withdrawn, much fatter, sallow and a bit 'crumpled'. He was immersed in his ideology, preparing plans for the dissemination and control of his new religion, not only throughout Germany but right across the rest of Europe including Finland, the Finns being 'true Aryans'. He was also flirting with the free Ukrainians: this, I suspected, was more of an anti-Russian gambit than an exercise in Nordic propaganda. He explained that he had delegated some of the conduct of foreign affairs in order to give himself more time to organise his priesthood, but he had retained the job of keeping Hitler personally informed about foreign press comment and had trained a public relations staff to deal with foreign press correspondents in Berlin.

One warm evening in our favourite little café bar on the Kurfürstendamm Rosenberg opened out about his plans. He told Bill and me that he had actually started to build a great cultural centre, rather on the lines of an enlarged Vatican City, in southern Germany. It was to be the centre of the Nordic cult throughout a 'unified' Aryan Europe. It was to have great colleges where the apostles of the modern ideals for survival would be instructed. I nearly asked him if it was to have a Stonehenge-type circle in place of a St. Peter's, but the poor chap was so carried away with his vision that I just kept quiet and listened.

Was Rosenberg's anthology made out of Nietzsche's works to become the Nazi bible? Perhaps this new Rosenberg, rather withdrawn, apparently lonely, often seeking out Bill to talk to in the little café, was preparing himself for his high priesthood and beginning to have doubts about his ability to carry it out.

Rosenberg wanted me to see something of the effect of his ideological ideas on the youth of Germany, so he decided to attach one of his young press officers to me to take me about wherever I wanted to go in Germany that summer. I, on the other hand, had got quite a few things that I wanted to check. We had received some useful information from Goering's 'bible' about an experimental station at Rechlin up on the Baltic, and from this information it appeared that new types of aircraft, including the Messerschmitts 109, 110, the Junkers 87, the Heinkel 111 and the Dornier 17, were all undergoing tests at this isolated station. I hoped to get more details about these from some of the young pilots in the Luftwaffe Club. But in case I was not successful I'd set in motion the possibility of one of our Baltic friends getting a fishing boat near enough to see what the prototypes were like. I was also interested in the question of the Nazis *vis-à-vis* the Army, and the timing the Nazis had in mind for their expansion adventures. I wanted to know for certain how they proposed to neutralise Western Europe before they went into Russia. Were they going to try diplomacy backed by force or were they going to stage a *Blitzkrieg?* Bill told me that he had made friends with an important Nazi called Erich Koch who was the Gauleiter, or Governor, of the province of East Prussia. Koch was also a friend of Rosenberg's, and I suspect that Rosenberg had suggested that I go up to East Prussia to see something of Koch's successful work in that province. Rosenberg was quite honest about what he wanted me to learn and openly stated that he wanted me to see for myself and not be influenced by propaganda.

It was a large programme. We arranged that Bill would tackle the political angle through Rosenberg, while I would get out and about and meet the people, not only the boys and girls in the street who, incidentally, were growing excited about the future and had a very good idea that war was inevitable, but some of the more influential Nazis who would, I knew, talk to me if they were given the go ahead by Rosenberg. I felt that the year 1936 was going to matter to England. If we had little chance of standing up to the Nazi war machine, we might at least gain some leeway by initiating a diplomatic game of chess. In the event of course we did neither, but at least we had a breathing space which enabled us to know exactly what we would be up against in the air.

Karl Boeme, the young member of his press relations staff whom Rosenberg had delegated to look after me, with instructions that I was to see whatever I liked, was also a useful cover. Any inquisitive outsiders, such as the anti-British Hearst Press of the United States, or other pro-Nazi hangers-on, could be told I was being given the usual courtesy of a foreign press representative.

Karl Boeme had just become Professor of Journalism, a chair no doubt invented for members of Rosenberg's staff. There is a German expression which literally translated is "a good Charles"—meaning "a good fellow"—so I used to call Karl "a proper Charlie": he felt more than complimented. He was a cheerful, good-looking young fellow of about twenty-seven or -eight, about 5 foot 10, fair, sporting well-cut shirt and breeches. He liked to be smart, and he was the joy of most of the barmaids on the Kurfürstendamm. He had a quiet, rather plump little wife who lived in Hamburg, and who sometimes came to Berlin in terrible tweeds with her wire-haired fox terrier. I gathered that wives were not encouraged to appear in official Nazi circles—this was a man's world.

The Nazis insisted that their members whose work entailed contact with foreigners should learn the appropriate language. Charlie was struggling with English; thanks to an extraordinary system by which they had to learn off by heart a hundred words of English a week, and then learn to string them together in the right order afterwards, he was progressing rapidly, and gratefully used me to practise on.

Rosenberg was due to visit Lübeck, that wonderful Hansa city on the Baltic, for a few days. He suggested that Bill and I should go too and that Charlie was to come along to ensure my complete freedom. It was hot midsummer in Berlin so we were only too glad of a chance to visit the sea. The drive up was rather dull; the country was flat and uninteresting and the roads at that time were not as good as those further south.

As usual, when a high Party official was due, forests of crimson banners festooned the city, ruining the lovely old buildings. I think these banners must have been transported from one place to another as required. I simply cannot believe that each town had such a large collection. There was not the same warmth or enthusiasm as further south. The Baltic folk have always been an independent lot and they were a bit cautious in their acceptance of the Nazis. Nevertheless, there was a small crowd waiting outside the principal hotel to see the arrival of Rosenberg; he therefore advised the canter technique into the hotel. This was the last time that I was asked to carry out this drill as the danger to the leading Nazis had more or less receded.

The following day was Midsummer's Day and Rosenberg proudly announced that he would take us to see the new Nazi version of the Festival of the Solstice. No doubt this was one of the main reasons for his visit but he had, I think, been a little nervous about telling us in case we found some excuse not to come. He was keen to show us some of "his own work" in the ideological field. Maybe he found the Baltic folk more interested in the pagan rites than the southern Germans. Worship of the sun-god probably fulfilled the primitive needs of our forefathers when it came to bad harvests and low fertility, so I thought we might be in for the sort of ceremony performed by the present-day Druids of Stonehenge, colourful reminders of our own pagan origins, or even some singing like the choir on top of Magdalen Tower at Oxford on May Day morning. Accordingly, I approached Lübeck's ancient fortress with great expectations. In the centre of the gravelled ramparts was the circular roof of the ancient keep; on it stood a circle of identical Hitler youths, shoulder to shoulder, exactly the same height and shape, fair hair, blue eyes, dressed in their pale khaki shirts and shorts, 'totally Aryan'. Rosenberg and his party, which included us, took our seats nearby and the battlements now echoed not with the clank of armour or the whistle of arrows but with centuries-old pagan litanies chanted by the circle of Aryan boys. At midday there was a shadowless silence as the sun hung for a moment directly overhead, and then a paean of praise rang out for the Aryan sun-god. The whole performance had been in deadly earnest. Here was no lighthearted compliment to tradition. Here the youth of Germany were being indoctrinated with a new creed, the creed of their own racial superiority; of the glory of their Aryan state reflected in the sun. This creed could only breed arrogance, and despite the ancient setting and the warm sunshine I did not like it at all. But of one thing I was quite certain: the youth of Germany would at this time have set up any false gods their Führer had asked them to.

We are told that even up to the time of our own King William II human sacrifice existed in England, though by then it was confined to the head of the state. When bad harvests made the plight of the people desperate, the flight of the arrow that slew the King in the woods was no accident. Was this Aryan nonsense going to revive the human sacrifice? As Rosenberg watched the performance with enthusiastic approval, I put the question to him. "No," he said, "the Nazi version of the festival needs no human or live sacrifice." But only recently he had had considerable trouble with an ex-General up in Schleswig whose fervour had induced him to seize and sacrifice one of his farming neighbour's best cart horses and then to lead a barbaric dance round the corpse stark naked. This was going too far, and much as the Party appreciated the distinguished military support, the General had had to be stopped, in the face of local disapproval. I gathered that the culprit was old General Ludendorff, who had given the Nazis so much support in the early days down in Munich. There was not a trace of humour in Rosenberg's voice or in his face when he told me this absurd story. How little time was to pass before human sacrifices beyond the comprehension of even barbaric pagans were being made in the gas chambers!

That evening in our hotel I tackled Rosenberg on the whole subject of his new—or perhaps re-hashed—ideology. I was already aware from his remarks when we were in Luther country in 1934 that he held the Christian religion in some contempt. I knew, too, that the rules of dictatorship demanded that all existing religions must be supplanted by the worship of the state. The Nazis had identified this with the Aryan race and it was a logical step to return to the paganism of their supposedly Aryan ancestors. Looking back I suppose I was rather critical of Rosenberg's new religion; maybe I went a bit too far, but I tried hard to point out to him that if he had any regard for history—and history has an uncanny way of repeating itself—then his plan to eradicate all the old beliefs and customs which had been used through the ages, albeit too often abused by ambitious priests, would surely alienate a large part of the older population who might otherwise go along with the Party. I was, as I have already stated, aware that a successful dictatorship must have both an internal and external enemy, the former providing an excuse for getting rid of anybody that you did not like, and an external enemy to rally the people against possible danger and form a good excuse to build up a large army. We had seen it in the USSR, where the spies and saboteurs were the internal enemies and the "imperialist reactionaries of the free world" the external ones. Now in Germany, under the Aryan cult with its fallacious theory of purity of race, the internal enemy was the Jew, and the external enemy the Communist; both were potential destroyers of the Third Reich.

It is probable that history, in the long run, will remember Hitler and his henchmen for their greatest evil—the murder of over six million Jews. This wholesale slaughter did not start until long after I stopped going to Germany. Persecution was at that time confined to the wrecking of Jewish property, like the jeweller's shop in the Kurfürstendamm which I saw sacked by a carful of howling young Nazis, or the extortion and confiscation of money. Lucky were those families who got away alive during that period.

I had argued the Jewish question with Rosenberg back in Berlin and had left him in no doubt that the Nazi policy of Jewish persecution was probably one of the main reasons why the United Kingdom would give Hitler neither help nor encouragement. He countered by accusing the British of having imposed their own government on half the world. But here I was able again to reinforce my advice about religion. I told him that the success of the British Empire had been primarily based on non-interference with the religions and customs of the people to whom we had given peaceful rule; missionaries yes, but that was peaceful persuasion. We had endeavoured to replace tribal wars with justice, but interference with religious beliefs, never. Rosenberg then went so far as to tell me, and I believe he was speaking the truth at that time, that he was trying to establish some sort of refuge for the Jews in Brazil. Of course it never came off. I find it hard to believe that the gas chambers were contemplated by the Nazis in those early days of 1935–6. I believe they hoped that the persecution they were adopting would force Jewish families to leave Germany. Figures have been given that suggest that about half of them did get away, but where could the countless others go? Maybe if the conquest of Communist Russia had gone according to plan, there would have been some sort of resettlement of Jews in that country. I think it was when their plans began to go wrong that the latent bestiality of the Nazis emerged. It is the old, old story of how unlimited personal power, unrestricted by the ballot box, will turn the human being into a tyrant and the failing dictator into a maniac. The killers amongst them went berserk. But I do not believe that either Rosenberg or Hess initially meant to murder; Rosenberg gave the killers their cue with his Aryan nonsense, so he cannot escape the collective moral responsibility of the whole bunch, while Hess, after his flight to Scotland, lost any authority he might have had over the bloodthirsty SS. But I do not believe that either started out with murder as their goal.

I had got a bit hot under the collar arguing with Rosenberg, so perhaps it was to try to cool me off that he suggested a day or two by the sea at Travemünde by way of relaxation. This resort on the Baltic Sea is an attractive spot in high summer and was evidently being used by some of the more senior Nazis for their holidays. There were a number of them there with their wives, families and girl friends, and the large modern hotel seemed full and well run. Whether it was part of the 'Strength through Joy' organisation I never found out, but it was gay with the girls in their summer frocks; there was dancing in the open air and cool drinks. In fact the whole place was quite human. It seemed as if everybody was enjoying the absence of the saluting and the banners, the marching and the other Nazi symbols of Berlin. Rosenberg had asked several Nazis with their wives and girl friends to join our party. Charlie was becoming a little restless; there was no selection of seductive blondes for his entertainment, nor was there any attempt to draw them across my path. However, I did notice one very striking girl of evident Slav origin who seemed to be attached to one of the officials, and I casually asked Charlie who she was. Charlie wasted no time; she was brought over and intro-

duced to me. We danced. Her escort was found some very
urgent business in Hamburg that very afternoon. Josephine
was a Yugoslav from Zagreb. She was well educated and spoke
several languages, including fairly good English. Her exquisite
figure, her dark eyes beneath raven hair, her gaiety and her
philosophy of Life with a capital 'L' had led her to the theatre
as a dancer in Berlin, where she soon became the toast of
the young Nazis. I don't think Rosenberg really approved my
non-Aryan choice.

It was at Lübeck that I made my first contact with the new
German Navy, which had been greatly restricted both at Versailles and in a treaty with Britain. Two brand-new destroyers
had just been completed and the Chiefs of Staff of the Navy
and of the Army were there to see them put through their
paces. Rosenberg represented Hitler—I imagine because of
Hitler's dislike of the sea. Other Nazi officials included the
head of the Armament Programme, but it seemed to me odd
that, to the obvious annoyance of both the sailors and the Nazis,
Werner von Fritsch, Chief of the Army Staff, and several of
his generals, had decided to come too. Rosenberg murmured
to me that the Army was there to establish its position as the
senior service over the Navy. I wondered if maybe it had something to do with Hitler's previous deal with the Army, who
were determined not to let the Navy get as close to the Nazis
as the Air Force had done under Goering. The situation was
tense. Even Rosenberg showed contempt for a young Army
officer (who happened to be a grandson of the great Bismarck)
as he slithered all over the decks in his incongruous jackboots
ordering the sailors out of his way.

Once out at sea the little ships raced about with great speed
laying smoke screens and firing dummy torpedoes. It was a
thoroughly good propaganda exercise for the young Navy. Rosenberg, anxious to escape having to talk to the Army on the
way back to port, took Bill and me down to the junior officers'
wardroom. These young men were mainly sons and grandsons
of German naval officers of the old régime, an entirely different
type from the Army types up on deck. Pleasant-mannered and
most talkative, we spent quite a while having drinks with them,

listening to their excited hopes for the new German Navy. Although great battleships had been banned under the Treaty of Versailles, Hitler had already flouted such restrictions and laid down the keel of a vast new battleship, the *Bismarck,* so the young officers were hoping for more of these in the near future. We had a lively discussion as to the weapons these giants should carry; it ended in a good exchange of views on the ship-versus-aircraft argument then exercising the minds of sailors everywhere.

Later that evening we were invited to another naval party in Lübeck where I met a most delightful elderly retired Admiral. A very courtly old gentleman, he began by telling me about the Kaiser, to whom he had been ADC for a number of years. The Kaiser had a passion for strawberries and used to start with a pilgrimage to Corfu in the early spring, gradually working his way northwards through Europe as the strawberries ripened, ending up in East Prussia or Norway in the autumn. The Admiral said he got sick and tired of the strawberries, but the Kaiser never did. As the evening progressed, he became increasingly garrulous. Soon he was telling me all about the design of the new battleship *Bismarck,* its gunnery control and unsinkability. He was expanding on the vast number of its watertight compartments when Charlie, who was with me at the time, panicked and raced off to fetch Rosenberg.

I had always been completely open in my conversations with other people when I was with Rosenberg, and I was so now as I told him what an interesting discussion I had been having with the Admiral about the new *Bismarck,* being careful to recap the discussion for him. Rosenberg was not in the least perturbed; in fact he seemed pleased that I had shown interest in Germany's latest achievement. His cheerfulness calmed Charlie's fears but the Admiral clammed up and was not to be drawn out further.

I always found that most information is usually to be obtained from people by just listening to them in an appreciative fashion. My axiom was never to ask a direct question and I only broke that code once in my entire time in Germany. Sharp ripostes and obviously loaded queries put people's backs up and make them wary. Most people are only too happy to talk to a good listener who offers the occasional intelligent comment, and they will ramble happily on with a few judicious promotings; the art lies in directing the conversational flow unobtrusively. Those who enjoy their profession are usually particularly happy to explain its intricacies to someone who seems genuinely interested, and the members of the new German armed forces were no exception. The enormous pride most Germans felt in their country's resurgence under Hitler made most of them keen to explain their latest ideas of warfare. I was always most careful not to appear too inquisitive, but to amass whatever information each person was willing to divulge. I would then add each scrap to whatever the next informant proffered, and so on. The fact that I was sponsored by Rosenberg meant that the many conversations I had with different Germans over the years enabled me to build up an amazingly detailed picture of what was going on in the country as a whole; how they were feeling, and what the general consensus of opinion was. It was a matter of listening, remembering, storing and collating. Each bit of information helped to fill in a piece of the mosaic, even if at the time it might not have seemed relevant. However, information could not always be garnered so easily. Sometimes one had to work at other ways and means of obtaining it.

One of the reasons why the Air Staff had been puzzled at the apparent 'target' for the build-up of the Luftwaffe was that they could not at first bring themselves to believe the figures of the German training programme that this sort of expansion would entail. It certainly needed a mammoth effort to train thousands of pilots and air crew, not to mention the vast ground organisation required for riggers, fitters, armourers and communication units, plus all the other ancillary personnel required for a very large Air Force, if it was to be completed in the time available. Pilot and air crew training was one of the items I had been very closely quizzed about at the Cabinet Committee meeting already described, and I lost no opportunity to see and hear personally all that I could on this subject when I was in Germany. Both I and my French colleagues

had deduced from the information which we had received
from Germany that the flying training programme was, with
true German thoroughness, standardised and spread over a
number of given aerodromes. Training for the Luftwaffe and
for the Naval Air Service seemed to be on parallel lines. All
this had emerged from the precise documentation in Goering's
Air Force 'bible', which laid down the whole organisation, with
the training, equipment and operational roles of each German
air unit down to squadron level.

There was a flying training school listed at Wannemunde
just across the canal which ran in from the sea at Travemünde,
and I made an excuse after we had returned to Berlin to take
Josephine back there for a few days' holiday. It passed all too
quickly, but as we lay on the sandy beach it was not difficult
to estimate the daily number of hours flown by counting the
number of aircraft in the air during most of the day. It was
of course much more difficult to estimate how many pilots
there were in training, but about a dozen aircraft were up
in the air from dawn to dusk. That one school alone must have
turned out fifty pilots a month during the summer.

During these few days at Travemünde with Josephine I
talked to ordinary young Germans, many of whom were enjoying a holiday by the sea, paid for by the state 'Strength through
Joy' organisation, while awaiting posting to some job either
in the forces or the factories. Charlie's smart Nazi uniform
had not, I felt, always drawn unbiased views from those we
had talked to, but Josephine thought it was all a lot of fun
and with her charm and gaiety soon got young and old chatting
about life in general under Hitler. That summer of 1936 she
and I talked to dozens of ordinary citizens not yet in uniform,
whether at Wannemunde or on the shores of the Wannsee
Lake near Berlin, in bars in the town, or in the cafés and
restaurants outside the capital. They were often intrigued by
this tall blond Englishman and his Slav girl friend, but one
incident reminded me forcibly of the ugly side of the Nazi
coin.

Josephine and I went out by the metro to the Wannsee Lake
for a swim and a sunbathe. We were lying face downward

on the hot June sand so that neither of us noticed a group of
bronzed young Nazis until they were close beside us. They
looked belligerent and I quickly realised that they had probably
mistaken Josephine's lithe body with its deep chestnut suntan
together with her raven hair as belonging to a Jewess.

As they stood over us, Josephine turned over and they saw
a broad grin beneath her little tip-tilted nose. Their embarrassment was enhanced when she told them I was a guest of Rosenberg, and she cleverly turned the whole incident into a laugh
with apologies from the young men. But it wasn't funny and
Josephine herself, I knew, had been frightened. As for me,
under different circumstances, I should have been beaten up;
I realised for a moment what it must be like to be on the
receiving end of the Jewish persecution. We had another swim
to cool us down.

When I finally left Germany that summer it was with the
conviction that the vast majority of non-Jewish Germans fully
supported the Third Reich. Perhaps the more elderly did so
for fear of the alternative, Communism, but the young gloried
in a new-found purpose, in the promised fulfilment of a dream
of a great German Empire in which each of them would have
a vital role.

From what one saw and read in Britain at that time, I do
not think that those whose job it was to keep the British public
properly informed about events in Germany put nearly enough
emphasis on this dangerous surge of patriotic fervour. Rather
were they too inclined to dwell on the misfortunes of the perse-
cuted minorities, on political manoeuvring and on external
trappings. Too often the spectacle of Hitler whipping up vast
audiences into evident euphoria with his extraordinary oratory
was made fun of; cartoonists exaggerated his comic opera en-
tourage. Funny it may have been to the outsider, but inside
Germany the promise from the new Messiah of a Thousand-
Year Reich flowing with milk and honey, backed up by Goebbels' subtle propaganda, could only lead to war. Why weren't
the British public told so more often and more forcibly?

From my conversations came little bits of information which
I strung together to try to assess the timing and the intentions

of the Nazis. Hitler and company were not building all these planes, tanks and bombs for fun, for defence or for a show of political force, but for aggressive action. The youngsters argued that there must be some bloodshed, obviously, in the great expansion of the Reich, but the whole conception of over-whelming military force would ensure that it would be minimal and that in the event Germany would be hailed as the saviour of Europe. The speed with which their armies would occupy the selected areas would be so great that it would be all over before anybody really knew it had started. *Blitzkrieg* again. The idea that they might have to fight the English had not occurred to many of them; most accepted the logic of their Führer that in the unlikely event of England being ungrateful enough for Germany's war against the Communists to enter the conflict against her, the matter would be dealt with quickly and almost painlessly.

A few, however, appeared to think otherwise. Josephine in-troduced me to one young man who had joined Goebbels' Prop-aganda Ministry just a few days before, for, as he explained to me, everyone had to join something. He hadn't wanted to go into the Army and as lots of extra people were being re-cruited by Goebbels, he thought he would prefer to go with them. We all sat drinking for a while in a café, then as I moved off to get some more beer, I heard him say to Josephine, think-ing I was out of earshot, "He seems a good sort of Charlie, it's a pity we've got to fight them." Had Goebbels not the same faith in Britain's possible neutrality as Rosenberg or Hit-ler? For a moment it made me wonder whether Hitler and Rosenberg's neutral-Britain policy was just a bluff to stop us rearming. If so, they need not have bothered.

The next time I was in the Luftwaffe Club I tried to bring the conversation round to whom the possible next war would be against but found the pilots cautious and divided on this point. On the whole I felt that Hitler had been genuine in his belief to me that we would not fight, and Goebbels equally honest in his expectation that indeed we might. It was some-thing I should have to learn more about.

Most of the talk in the Club was about the pilots' training

programme, their "crash courses", as they called them. So I thought I would look at one of the aerodromes where these took place. While I was trying to organise this I received a note from the Air Attaché asking me to go to see him. Events had taken a bizarre turn.

Hitler had decided to order real détente between the Luftwaffe and the Royal Air Force. He had, he said, been worried by the exaggerated reports on the Luftwaffe build-up in the British press, and now he asked for two senior officers from the Air Ministry, together with their aides, to come to Germany where they would be shown exactly what the Luftwaffe was doing. The Attaché told me that the invitation had been issued by Erhard Milch as the Secretary of State for Air, and that the Air Ministry were going to reply shortly with the names of the people they would send. There was a note for me on this from Archie Boyle saying that he thought it would be better if I kept out of the way of the delegation since this was an official visit, which would be carried out in full uniform.

I came to the conclusion that Hitler must be getting desperate about British neutrality; he evidently must have thought that if he could make official contact with the Royal Air Force and show them some of the might of the modern Luftwaffe, it would pressurise the British Government to keep out of the coming conflict. I was anxious to hear Rosenberg's reaction to this latest move by Hitler. I hadn't long to wait for he soon sent a message round asking Bill and me to go to see him in his office. Rosenberg was cross, he said, because he hadn't been consulted on this move and Hitler had gone over his head straight to Goering. It was, incidentally, interesting to note that Goering hadn't sent the invitation. He probably didn't approve of it but had to do what Hitler ordered and so passed the job on to Milch, no doubt so that he himself could escape any criticism that might arise later.

Rosenberg asked me if I had any official information about the visit. I told him that the Air Attaché had informed me, but as this was an official communication between the two air forces I didn't propose to butt in. Instead, I was making arrangements to go up to East Prussia. Rosenberg pointed out rather bitterly how thoughtless it was that the part both he and I had played in founding this understanding between the two air forces had been disregarded; now we were apparently both to be left out of it. I told Rosenberg that this seemed to be the way of the world, that those who started something good usually found that someone more ambitious came in half-way and reaped the benefit at the finish. He remarked that perhaps both he and I ought to be a little more ambitious. I could hardly explain to him that ambition didn't fit very well in my line of work except in so far as I wanted to find out what the Luftwaffe was doing. Nor could I explain to him that I didn't expect personally to get any kudos out of this détente. True, I had started it, but now it was being taken over and at last the Air Staff would be able to see for themselves that I had not been talking nonsense.

Two air marshals accompanied by two more junior members of the Air Ministry staff duly arrived in Germany and I was to learn later on in London exactly what they had been shown. They visited the Air Staff itself and the Air Staff College. They were shown the new Richtofen Fighter Wing, now in the summer of 1936 equipped with the ME 109. They were shown the production line at Heinkel's factory on the Baltic coast and the newest aircraft, the Heinkel 111, the Junkers 86 and JU 87, and the Dornier 17. Bombers and dive-bombers were demonstrated to them and they were given the performance figures, which must have frightened them somewhat. However, this didn't satisfy Air Marshal Courtney, who asked Milch for his production programme, upon which Milch produced his 1934 programme which he said was due for completion in 1938. It comprised thirty bomber squadrons, six dive-bomber squadrons and twelve fighter squadrons, some 2,340 aircraft in all; and he then said that to date some fifty percent of the programme was completed, meaning 1,116 first-line aircraft. However, because these figures did not agree with those I had given the Air Ministry, Courtney said that he was under the impression that more had already been built. Milch admitted the error and told him that the figures he had given had been completed nine months earlier. Thus, at the end of 1935 they already had fifty percent of the programme complete.

I was to learn from Rosenberg later that Goering had been

wise to keep out of this détente because now Kesselring, who became Chief of Air Staff in 1936, openly denounced Milch for giving away the Luftwaffe secrets. In fact, Rosenberg gave the impression that there was a good deal of in-fighting going on between Goering and his principal officers. Rosenberg was still disgruntled when I came back from East Prussia and went on down to Nuremberg. However, I think I had done well to keep clear of the official mission because Kesselring, now Chief of Air Staff, welcomed me with more than usual courtesy. Two weeks after the mission returned to London, the newly promoted Major General Wenninger was given similar details of the Royal Air Force, according to current planning. This showed that the RAF would have 1,736 first-line aircraft plus an immediate reserve by the end of 1938.

There was, however, one particularly interesting point about this détente: Milch not only asked our delegation in Germany not to take any notes, but he also asked them not to pass the information to the Foreign Office because he did not wish it to be passed to the French. He obviously felt that once it was outside the hands of the Air Ministry it would somehow be given to the French. When Courtney told me of this provision laid down by Milch, it struck an immediate chord. I knew that Milch, when he had been chief of the civil airline Lufthansa, had been very friendly towards Britain, and the outcome of this détente also made it clear that he did not wish to go to war against us. None of the planes we had learned about so far were long-range bombers, so it did not look as though Milch had built an Air Force with Great Britain in mind. Had he, I wondered, been the source of my photographs from Goering's 'bible' with the similar request that it should not be passed on to the French? It seemed quite possible now, and the fact that Kesselring was denouncing Milch for giving us information fitted the picture; there seemed to be a Goering-Kesselring faction who were bloodthirsty for revenge against England, while Hitler, Milch, Rosenberg, and, I suspected, Hess, and maybe other members of the Nazi hierarchy, were playing for British neutrality. Goebbels was evidently preparing for either.

10
East Prussia

Hitler's act of détente had taken a great load off my shoulders, for now we knew the performance of the German aircraft which would make up the Luftwaffe and the Germans' own estimate of their production programme. At long last our civil servants and politicians were beginning to understand what was happening and seemed likely to look more kindly in future on the information which I might be sending them. My facts and figures had proved approximately correct, so those in power above me might perhaps trust my reports from now on—or was that hoping for too much? It was just as well that Hitler's splendid act of open showmanship had occurred when it did, for obtaining information was proving increasingly difficult. In addition, Rosenberg had been squeezed out of the Foreign Relations Department by Ribbentrop. However, it would still be possible to obtain data on factory and aeroplane production, although this would now be hived off into Desmond Morton's industrial output section. My job would be to find out more about the general efficiency of the Luftwaffe, its training and tactics. I would also keep a watching brief on dive-bombing training, aircraft armament and performance and the possible production of any new type of gun or bomb. As always I would be listening for the slightest whisper which suggested that a new secret weapon had been invented, for news of their radar research, and for any murmur of advances in their development of aerial photography and code techniques. But first I would have to concentrate on discovering more about the Germans' intentions against Russia, endeavour to gain a clearer idea of the dates when they were likely to begin war operations and the probable order of procedure.

With Charlie Boeme once again detailed by Rosenberg to look after us, Bill and I set off for Königsberg to meet Erich Koch, the Gauleiter of East Prussia, from whom we hoped to obtain data about the Russian front.

As a special JU 52 had been laid on entirely for our benefit, I asked Charlie if we could see as much of the country as possible. It was an amazing land to the east of Berlin, densely covered with forest interspersed by small lakes. From the air the little areas of water glistened in the sunlight like so many mirrors nestling in the deep green velvet forests which stretched away to the horizon. There seemed few areas of good land, and it was here in the east that I knew that a number of military aerodromes had recently been carved out of the forest, so I asked the pilot to see how many of these we could count. He happily found and flew over five or more of them within reasonable range of our direct route. I found that these aerodromes were all precisely the same pattern, designed to hold about two squadrons. But now the skies around us were filled with operational aircraft, a considerable advance on those I had seen at Wannemunde; proper military types which seemed to make our old Junkers machine look as if it were standing still. This was certainly an opportunity I would not have missed; it was the visual proof of the information from Goering's 'bible' which had been backed up by our other sources. If what I had seen was being duplicated all over the country, the present effort in Germany would certainly be able to meet Milch's programme and supply a large pool of fully trained pilots in reserve.

We had to land at Danzig for customs. It was not difficult to imagine the irritation of the Germans at this restriction, one of the less sensible provisions of the Versailles Treaty. Nevertheless, the famous Danzig Geldwasser, a sort of Cointreau liqueur with specks of gold leaf floating around in it, was very welcome, and the blonde Polish barmaid was duly noted down in Charlie's little book. On leaving Danzig we flew on along the Baltic coast and up the long canal leading from the sea at Pilau to Königsberg some miles inland. I noted the range of new concrete shelters for U-boats under construction at Pilau.

Erich Koch was at the aerodrome to welcome us with his broad smile and noticeable lack of 'Heil Hitlers'. We joined the waiting cars at an ordinary walk. The tension so evident in Berlin seemed much less, just a hint of anti-Russian feeling which was understandable if one lived next door to a nation that had recently slaughtered hundreds of thousands of its innocent fellow-countrymen and seemed determined to destroy the form of free enterprise socialism so dear to Erich Koch's heart.

Erich turned out to be a veritable cock-sparrow of a man; he'd been born and brought up in the Ruhr, a railway worker by trade, and he was a passionate Socialist. He had, however, seen no future in trades unionism under the Nazis, so had wisely decided to achieve his ambitions by joining the Party in 1925. A natural organiser, whose stocky 5-foot-6 frame exuded energy, he survived the in-fighting in the Party and managed, when Hitler came to power, to be given the job of Gauleiter of East Prussia, an area cut off from the rest of Germany by the Polish Corridor. Here he hoped to carry out his Socialist plans with little interference from Berlin. I liked this enthusiastic man as soon as I met him, for he had none of the arrogance of the jumped-up Nazi yet was close enough to the hierarchy to know a great deal. He was clearly a close personal friend of Rosenberg's, although I gained the impression that he used this friendship to enable him to obtain what he wanted for his beloved province; it was not based on admiration for any of Rosenberg's "theories", as he called them. In Berlin Rosenberg had already given me some idea of Koch's passion for his resettlement scheme in East Prussia for the overcrowded families of the Ruhr, so I was not surprised when he offered to take us to see his special planning department, run, surprisingly enough, by a young Jew. As Koch explained in detail all the plans he had for the future, he bubbled over with zeal.

He had soon found out that practically the whole of the agricultural land in the province was in the hands of the old Prussian families. But these gentlemen had not bothered to make their estates pay; in consequence they were all heavily mortgaged to the state. There had been some sort of fiddle by which the landlords did not even pay any interest. It was therefore easy for Koch to foreclose these mortgages and take over the land. He did, however, leave the barons enough land around their houses to run a home farm and to continue to use their titles. At least this is what he told me, and I certainly saw some examples of it. It was a wise move, for the barons did not mind very much as long as they had somewhere to live; many, I think, were relieved at not having to worry about their lands and their mortgages.

One family had certainly got things straight. Koch took us to spend the night at a plain, square-built baronial hall not far from Elbing. We arrived late in the evening; Koch told me that the Baron was away but that the Baroness would look after us. I envisaged a legendary stretch of high-necked, tight-busted, ankle-length black alpaca between buttoned boots and a scraped-back bun. The stout doors were opened by an aged retainer in knee breeches and as we were ushered into the lofty, softly lit, heavily panelled hall a very beautiful woman in a white gown, which had not stopped on its way from Paris, greeted us. At first sight I thought it must be Marlene Dietrich herself, so alike were they; later she told me she was Polish, which explained both her elegance and her vivacity.

I do not know whether the Baron was away permanently, but the house had turned out to be a 'welcome home' for a select few of the higher Nazis when they came to East Prussia. Goering used it as a hunting lodge when he came up after moose and deer. Hitler himself had been to stay, and Erich

Koch seemed quite at home there. I felt sure my extremely attractive hostess looked after them very well. It would have been interesting to hear more from her about her guests, but alas I did not have the opportunity of talking to her alone. We dined and wined from the very best, and Koch did more than justice to his second helpings.

There was a son of the house, a swarthy boy of about fourteen, totally unlike the Baroness; I think he must have been the son of a previous wife. He had evidently been trained by his father. Once, when the old retainer had not jumped to his command, he sent him flying through the baize door with a kick and a curse. The Junkers still thought they were in charge in some places.

I slept in the special bed which had been built to hold Goering; at least there was plenty of room to move about.

When Koch had chosen a site for one of his settlements, instead of building the houses in the middle, he put the factories at the centre on the railway or river. Most of the light industries, some of which were evidently connected with the rearmament effort, he brought out from his native Ruhr, together with the people who already knew how to operate them. The houses, shopping centres, sports grounds and swimming pools were then located outside the factory area with plenty of roads leading in. The houses, in this way, could be planned on a garden suburb principle with all their amusements close at hand.

Outside the housing belt again there was a ring of small holdings for those small farmers who preferred to produce vegetables and perishable produce. These holdings had only to deliver into the housing belt and need never penetrate the industrial centre at all. Outside these small holdings again were the larger farms growing grain and livestock. Such a set-up could never have been attempted unless whole areas of land had been available from the start; the idea seemed good and Koch was immensely proud of what he was doing.

There was no false showmanship either when we visited a number of houses without any warning; the new tenants were genuinely delighted to see Koch. He admitted he made the initial mistake of putting the bathrooms downstairs. The old habits of keeping the coals in the bath die hard, and so upstairs went the baths where it was too much trouble to carry the coal anyway!

It was summer time and the sight of so many kids from the black Ruhr enjoying the open-air swimming pools was refreshing.

Elbing is a typical small, old-fashioned East Prussian town, built on three sides of a large gravel square, perhaps two to three hundred yards across, all the houses whitewashed and with red-tiled roofs. At the far end stood the stalwart building of the town hall with a few other three-storey buildings, one of which was the local hotel. It was here we came to have lunch on our way to see the historic Hanseatic Castle of Marienberg.

As usual our party—Koch, Bill, Charlie, myself and one of Koch's boys from the Planning Department—arrived without notice. However, the hotel readily agreed to put on lunch. The landlord, anxious to honour the Gauleiter, promptly told the mayor, and the mayor and corporation insisted on coming too—all three of them! This, in turn, meant getting an extra waiter. The one they found was out of practise and in his nervousness spilt the soup all over my suit. There was panic! I think the mayor suggested shooting at dawn, the landlord just a year in gaol; however, my assurance that no harm was done together with a tip to the waiter seemed to rectify the situation.

Marienberg was originally built in the late thirteenth century, about 1280. It was enlarged in the fourteenth century and was the seat of the leader of the Teutonic Knights. In the great hall were a series of richly painted murals showing the history of this Hansa outpost which was half trading post, half fort, much as the old trading posts of the East India Company used to be before the British Government took over India.

Our guide was an ex-Prussian officer of the First World War, still very stiff and correct, complete with eye-glass and duelling scars. The first mural showed the Prussian peasants in the days when Marienberg was originally built. To my surprise they were wearing only bearskins and carried wooden clubs; even our rural population of the thirteenth century was becoming slightly civilised and I pointed this out to our guide. He nearly exploded; his stiff collar just managed to contain the reddened, swollen neck. At last, unable to insult me in front of Koch, he turned on his heel very precisely and strode off. I had no idea the Prussians were so touchy. Koch burst out laughing, which did not improve matters.

However, we found an old caretaker who showed us over the rest of the castle. One could imagine those early traders watching from the battlements, looking down the river for the approach of the stout Hamburg ships. Marienberg must have been a very isolated place in those days.

When we returned to Königsberg, we found the town a forest of red banners in honour of·Hess, who was staying at our hotel. He was his usual quiet self, and, no doubt due to the calmer atmosphere of Königsberg, a little more relaxed than when I first met him in his spartan office near Hitler's in Berlin. As I was leaving the sports display given by the local Hitler Youth and rows of buxom young women, I kept a few paces behind Hess and I found myself in a broad corridor of grass between a living, impenetrable wall of six-foot-tall, black-uniformed, white-gloved, steel-helmeted giants standing shoulder to shoulder. I marvelled at the security technique which the Nazis had worked out, and I remember thinking how different was this man strolling rather shyly towards his waiting car from the ordinary run of strutting, saluting service men and SS who now seemed so thick on the ground back in Berlin.

We went to the play that night, and I was given a seat next to Hess. The local company had chosen the play *Coriolanus,* principally because every few minutes somebody gave someone else a Nazi-type Roman salute. It seemed to amuse Hess, but he turned to me and said very quietly, "You know, it isn't really necessary." He was much more interested in opera and talked of music which he evidently enjoyed, though I gathered he did not share Hitler's passion for Wagner.

There were a number of naval officers up from the submarine base at Pilau for this occasion in order to meet their Deputy Führer, and after the show the Commander of the base suggested that I might like to go down the next day and see the place. He promised me a rousing evening in the mess. This was a bit tricky because I had already learned before I left London that a secret submarine base was being constructed at Pilau, and ever since I started coming to Germany I had made up my mind to act as a normal person would do, being careful not to appear too inquisitive but always interested in what I was told. After all, I was in reality a spy; so once again, as I had done in Weimar, I made up my mind quickly not to go to Pilau just in case someone in the German Navy should get suspicious. I thanked the Commander but said that I knew that the Gauleiter had arranged something else for me, so, much as I would have liked to come and meet his officers, I was afraid it would be impossible. If Rosenberg had been present he would probably have encouraged me to do so and I would then have gone, but Charlie was with us in Königsberg and I'd seen how he'd panicked when I had been talking to the old Admiral about naval affairs. It was a pity because I would very much have liked to have seen inside one of those new bomb-proof submarine shelters. I noticed that Bil! had been watching me rather anxiously and no doubt he too thought it would be too risky to accept. As it was, the whole party went back to the hotel and we had some drinks together. I think too that Hess was relieved I had refused the invitation. He bade me a friendly goodbye as he went off to Berlin.

Koch had suggested that I might like to go to see an amber mine, one of the very few in the world. Apparently the reason for the amber's presence was that long ago when this whole area, together with the Baltic Sea and Scandinavia, had been covered in great pine forests, some giant storm or meteorite had felled a wide swathe of trees from East Prussia to Sweden. The pines, cut down in full vigour, had oozed great lumps of resin which in due course had been buried and turned into amber. That part of the amber bed which now lay under the Baltic was continually washed by the sea, which accounted for the bits of amber we used to pick up on the beach at Felixstowe on the East Suffolk coast when we were kids. It was uncanny to see ordinary flies and mosquitoes encased in great lumps of transparent gold and to realise that they were millions of years old. There does not seem to have been very much evolution in those species since then; maybe they had already reached their full state of usefulness as scavengers before man evolved.

Amber in large lumps like potatoes must always have had rarity value, but I was astonished to find that the mine had such strong police protection. The manager seemed nervous as he showed us round, and when we returned to the cleaning and processing plant, after visiting the great open-cast mine, he became increasingly worried. Finally he took Charlie aside and asked if it was all right for foreigners to see what was now a war factory. Charlie gave him the OK and laughed with us over the idea that we might be seeing anything we should not. The manager explained to us that the amber was melted down and purified to make particularly fine resin which was used for covering electrical wiring. I did not go deeply into the matter in order not to appear too interested and so embarrass the man in charge. Instead I suggested that it seemed such a waste of a lovely material which was so valuable for necklaces and beads, especially esteemed in Moslem countries, whereupon he assured me that the market for necklaces had been cornered by the British and that the resin was unique for certain classes of insulation at extreme altitudes. The final answer to that one came in 1944 with the 'V' weapons.

There was one other place in East Prussia I wanted to see and that was the great stud farm at Tracheneu. Before the First World War this used to supply nearly all the horses for the German cavalry regiments; goodness knows how many mares were kept in those days. In 1936 this lovely stretch of rolling grassland was only partly occupied. The vast paddocks with their white wood railings were dotted with clumps of oak and pine for shade. In the centre of the farm were the stud buildings erected round an enormous quadrangle. The whole scale of the place was prodigious.

Even now a number of paddocks were full of the most lovely horses. Four colours were bred here—chestnut, grey, bay and black—and I suppose there were about fifty mares of each colour running with their foals of the year. Other paddocks held the yearlings and still others the two-year-olds. I gathered that there was some system of putting them out on farms as two-year-olds until they were fit to go to the few remaining cavalry units or perhaps to private ownership now the cavalry was all but finished. Any one of the horses I saw would have made a good hunter. The stallions were mostly imported either from the United Kingdom or from Ireland. To anyone with a love of horses it was a wonderful sight.

I had noticed that since Hess's visit Koch had been rather quiet and subdued. He in turn noticed my concern and said that Hess had told him there were going to be a number of generals from the Army visiting his province in the near future. He looked somewhat surprised and even alarmed when I said that I supposed this was in connection with the Russian invasion. However, I went on to tell him what Hitler had told me and about my conversation with von Reichenau in Berlin. Then he let himself go; he said that just as he was trying to get his province into some good working order, the whole place was going to be over-run by the military, who were going to build concrete this and concrete that and railways and spoil this little province. He told us that he had decided to come back to Berlin with us if we would give him a lift.

I was sorry to leave East Prussia. Here was a little enclave, untroubled up to now by racial bitterness or by extreme Nazism, being transformed from its feudal harshness into a well-planned Socialist state under a benevolent dictator; a man who put people before things. And now as we flew back over the sand dunes which divide a large inland lake from the Baltic Sea, both Erich Koch and I felt sad about what was in store for this land. We both knew. He asked me to come back again. Not only had my visit to East Prussia produced confirmation about the Pilau base, even if solely from the outside, and a small clue regarding resin which might come in useful; but I now had a good friend in Koch, who would, I felt sure, talk more freely another time. I certainly intended to return.

11
The Vital
Question

The détente between the Luftwaffe and the RAF continued in 1937, a year in which I tried to complete the jigsaw puzzle of the Luftwaffe, fitting in all the small items which were now coming in freely from our various sources in Europe and the bigger pieces from the photos of Goering's 'bible' which were still arriving from Berlin. The Luftwaffe itself was beginning to flex its wings in public. In July Ernst Udet, who was evidently responsible now for aircraft production, came over to the Hendon Air Show; and both Milch and Udet were seen at Zurich in Switzerland showing off their ME 109 fighters and the DO 17 bomber, which proved, in the international field, to be faster than the fighters from the various countries that took part in that air display. Also on show there was the new Daimler Benz 600 aero-engine.

In July the principal designer of the Bristol aero-engine, Roy Fedden, was invited to Germany for a tour of the Messerschmitt aircraft factory. When he came back he told me that he'd never been so frightened in his life both by the rate of production and by the performance of these latest German

fighters, the ME 109 and the twin-engined ME 110. No doubt
that was the object of the exercise.

As the summer wore on, Desmond Morton started to get
very interesting information about German shortages of those
materials necessary for any rearmament programme. Apparently not only steel but aluminium were now scarce, and a
contact in one of the aircraft factories advised us that the target
for 1938 would not now be completed until the spring of 1939.
This was indeed good news. No doubt it accounted for a number
of contradictory reports we began to receive about the total
first-line aircraft which would eventually form the Luftwaffe;
they had obviously run into difficulties.

In September of 1937 the Germans held fairly large-scale
manoeuvres to which some foreign military and air attachés
were invited, and according to the information given to them,
the Germans fielded over thirteen hundred aircraft, all new
and modern machines. For the first time the Stuka dive-bomber
was seen in action. As it dived out of the sky it cannot have
seemed all that menacing, for it did not alert any of the military
as to its potential; at that time it was not fitted with its screaming
siren device. None of the senior French nor British officers
watching recognised it as dangerous. They did not seem able
to envisage the effect it would eventually have as it screamed
down like a demon to drop a large bomb directly onto the
troops and guns below. Perhaps it was the absence of a spearhead of advancing tanks crawling along the ground at the manoeuvres which lulled them into apathy. But when I heard
about the Stuka demonstration I remembered all that Hitler
had said to me and felt the old familiar desperation at the
blindness of our senior officers.

The Nazis sent a special aeroplane over to Britain to pick
up a number of visitors who were invited to the Nuremberg
Games in September 1937. I was one of those chosen. Bill
and Charlie came to meet me at Nuremberg and we went
off to the hotel rooms which Rosenberg had reserved for us.
Apparently Rosenberg was unlikely to be at the rally himself
and I later found that he had been down to Austria, no doubt
preparing his Aryan propaganda for Hitler's coup in 1938. I

watched the parades in the stadium with growing unease and gazed with my usual surprise at the frenetic exhortations of the Führer, but the most interesting part of my visit was lunch at an *Arbeitsdienst* camp.

After they had finished their spell in the Hitler Youth organisation, young men between fifteen and eighteen years of age were drafted into these camps, where they undertook to improve Germany by building roads and reservoirs and carrying out drainage and forestry operations. It was a form of pre-military training destined to keep them fighting fit and out of mischief under firm discipline. The ones I saw were a magnificent bunch of boys, with their sun-burned and muscular bodies stripped to the waist as they laid draining pipes along a mile-long trench. I had lunch in their mess room with the young Commandant, who must have been all of twenty-three years old, and I asked him what was the secret of their apparent enthusiasm for their work. He explained it quite simply. He said that these young people had a cause which had been handed to them by the Führer. They knew quite well that shortly they would be drafted into the armed forces and that they were going to be part of the great new German Reich. "It's exciting for them, you know", he said. I remarked that it must be a bit of a job keeping such a high-spirited bunch of youngsters under control. He evidently mistook my meaning because he replied, "One teaspoonful of bicarbonate of soda per head per day, and sex doesn't even start to rear its perverted head." I was to see them in their thousands giving a display at Nuremberg the following year.

On my return to London I discovered that the Air Ministry had issued an invitation to Milch to come over and bring with him a delegation on much the same lines as the one which we had sent to Berlin the year before. Milch and his delegation turned up in England in October in one of their new Heinkel 111s and were shown our own Air Staff College and some of our units which had not yet been equipped with modern aircraft. We were particularly careful not to let any of them see a prototype Spitfire, for that was indeed our top-secret weapon. However, by now we wished to make it clear to the Germans that although we were not prepared or preparing for war, we were still alert to the possibilities and not completely vapid, so we took them to see one of our new shadow factories to indicate that we could expand our production of aircraft at great speed should we be required to do so.

The game of bluff and counter-bluff which we were playing with the Germans was often a very close-run thing. At one party given by Fighter Command for the visiting Germans, Milch asked how we were getting on with our development of radar, which caught his hosts completely off balance, for this particular invention was still high on our secret list. How much did the Germans know about radar themselves? How much did they know about our experiments? We were fairly certain that we were ahead, but this hunch was not yet proven. Early in 1939 a small radar saucer with a central aerial was seen near the Baltic Sea by one of our contacts, and it was this discovery which alerted the Air Ministry to call a special meeting, with scientists Robert Watson-Watt and Henry Tizard present, to find out what I could do to penetrate any German experiments in this direction. At this meeting it was decided to provide me with a young scientist to assist me in this sort of scientific work and so R. V. Jones became attached to my section—a partnership that was to have such excellent results later on. When war broke out we discovered to our great relief that the Germans only had a very short-range experimental radar outfit, which did not become efficient until we started our retaliation bombing later.

Milch had no sooner returned to Germany than Charlie Boeme came over to stay with me. I had invited him while I was at Nuremberg. I wanted to show him what life was like in Britain and to entertain him in my house in the country. I felt it would do no harm and might knock a little bit of the Aryan nonsense out of him. I showed him some of our country pursuits, taking him out shooting and to a Meet of the Cotswold hounds. I myself was riding and Charlie seemed very amused at our pink coats and top hats, which he considered very Old World stuff. Nevertheless, he got thoroughly excited when we found a fox. He was amazed at the good roads that we had in Britain and he said he didn't know that we'd built autostrades everywhere. I explained to him that this was the ordinary London to Gloucester road and that we hadn't yet gone in for the German type of motorway.

When Wenninger discovered that Charlie was in England, he asked us both out to dinner. Major General Ralph Wenninger was now a person of some importance. Since the détente he had become a considerable figure in the politics of the Reich *vis-à-vis* Britain. We went to his flat for a drink and then he and his wife took us on to the Savoy for dinner. Wenninger himself seemed a little nervous and I thought perhaps he'd been advised by the German Air Staff not to talk to one of Rosenberg's men. However, the dinner went through quite happily until the bill came at the end, when poor old Wenninger found that he hadn't brought enough money with him. I came to the rescue, but I could see there was trouble brewing with his wife. Charlie excused himself and I found him eventually, chatting up the cloakroom girl. But before the three of us had left the table, Frau Wenninger had torn a terrific strip off her poor husband. I suppose she thought that Charlie would report it all back to Rosenberg, who would enjoy a chance to have a dig at Goering. Wenninger then asked us back to his flat, where he not only repaid me the money but also gave me another bottle of wild raspberry liqueur, so honour was satisfied.

Just before the end of the year Hitler started to make speeches about how oppressed the German minority was in Austria, saying that it was high time that Austria returned to the Fatherland. These were recognisable tactics: it was clearly just a matter of time before he moved in to collect Austria under his wing. But I knew that when that happened it would be the end of détente between the RAF and the Luftwaffe.

It took longer than I expected for the occupation, as the *Anschluss* did not take place until March 1938. It had been preceded by much ineffectual diplomatic activity which, as I had imagined, knocked détente on the head. Had it perhaps now occurred to Hitler that we were not amused and that there was a distinct possibility that we might in the end fight?

By May of 1938 Bill advised me that everything pointed to some more definite decisions being taken on the timing of the 'expansion'; also that security was being tightened up. All this made it imperative that I go to Berlin, despite the fact we were getting a good deal of data about the Luftwaffe. The crucial knowledge of 'when' and 'where' we could expect to be attacked was not the sort of information that was readily available to ordinary sources. The other question was whether I should be welcome in Berlin, or whether I should now be *persona non grata*. I realised I had had a good innings from 1934 to 1937, and also that Rosenberg's position in the hierarchy was getting weaker as the war clouds gathered. I put the question to Bill: should I be running too great a risk if I came over? Rosenberg had issued no invitation but I had one from Erich Koch to revisit East Prussia. At the same time I didn't want to involve Bill in any trouble. His presence in Berlin would be vital to us and we had already made arrangements to evacuate him to Switzerland if things got too hot. I would have liked to let things cool down a bit after the *Anschluss*, but again the longer I left it the less welcome I might be in Germany.

Bill's reply was reassuring. He himself was still considered an essential English contact by Rosenberg, and he didn't believe Rosenberg or Hitler, who still wanted to maintain contact with the RAF, would consider me unwelcome. I should have to tread carefully, but if we went to East Prussia, we might learn what we wanted to know without appearing too inquisitive.

I decided to go to Germany. I had to know how the *Anschluss* had affected their plans. Was it still to be a Western mopping-up and silencing operation and then the invasion of Russia? Which personalities in the German High Command now carried the most weight, who was applying pressure to whom, and who was Hitler listening to? Were those intent on revenge for the defeat of 1918 winning over the 'leave Britain out of it' faction?

So in the summer of 1938 I returned to Berlin. I reckoned that by this time, if there was going to be a war in the near future, the signs would now be obvious. I was right. In what one might call official circles, in which hitherto I had moved fairly freely, I was now being treated much more carefully. By contrast the pro-Nazi American press and visitors were being given the full VIP treatment. Young William Randolph Hearst of the Hearst Press, already very Anglophobe, was the object of a great deal of attention by Rosenberg's Foreign Press Department. The military seemed more sure of themselves, and the new German Air Force was too busy, no doubt getting their units organised, to entertain visitors. However, having successfully negotiated the open-fronted, non-stop lifts of Goering's new Air Ministry, I was courteously received by the officer in charge of foreign liaison. He was polite but evasive, fobbing me off with bland generalisations. In 1936 I would have been encouraged to go along for a drink at the Luftwaffe Club to meet the pilots. But this time no invitation was forthcoming, so I decided to go along anyway. There was a difference here too now; they seemed aware of my Englishness and were politely noncommittal.

The only inquisitive person was Charlie Boeme, who seemed naïvely curious about what was going on in Britain. I was in his office one morning when rather over-casually he asked me what slogans the English would use in the next war. He was not a very good actor and it was evident that this was a leading question which he had been told to ask by Goebbels' Propaganda Ministry; he had passed the question on to me exactly as he had received it in all its baldness. It was useless to tell him that we did not work out these things in advance and that anyway, His Majesty's Government did not recognise the possibility of war. I was sure that Charlie did not believe me when I denied any knowledge of such plans, and no doubt Goebbels' worst fears were later realised when their own Beethoven gave us the incomparable 'V for Victory'.

Rosenberg himself was out of Berlin and Charlie apologised for his absence. Apparently he was down south somewhere either in Austria or looking after his new 'Vatican'. So I decided to go up to East Prussia as arranged and revisit Erich Koch. I felt that he might be the one to give me some concrete information. Charlie offered to come along, but I told him that as long as he could provide an aeroplane for Bill and myself to go up to Königsberg, there was really no need for him to come as obviously he was very busy in Berlin looking after the Americans. I felt sure he'd been told to do so by Rosenberg and he seemed relieved that we didn't want him to accompany us to East Prussia, but he looked a bit askance at my remark.

I had asked Charlie to alert Erich Koch to our visit, and he came down to the aerodrome to meet us. There was not quite as much bounce about him as there had been the last time I had seen him. He seemed preoccupied and I soon realised that the Army were in his province in large numbers, also that most of the senior officers were staying in the one good hotel. Koch told us that he thought it best that he should take us to one of his little hotels by the Mesurian Lakes, where at least we should get peace and quiet. Also, as he explained, it would save the embarrassment of having to introduce me to a number of generals, who might think it a bit odd that I should be up there at this moment.

Koch appreciated the strange beauty of these long, narrow, dark green waters which lay between steep pine-clad hills where the trees ran right down to the water's edge. I have seen similar scenery on the Wanganui River in New Zealand, but instead of the pale greenery of the New Zealand tree fern, here was nothing but the deep blue-green of pines reflected in the still lakes, whose quiet calmness seemed remote from the mad turbulence of Europe. Erich Koch had built several small hotels by the lakeside, for he had plans for opening up the area as a holiday resort. The only people around were locals from the sparse villages, and it was possible to wander peacefully from one lake to another; sometimes on a sandy road through the narrow gorges; at others in a boat through a modern lock which had replaced some old rapids.

It was a fisherman's paradise, too. The fish were a cross between fresh sardines and brown trout, quite unsophisticated but good fighters. I think they tasted best smoked over a fir-cone fire—a trick I had learned with trout on the shores of New Zealand's lakes.

Did I think the English tourists would come to East Prussia? "Yes, of course they would", I replied. "Well, some time perhaps in the future." What a waste of good holiday material that was!

We spent several days in these idyllic surroundings and it was here that, as I had hoped, Koch unburdened himself. Evidently plans were now well advanced for the great drive East, and East Prussia was, of course, going to be the launching pad. What was going to happen to all his plans for his people? Now flocks of generals swarmed over his beloved land, organising digging here, cutting down forests there, pouring masses of concrete everywhere, tunnelling, laying railways to nowhere: all was destruction and noise. It was heartbreaking.

He didn't know which he disliked the most, the Russians or the generals, and to prove his point he took me round to some of the massive earthworks on our way back to the capital. It was one such bunker that was destined to be Hitler's headquarters for the Russian campaign, and it was here the Führer nearly died when the Army tried to assassinate him in 1944. The military were certainly spoiling the countryside, and the timing of all this construction coincided with the other indications I had seen in Berlin that by 1938 Hitler's plans had been decided upon. I found Koch looking a little sideways at me now and again as if he knew that we were both going to be in for trouble, and I judged that this was probably the moment to put to him the question which I so badly wanted answered. I asked him how long he was to be burdened with these Army people. He smiled and said, "That is in the nature of a leading question." As he turned he looked me straight in the eye and said, "But I have no doubt your Secret Service knows all about it." It was a bit of a jolt but I think by that time I was sufficiently shock-proof to make an immediate disarming reply, "Maybe. I believe they're pretty good but as I have some admiration both for you and your province, I'd rather like to know for myself." Nevertheless, I wondered whether the Nazis had received some warning about me or was the clamming-up in Berlin just a general tightening up by the security services? Koch reflected for a little while, then he turned to me and said, "In my opinion it will take at least three years to complete all their construction, and by that time my poor country will probably sink under the sea from sheer weight of concrete."

So it was to be 1941 at the earliest in the East. This was the first and only time I ever asked a direct personal question of any of the Nazis. I felt that the matter was of such vital importance and that, as it now seemed unlikely I would be able to come back to Germany very much longer, I would take the risk. In any case I persuaded myself that the whole subject of the invasion of Russia was one which Hitler himself had taken pains to see that I was informed about. It was to me the key to the timing of any *Blitzkrieg* in the West.

On our way back to Königsberg, along one of the rather narrow roads, there was a repair job being done, no doubt in order to carry some of the heavy lorries. The whole scene reminded me of my boyhood; piles of broken hard stone being spread by hand and rolled in by an old-fashioned steam roller. There was no room to pass so we waited for a while, and when the driver of the steam roller just went on with his job Erich Koch got out and had a word with him. But Gauleiter or not, the driver was going to finish the job before he moved out of the way. Erich Koch came back to the car laughing. He turned to us and said, "Now that's what I like to see, it's almost English. There's far too little independence among us Germans." There was no belligerent impatience about this man.

I had spent quite a while with Erich Koch. His character was not complex; he was not a racist and, in the true sense of the word, I doubt if he was a real Nazi. He did, however, loathe the Communists, for he hated their genocide, their propaganda, their secret police state and their proximity just over the border. One thing I felt quite certain of was that Koch had not been guessing about the date, nor had he tried to bluff me. He wasn't subtle enough for that.

In my hotel room that night I worked the times out backwards: if the Russian invasion was to start in 1941 it must begin in the spring as soon as the snows melted in early May. That in turn meant that if the Germans meant to have a *Blitzkrieg* attack on France and the West they would have to complete it by October 1940 in order to give themselves time to refit their divisions and re-deploy them from the West to the east Russian front. The Germans always liked to attack in the spring so that they could deprive their enemy of any harvest and more than likely reap it themselves, so we should have to look for signs of a *Blitzkrieg* in the West in the spring of 1940 at the latest. It was now high summer of 1938. That would give them another eighteen months to get their Air Force into shape—which meant for me another eighteen months to try to complete our knowledge of the Luftwaffe. Looking back on it all I often wonder if my conclusions, which I rendered to my office when I got home, were ever seen by Churchill or any other politician or senior military commander. Certainly I was not the only one to hold the views I did, so I only hope my information helped to reinforce the views of those who understood that war was coming. My bosses and my senior colleagues in the Air Ministry certainly agreed with my suggested timings, and it was partly the knowledge that the Germans had to invade Britain before the end of September 1940 or not at all, because of their Russian commitment, which helped us to recognise the Battle of Britain, when it came, for what it was: a crucial turning point with a definite time limit for the Nazis.

Erich Koch came back with us to Berlin to attend the annual rally at Nuremberg. Rosenberg was also in Berlin on our return and we all had lunch together the following day. It was the last time I was to see Erich Koch. In the great German retreat before the onslaught of the Russian armies in 1944 he refused to abandon his province or his people, and in 1945 the Russians took him prisoner. After the war I heard a story that the Germans had stripped a famous tortoise-shell panelling from one of the well-known Russian palaces during their advance into Russia in 1941 and that the loot had been buried somewhere in East Prussia. Perhaps the Russians thought that Koch knew where it was and when he refused to co-operate they threatened to kill him. Knowing him as I did, I am quite sure he would have told them nothing even if he knew.

12
Exposure

When I had been in Italy in August 1936, I found myself shadowed the entire time by the Italians. They kept tabs on me right up to the last moment when the Paris Express from Rome crossed the border into France. This had aroused my suspicions, so when I was back in London I looked into the information available about the various tie-ups operating between European countries. There seemed to be a fairly close Intelligence link between the French and the Czechoslovakian Intelligence Service in Paris. The Czechs had taken advantage of close Anglo-French links to try to penetrate the British Secret Intelligence Service, and had even been reported as watching the house where 'our man' in Paris lived and where I used to stay when in France. Added to this the Czechs had some kind of Intelligence tie-in with the Italians. Would the Czechs have learned about me from their French connections, and had they in turn passed on their information to the Italians? Might the Italians in their turn offer it to the Germans? It seemed to me that too many people were learning too much for safety. Knowledge of this kind is always worth cash to someone; sooner or later the Germans must surely come to hear of my professional role. By 1938 I felt my days as Rosenberg's guest in Germany were probably numbered.

Now, over our lunch together with Erich Koch in August 1938, Rosenberg gave me no encouragement to talk and was himself studiously uncommunicative. Still he had asked Bill and me to dine at his house the evening before we all went down to Nuremberg, so I felt relatively safe for a few days yet.

I spent these next few days wandering round Berlin trying to assess the mood of the people. Security seemed to be tightening up all round to judge by the number of SS personnel on the streets, and there was an air of mounting excitement everywhere; an air of expectancy, of heightened awareness, as though they were all waiting. This was especially marked amongst the young people, who seemed tense, alert, ready to spring off at a moment's notice. The pavements, cafés and restaurants on the Kurfürstendamm were crowded and the Kakadoo, with its large semi-circular bar and its alternate blonde and brunette barmaids, was doing great business. We met the Wenningers by accident outside the Kranzler restaurant and they invited us in to have dinner with them, but not a word was spoken about détente, about the Luftwaffe or about the future. The meal of blue trout from the Black Forest, fresh from the large tank outside, was excellent; but I felt uneasy throughout.

Rosenberg had asked us round to his house the following evening at about six o'clock to have a good long chat with us. He had installed a television set, even though it was only 1938, but it may well have been some sort of closed-circuit affair wired to the radio station close by; however, it worked well, for the picture of a ballet was good.

There did not seem to be anyone else coming to dinner besides Bill and me. Indeed, I never met his wife and daughter, nor the red-haired Jewish mistress he was reputed to have kept in Berlin; as far as I could make out he seemed to be living all alone in this big house, apart from an elderly couple to look after him.

First we had champagne, then for dinner fish and meat embellished with estimable hock, followed by fruit. He had obviously gone out of his way to lay on a first-rate meal, which lasted nearly two hours. Each course was accompanied by a lengthy monologue from Rosenberg, who certainly was not his usual self. Finally, with some ceremony, he produced a tall bottle of sticky, sweet green liqueur from a locked cupboard. By this time it had become obvious from his conversation that he was trying to warn me in some way. I sensed too, from the whole set-up, that this was probably the last time Bill and I would see him alone on the old basis of friendship. Somewhere in the back of my head a red warning light of personal danger lit up. How much did he know?

I began to search my memory to see if there was any way in which I had slipped up. Had someone given me away? The Italians, for instance? But barring my recent direct question to Koch in East Prussia, I could remember no time when I had done anything which would constitute direct espionage in their eyes. My actions had always been beyond suspicion, my conversation simple. They had done all the talking.

Rosenberg had learned a great deal about diplomacy since the days when we had first met him, but this evening, perhaps because of the liqueur which I found undrinkable but to which he did ample justice, he let his hair down and began to talk of our special relationship. This was most disconcerting, for surely I had proved a great disappointment to him in my supposed role of persuading influential people in Britain to see things the Nazi way. I had not been seen to have influenced anyone of importance, so why was he being so effusive?

In his monologues Rosenberg repeated Hitler's declaration to me that three super-powers should govern the world, and the Nazis' hopes of bringing this about despite England's present refusal to co-operate and her apparent lack of any definite policy towards Germany. He reminded me that Hitler was convinced, and all those in close contact with the Russians must believe, that unless Communism was crushed now the world would degenerate into chaos, inflamed, as he put it, by the envy and hatred of the Communist doctrine. He reiterated with some force that the Third Reich would crush this menace and was prepared to go it alone if Britain was for once able to keep her nose out of other people's business. He said this with one of his rare smiles, but I couldn't help feeling that he had accurately summed up the occupational disease at that time of so many of those who talked so much but did so little to save Europe in the late 1930s. He assured me that the German Army and the German Air Force were becoming the most powerful weapons ever known in Europe, and finally he put in his own little bit about the Aryan races being the only ones who could rid the world of corruption. What more did England want?

Despite the friendly manner in which he told his story and the generous draughts of wine and liqueur, I think Rosenberg must have prepared himself carefully for this lecture and had summed up with some skill the policies that the Nazis had been trying to put across to the British Government with a mixture of bluff, persuasion and threats for the past four years. It was not surprising that the Nazis had been puzzled by the lack of reaction in Britain; there had been none.

The meal was over, but Rosenberg still had a final message to deliver. Perhaps I had seen a number of Italian officers around in Berlin? Well, he would like to inform me that now that the Rome-Berlin axis was in full operation, the Germans and Italians had become very close indeed; so close, in fact, that they were exchanging Intelligence information. Under the circumstances, he felt that it might be better if, after the Nuremberg Rally, I were not to come back to Germany.

I looked completely blank at this suggestion, as if I did not know what he was talking about, but of course I realised that he now knew I was connected in some way with Intelligence. So my impressions at the beginning of the meal had not been so ill-founded after all. Still, he had told me that I was exposed in the most delicate and gentlemanly manner, so I did not feel that an order for my immediate arrest was likely. I believed that Rosenberg was genuinely sorry that his connection with me would have to cease, but I also felt reassured by his manner that the precautions I had always taken not to appear too inquisitive and my seemingly great efforts towards détente would mean that the Nazis would not take action against me provided that I left quietly.

I could foresee no useful role for Rosenberg in a war and suspected that even now he was probably over the peak of his power; he might well be inclined to back both ways in case the great Nazi dream did not come off. All this gave me considerable comfort and offered hope that there would be no public disclaimer of myself. An open showdown would have been too damaging both for Rosenberg's reputation and for all those who had given me their confidences and protection. Many of them had been seen to entertain me openly; they would look foolish if it were widely known that I was a spy.

During the remainder of the dinner party my mind raced back over everything that I had done in Germany to see if there was anything which they could pin on me, but I had done a great deal more listening and looking than anything else. Rosenberg had made no accusations against me. It seemed as if my bogus reports which had been leaked back to Berlin had always convinced him right from the beginning that I was playing it straight. I did, however, wonder whether it would be advisable to go to the Nuremberg Games even if I stuck close to Rosenberg; might it not be better to make a dash for home while the going was good?

Rosenberg had been drinking pretty heavily towards the end and by the time we finally came to say goodnight he was really sloshed. He found difficulty in standing upright on the pavement when he came to see us off and was morose and sad. I was sorry to say goodbye to him like this but at the last moment, just as he turned to stagger indoors, he asked us to come with him in his car to see a little of Bavaria. Then I knew that whatever he had heard of my real activities, he was not prepared to take any action and I could go out as I had come in, a guest of Rosenberg, sponsored by the Führer himself, and no questions asked.

After all was said and done, Rosenberg had always been very fair with me; he had always given me the full VIP treatment when I was in Germany, and he had enabled me to see a great deal of the countryside, to meet the people and so to weigh up the mood and the feeling of the Germans themselves. Over and above this he had unwittingly given me every opportunity to check for myself much of the information that I was getting from various sources in Germany and to sift the wheat from the chaff. This latter point was particularly important, for there was a vast amount of chaff pouring in from refugees hoping to make a little cash, and this was to increase steadily until 1939. In addition I had been able, through close contact with the top men and with the help of Bill de Ropp, to obtain a fairly accurate impression of what was shortly going to hit us.

We drove through Bavaria in Rosenberg's limousine with Herr Schmidt at the wheel. He had driven me a great deal on various excursions around Germany and so at Bill's suggestion I had bought him a small gold cigarette case as a present. Schmidt was a little embarrassed and almost sentimental. He may have guessed that I should not be seeing him again. We drove straight to Munich and did the 370-odd miles in time for a four o'clock pint of that wonderful dark brown Munich beer, swallowed ice cold at a little café in the shade of the great cathedral. First impressions are often best. It was hot, the beer went down smoothly and nothing could dispel the charm of the place. Parts of the new motorways, the plans of which had once preceded me at my first meeting with Hitler, were now operational. We drove on down into the Bavarian Hills to a favourite lakeside holiday haunt of the Nazi hierarchy, the Tegelsee. Much to the disgust of the locals the large and prosperous Gauleiters used to wear the traditional Lederhosen and Tyrolean hats, which is much like a Londoner donning the kilt and bonnet to go to Scotland for his holiday. The pants did not suit most of their figures either! Nevertheless, the country was magnificent. We met several of Rosenberg's friends taking a refresher before the Nuremberg show.

We went back to Nuremberg by way of the medieval walled city of Regensburg, now deservedly a tourist attraction. All was bustle in the town of Nuremberg when we got there. A new hotel had been built to accommodate the principal guests and Nazis of importance for the rally. Companies of 'Brown

Shirts' from various parts of the Reich were arriving and marching through the streets to those short, staccato German marching songs. They would be lining the routes for their Führer
during the next week. The whole city was as usual a mass of
crimson banners. Every now and again a well-known leader
would go by in a large black car and the crowds would give
him a 'Heil'. Especially popular was the town's own leader,
Streicher, who was the main Jew-baiter. He was a really nasty-
looking type who took his ill-gotten popularity with evident
joy. Despite the grimness behind all the bustle, what with the
multitude of odd-shaped brown-shirted Teutons, the crimson-
bannered streets and the spotlights, I felt we were getting
right back to the comic opera atmosphere once again. The
Nazi showmanship was by now terrific.

Streicher had fitted up an anti-Jewish exhibition. It had large
photographic murals of a well-known Jewish film actress in
all stages of nudity and love-making around the walls. This
'decadence exhibit', as it was called, made the place almost
impossible to get into or out of, so thick on the ground were
the gawping young Aryan males. Apparently some foreigner
had taken away one of the crudely illustrated propaganda book-
lets, and when I got back to my hotel room I found a tall
blonde dressed in a smart blue uniform quietly going through
my luggage. She got up from her knees, quite unembarrassed,
gave me a sweet smile and explained it was just routine control.
Needless to say it was not I who had taken the booklet. We
parted good friends, but obviously everyone was being carefully watched. Bill confirmed this, and we took good care not
to talk privately in our rooms, which were no doubt 'controlled'
by microphones in this new building.

This year, for the first time, the whole place was full of Italian
officers in white uniforms and gold tassels. Their free and easy
manners in the hotel, where they used the lounge for lounging,
offended the strict 'correctness' of the Nazis and I doubt they
would have been so happy if they had understood the Nazis'
ill-concealed displeasure. However, Charlie, Bill and I found
a small bar with only Himmler and a few of his pals propping
it up. The pretty blonde barmaid was just what Charlie was

looking for. There was an entrance to this small bar from the street; it was carefully guarded and one of its double doors was shut with a bolt into the floor. All at once there was a clatter of side-arms and a curse, and there, stuck in the single doorway, was Goering. The quickness of Charlie saved the day. He slid up the bolt of the second door and the bulk flowed into the bar beaming.

One trick I always enjoyed, and that was the way the 'leaders' were both divested of, and re-equipped with, their Sam Browne belts complete with daggers and revolvers, their hats, and lastly their gloves and canes. One of the leaders had only to enter a hotel or other room from out of doors when two arms would come round his waist from behind, undo his belt buckle and shoulder strap, and deftly slide the whole thing off from the back. Another pair of hands would remove his hat and then take his gloves and stick. I once timed Himmler being re-dressed in this way: five seconds flat!

Himmler looked at you with his beady eyes through his thick-lensed, rimless glasses, yet never seemed to see you. Perhaps he was only locating the jugular vein for future use. His hand-clasp was cold; his black uniform befitting the poisonous beetle that he was. He had no social graces whatever. .

Rosenberg had arranged a luncheon for some of his more honoured guests at Nuremberg. The table was long and narrow and I was seated just opposite Himmler. After the usual heel-clicking introduction and cold handshake he spoke not one word to me across the two feet of tablecloth during lunch. I wondered whether he had now got a dossier about me in his pocket. It was like eating opposite a cobra!

Each day of the Nuremberg Rally there was a show put on in the sports stadium, both for the benefit of foreign visitors and for internal propaganda. The Nazis, as usual, performed en masse. I think one of the most significant demonstrations I saw was the parade of the young men of the *Arbeitsdienst.* They drilled with polished spades instead of rifles and it was quite a spectacle to see several hundred thousand of them flashing the symbols of their work in the bright sunshine with faultless precision. Hitler was present at this particular parade, and Bill, Charlie and I had been given seats in the 'Royal Box' set high above the stadium. Hitler greeted us cordially, which was a great relief and probably meant that whatever Rosenberg and Himmler knew about me, they had not passed it on to him. We found ourselves sitting only a couple of rows behind him and slightly to one side. Charlie, who was sitting beside me, seemed, that afternoon, to be completely hypnotised by his Führer. His eyes never left the little man, and from time to time he would interrupt my attention from the weaving and flashing of the spades with such words as: "Look, the Führer smiles, look, the Führer laughs, look, the Führer waves his hand!" I could see it all myself and I simply hadn't the heart to say to Charlie, "So what?" I had never encountered this sort of absolute hero worship before; I thought then that if Charlie could so lose himself in the worship of this little man, no wonder the youth of the nation were ready to go through fire for him. I certainly could never see the British youth going overboard for a political leader, but then circumstances can alter cases.

The flashing spades came to rest and then it happened. The Führer got to his feet to make his speech and there was a roar from half a million throats. As he stood there in front of the microphone, I saw the same thing happen that I had seen the very first time I met him: the back of his neck went red, his eyes started to bulge, his face flushed, and then he started one of those diatribes into the microphone that are now so well known. This time it was considerably more belligerent, which made me think that time was really running out. The Third Reich was going to take its place in the world. The Aryan race was going to predominate; there must be room for every German to live and live happily; and all the rest of it. He never repeated himself, but gradually one could see the vast army of young men below us in the stadium starting to sway with crowd emotion. I wondered if Hitler would stop before it became hysteria. He gauged it just right. He whipped the whole of the assembly up to a frenzy and then he stopped. His neck returned to a normal colour; his eyes went back into their sockets and his face became calm. I had been fascinated

not by the speech, which obviously left me cold, but by the
extraordinary hold this little man had over his audience and
the way in which he could switch on and switch off this strange
performance. Was it possible for a human being to be possessed
by the reincarnated spirit of some medieval monster? I looked
along the row of chairs to my right to see how other people
were taking it. I noticed Franz von Papen in civilian clothes
sitting towards the end of the row, his Homburg hat well over
his face. He was fast asleep.

We descended the steep steps which led up to the dais on
which we had been sitting, and made our way back to the
hotel. Here Rosenberg informed us that he had got special
passes to take Bill and me to the Party meeting the following
afternoon; we were getting the full treatment. The Nuremberg
Nazi Party meeting had become an annual festival of remem-
brance for those who were killed in the early days of the movement. It was held in the new Party Hall in Nuremberg. Under
one of the two pillars of the doorway had been buried a copy
of *Mein Kampf,* and under the other a copy of Rosenberg's
The Myth of the Twentieth Century—probably the best place
for both these books. The hall was not very large and only
selected early Party members and their womenfolk had been
given tickets. I think Bill and I were the sole outsiders and,
as Rosenberg's guests once again, had been given seats in the
front row. On a raised platform, just a few feet away from us
and facing the audience, sat the leaders.

The ceremony started soon after we had taken our seats.
On the roll of the drum everybody stood up and along the
aisle from the back of the hall came the slow procession of
banners. The square storm-troopers in black uniforms, their
square heads engulfed in square black steel helmets, each man
carrying a square black and silver banner of his district sur-
mounted by the inevitable vulture, slowly filed past the leaders
to take up their stand behind them. At last the final banner
was in place, making a great black and silver curtain behind
the line of chairs on which the leaders sat.

I had never before seen all the top Nazis together, and now
here they were facing me, all sitting in a row on hard wooden

chairs not a dozen feet away. I had a feeling it just could not be true; surely they did not really look like that. It was almost like being in Madam Tussaud's waxworks! What was so odd about them? Of course, none of them had their hats on. I had met a number of them without their hats from time to time but never the whole bunch sitting in a row. What an enormous difference the German military-type hat with its high front made to the wearer. But here, amongst their closest followers, they were just fellow-Nazis; no pale blue uniforms and rows of medals for Goering; now they all wore plain brown shirts, buttoned at the wrist and neck, with a plain black tie.

I suppose any line of middle-aged men all dressed alike but so different in size, shape and face, would look funny. I managed to keep my face straight by reminding myself that these men would soon be responsible for waging yet another war, in which it now looked as if we should inevitably be involved, along with goodness knows what suffering, and I remember wondering what would happen if some fanatic or would-be martyr could liquidate them as they sat there together—Hitler, Hess, Rosenberg, Goebbels, Himmler, Goering, Heydrich, Ribbentrop, von Schirach, the lot.

Only Hitler and Hess seemed to me to be really at ease. The former had achieved a great measure of poise, but now, as he came to the lectern to read the names of his dead comrades, he looked not four but fourteen years older than when I had first met him. The pockets beneath his protruding blue eyes were deeper, the face sallower; but his voice was strong, and as with other men whom I have seen fulfil their destinies in a short space of time, one sensed an authority which had grown with power over the past few years. There seemed little doubt that he had been the undisputed leader of this new Party right from the start; now all who saw him knew it.

Sitting on Hitler's right was Hess, the ever-faithful shadow, self-effacing, quiet-mannered, a dreamer, and yet, as he proved later, a man of decisive action if the need arose. I cannot think that Hess, a little fanatical perhaps where the welfare of his leader and his country was concerned, was basically evil like some of his comrades. His solo flight to England during the war, at enormous risk, fitted his character and was his last desperate act to save his country from having to wage a war on two fronts. As he sat, quietly smiling, next to his leader, his arms folded and the well-shod leg thrust out in a typical pose, he too was relaxed. But there was always a slightly wild look in his eyes below those bushy black eyebrows.

Alfred Rosenberg, who sat next to him, evidently found his seat a bit hard. I had noticed he often adopted the forward leaning position, which he now held, one elbow on the knee and chin in hand. This somewhat unpredictable man, whom I had watched since 1932, seemed to have lost his enormous enthusiasm and to have turned into a rather unhappy individual, as if he found the foundations of his Aryan religion less solid than he had hoped. Nevertheless, he had amply repaid me for his first visit to London, and when in Germany I had always been given a place of honour at official functions. His hair was beginning to thin on top, his face had lost any youthful look it ever had and was now lined, pasty and flaccid. He seemed to be looking inwards these days, perhaps not quite liking what he saw; after all, he was much more concerned with the long-term picture and now that the moment of truth was coming nearer the stakes were not quite so neatly arranged as he and his Party had hoped; maybe he was calling on his pagan gods. I wondered how long he could hold down his job and thought that perhaps he had wanted me to see him in the seat near his Führer, albeit for the last time.

Joseph Goebbels I never knew. He looked like an evil gnome, yet they say he was passionately fond of his family; a master of his art, his task grew too big even for him. He sat down, his bright dark eyes darting from face to face. Perhaps he was trying to get some inspiration for a new slogan; maybe, after Charlie's failure, he was trying to read my mind. At least he stood by his leader to the end. Unless you are insane, it takes guts to sacrifice your whole family and die with them.

Goering: now when you are as vast as Hermann and have short legs into the bargain, it is not easy to sit for long on a normal-sized, hard wooden chair and keep smiling. Despite the carefully arranged gaps on either side of him, he bulged against his comrades and seemed to look to them to keep him upright. He fidgeted, scowled and smiled mechanically from time to time. He also got overheated and had to mop his great slab of a face. Signs of too-good living were obvious; I would say that Goering, unlike Rosenberg, lived for today and possibly tomorrow and, as we know, he did it in style. He was one of the great swashbucklers of all time. Nero must have been one of his heroes; and yet here in his vast brown shirt below the sweating face, he looked more pathetic than ridiculous. Power had sapped his better judgement; he seemed nearer to the point of demoralisation than his comrades.

Himmler never moved. He sat solidly, rock-like, his arms folded; only his eyes were never still. I suppose this was from force of habit, in much the same way as we fighter pilots in the First World War kept looking around to see who was getting on our tail. I never saw Himmler smile; always the cold, sinister, rather flat, round pasty face with a bluish chin. A man who, in his youth, had been considered mentally subnormal and had been unable to hold down a job; it must have needed the unholy inspiration of his leader to enable him to build up the black-uniformed storm-troops as Hitler's personal army and Himmler's own instrument of evil.

Next to Himmler was Reinhard Heydrich, tall, fair and good-looking. One would not guess that it was this man above all others who would uncover and nurture the beast that was never far beneath the surface of that band of subhuman monsters.

Joachim von Ribbentrop always looked out of place amongst these men; the sort of man you would never look at twice in ordinary circumstances, except for the uncontrollable twitch of his face; a man who showed himself during his time as Ambassador in London as quite inadequate to fulfil any job requiring intellect, tact, or diplomacy, which after all was what he was supposed to have.

This was the last time I saw any of these men except Rosenberg. Somehow the comic opera had turned to sinister melodrama. The presence of such a concentrated dose of Nazis left me thoroughly depressed and I was thankful to get out into the sunshine and fresh air. Bill and I thought a drink was indicated.

That evening Rosenberg was waiting in the hall of the hotel as Bill and I came down before dinner, and one of Rosenberg's aides informed me that he wished to say an official goodbye. So this was it. Rosenberg was now a Reichsleiter, ranking second only to the Führer himself. At the far end of the hall he stood erect, flanked by his staff and his bodyguard, wearing a new, well-cut uniform with his badges of rank at the collar. He appeared to be at the peak of his career, one of the most powerful men in the new Reich. He had obviously made this a somewhat public occasion, maybe in order to show that I was now finished with. Shaking hands, he bade me a solemn farewell. I detected a little sadness in his voice and I felt a twinge of sorrow at having used him in the way I had. Utterly misguided he may have been, but he was honest in his own belief in what he was doing. Alas, the revival of the Aryan gods had let loose passions which we hoped had been buried in Western civilisation. How deeply, I wonder?

Both Bill and Charlie came to the station at Nuremberg to see me off as I caught the night train for Paris. Poor Charlie. Everything was going his way; no wonder he became a little overwhelmed by his success. Here he was in his thirties, already a professor; his wife safely tucked away in Hamburg with her wire-haired terrier; all the girls in Berlin crazy for him; the wine plentiful and even the German champagne drinkable.

It was the German champagne that was eventually his undoing. I heard, some time after the war started in 1939, that Charlie was as usual at one of the cocktail parties for the neutrals in Berlin. Russia was now a German ally, but I think that neither the Germans nor the Russians were under any misapprehension as to who was fooling whom. Charlie had too much to drink at the party and spilled the beans to a neutral of the plans for the great assault on Russia.

The word got back to Rosenberg of this unforgivable indiscretion, so Charlie was packed off as a private in the Army under orders to be sent to the Russian front when the time came, to put matters right. I expect he was in one of the penal battalions; anyway, I only hope for his sake that he did not last long. Life in those battalions on the Russian front must have been absolute hell. Bill, who was in Switzerland during the war, heard all this from contacts over the border.

It is difficult to describe the atmosphere when I left Germany in that summer of 1938. On one hand, supreme confidence among the Nazis and the generals; on the other, a feeling of solemn foreboding among the older citizens who had been through World War I. A third reaction among the young was a subtle froth of suppressed excitement; had I not felt the same in 1914? All this made me realise that it was time to try to piece together all the big and little events and conversations I had witnessed and taken part in over the past four years. If I could do this I ought to arrive at some fairly accurate conclusions as to the objectives, the methods and the timing of the Nazi cum Army set-up which we should assuredly have to fight soon—and fight with one hand tied behind our backs if our politicians continued to bury their heads in the sand. On new types of warfare perhaps part of my summing up could be labelled as intelligent guessing, but it was founded on well-formed impressions, and impressions are important. All too often those responsible for assessing information are inclined to insist on chapter and verse in black and white. But intelligent impressions formed over some years of close association with the people concerned—a turn of phrase, the odd remark at the end of a good evening, the odd silence when something should have been said—all these are, in my opinion, often of more real value than collated items of somewhat doubtful origin.

As I rocked sleeplessly in the overnight Paris Express I made a mental list of the outstanding impressions I had gained. First, of course, there was the enormous striking power of the new German war machine with its *Blitzkrieg* tactics. Secondly, there was Hitler's obsession with the conquest of Russia and the crushing of Communism. Then, thirdly, there were the tremendous efforts which had been made by the Nazis to keep Britain out of the coming war. And perhaps lastly, the sinking morale of the French nation and its armed forces. These were the impressions which I had plugged back in London over four years. Would they never be accepted by our General Staff? If only our generals had accepted the writings of forward-looking soldiers back in the early 1930s and reorganised our Army on a basis of tank divisions backed up by mobile anti-tank cum anti-aircraft guns similar to the German 88! If only the Government had allowed real expansion of fighter and fighter bomber squadrons of the RAF, surely we could, with the additional bargaining power of our neutrality, have 'persuaded' Hitler to go East instead of West. I woke up in Paris.

13
Flying High

Georges Ronin looked unhappy as he sat behind his bare wooden table in the wooden hut which was his section of the French Secret Service (Deuxième Bureau). The hut was too hot anyway in August 1938, so I suggested that we might discuss our troubles with greater ease under the awning of some café across the other side of the river. He readily agreed and we strolled across the bridge.

The Chief of the French Air Force, General Joseph Vuillemin, had recently returned from a visit to Germany and Georges had produced a splendid report for me about it all. As in the extraordinary détente with the RAF in 1936 and 1937, the General had been given a conducted tour of the Messerschmitt, Junkers and Heinkel factories where he had been shown all available sheds stuffed full of aircraft. He had been shown the latest aircraft coming off the assembly lines and had also seen a massed fly-past of fighters. The speed of their bombers had been prodigious; their Heinkel bomber could outstrip any fighter aircraft from other nations. All of which added up to a totally destructive offensive war. The tour had been meant to frighten him, and it did. Whether there was any more sinister reason Georges did not know, but Vuillemin had stated that the French Air Force could not last a week against what he had seen.

That the French were not in a position of strength was already known to us. We had always been told that in case of war they would be able to produce sixty divisions in the field. We never, of course, carried out espionage against our French ally, but when war seemed imminent it had been decided to send Desmond Morton over to Paris to find out whether this figure was correct or not. He had returned with a somewhat gloomy picture of a bare twenty divisions being available immediately, with a possible build-up of a further twenty divisions over several months. It had become clear to all of us in our office that if a *Blitzkrieg* attack occurred in 1939, France would scarcely be in a position to mobilise forty divisions. Personally, I had always had a hunch that the French might at the last possible moment reach some accommodation with the Nazis, somewhat in the style of the Munich Pact, so I was rather careful what I said to Georges at this meeting.

I explained to him that there was every sign of a complete clamp-down on information leaving Germany and that secret agents were terrified of quick execution. I told him that I was unlikely to be able to go back to Germany myself any more. He did not seem surprised at this; instead, he stressed the need for caution in every aspect of our work. I asked him what he meant by this. He seemed reluctant to answer, but intimated that we didn't know whom to trust even in our own country. However, he agreed that we had gained a fair idea of the proposed strength and composition of the new German Air Force over the past four years. What we now particularly needed to find out was the continuing production figures of the various types of aircraft and the performance of any new ones that might come out. We also needed to know of any expansion of the aircraft factories and the sites and capacity of new aerodromes in the West.

Up to about September 1938 it had not been too difficult to get agents to observe the numbers of aircraft put out on the tarmac outside the aircraft factories before they were flown away to squadrons, and this gave us a reasonable idea of the production line; but without such observation reports we should now have to use other methods.

Georges told me that out of desperation he had got hold of an old aeroplane, into which he had fitted a large wooden camera, and that it was being flown up and down the Rhine by a civil pilot, an old friend of his. The camera was operated by a splendid old man with a flowing beard who was normally a portrait photographer in Paris. They managed to get a few good photographs and to keep track of some of the fortifications on the German side of the river. Couldn't this sort of exercise be profitably extended?

I mentioned right at the beginning of this book how I, myself, became a casualty escorting photographic planes in the First World War and I explained now to Georges how I had also been making enquiries of the Royal Air Force as to what progress had been made in aerial photography. But it appeared that although technically the cameras had been vastly improved and automated, it was still impossible, some twenty years later, to take aerial photographs at all times of the year above 8,000 ft. because the camera lenses got fogged up with condensation from the cold air. It would obviously be impossible to cruise around even in a civil aeroplane in peacetime at this height taking photographs over Germany. They would very soon discover what we were up to, with disastrous results. But it was even more frightening to think of what might happen in time of war, and as it now seemed quite possible that we should be involved in another war with the Germans, we both agreed that, at 8,000 ft., up against modern German anti-aircraft guns and ultra-modern enemy fighters, aerial photography would be sheer slaughter for the pilots and air crews. Georges also pointed out that, with the rapid movements of the *Blitzkrieg*, aerial photography and lots of it would probably be the only way left to us to know what the enemy was doing. Desperate remedies were now necessary. We both knew that we should get the dirty end of the stick if Intelligence about the enemy dried up at this critical juncture.

It seemed unlikely that we should be able to produce something that the air forces of both our countries had not succeeded in doing. However, we considered that if we could get hold of an American executive-type aeroplane with a proper cabin for four or five people, we could at least carry out some experiments and probably take it for legitimate flights into Germany on some commercial basis or other. It might be possible to fit a hidden camera into this aircraft and if we could produce sufficiently good cover for a pilot, get some photographs that were worthwhile. Meantime we could experiment to see if we could raise the altitude at which we took the photographs. We decided on an American Lockheed 14, a new and very handy type of twin-engined executive aircraft. It had a heated cabin with room for four or five people as well as the pilot and co-pilot. It was all very up to date by European standards at that time. The next point, of course, was how to get hold of one, and Georges suggested that if I could manage to buy one in America he would do the same and we should then each have one with which to experiment.

It was, alas, evident that however much co-operation we might receive from our respective Air Staffs, this was bound to take some time and time was now running out. Back in London I put the whole proposition to my Chief. He liked the idea but said that the Air Ministry would have to supply the aeroplane and that I had better go over to see the Chief of Air Staff, Sir Cyril Newall, and talk him into it if I could. I explained the whole scheme to Sir Cyril. He was extremely sympathetic and went so far as to say that he was in France at the same time that I was in the First World War, where he too had been appalled at the wastage due to photographic reconnaissance. He gave me permission to order a Lockheed aircraft, provided I could get it imported into the country as a civilian machine, and he suggested I should get Imperial Airways to do the job for me. I explained to him that the French also wanted one and that by buying two we might get them a bit cheaper. He asked me to let him see the plane when it was over here and ready for operation, adding that the more we could do to improve the altitude of air photography the better. I took the opportunity to ask him if we could borrow

cameras and camera equipment from the RAF, and he said
that he would see that we got what we wanted. I was of course
delighted and let Georges know at once. Imperial Airways were
extremely helpful. An order was placed that very week for
two Lockheed 14s; Imperial Airways would order them as their
own machines and the bill would be paid by the Air Ministry.
Unfortunately, these sort of aircraft couldn't be bought off-the-
peg, and we were advised by Lockheed that they could ship
one aircraft to be erected in England within two or three
weeks, but the second aircraft would not be available for several
months. This was a bit of a blow, but I am afraid that I made
up my mind there and then to have the first one for ourselves
and I warned Georges Ronin that there would be some delay
in getting his aircraft.

So far so good; now I had to find somebody to fly the aircraft
for me, and it had to be somebody who was willing to carry
out experiments in high-altitude photography and indeed to
take the risk of flying with a camera aboard over Germany. I
mentioned to one or two of my friends, both in the Royal
Aero Club and in the Royal Air Force Club, that I was looking
for a pilot to do some special work. It would have to be someone
totally unconnected with the RAF and able to develop some
business interest in Germany.

While I was looking round for the right type of aerial 'James
Bond', someone put me in touch with Sydney Cotton, an adven-
turous type who had done a great deal of flying out in New-
foundland and who had invented the Sydcott flying suit, which,
when sealed at wrist and ankle, kept the natural body warmth
intact. I talked my proposition over with Sydney, who seemed
extremely keen to go ahead. At least he was a good pilot with
considerable knowledge of photography; more useful even than
that, he was connected with a firm which was trying to expand
the development of colour photography in England and Germany, so he was not only well versed in the whole subject
but also had good commercial connections which would enable
him to fly into Germany without arousing suspicion. I gathered
that the firm was not doing too well and that the extra sum
of money I could offer him would be very welcome. So it was

that Sydney Cotton came on to my payroll.

It was unfortunate that the Lockheed for France would be delayed, but I promised Georges that we would co-operate and that I would give him all the results that we obtained from our experiments. In the event the French aircraft only arrived in time for us to get it across to them in October 1939, just before the cold war broke out, so they had little time to make much use of it before the fall of France. To my surprise I received in return for sending it over a large sack full of high-value French bank notes instead of a cheque. The French Secret Service were cautious.

Our aircraft duly arrived in large crates and I had to rush down to the docks with a note from the Treasury to the Chief of Customs so that it was passed through without having to pay a vast amount of duty. I had arranged with my friend Nigel Norman to hire an isolated hangar at Heston aerodrome where I finally got the aircraft assembled with the aid of some of the Heston mechanics. It was an exciting moment when we wheeled it out for its first test flight.

Sydney Cotton was an aeronautical enthusiast. He flew the Lockheed around as if he'd been piloting it all his life. I went up with him for the second test; it was certainly a very smooth aircraft. We tried it out for height and obtained a ceiling of about 22,000 ft. Fortunately it was fitted with oxygen. We realised that if ever we were to get the cameras to operate at high altitude, this would be a wonderful flying laboratory. The heated cabin, too, was an absolute joy. Nigel Norman supplied me with a first-rate mechanic, who also came on my payroll and was sworn to secrecy; and once again through my friend in the customs I arranged that flights of the Lockheed in and out of Heston should not be subject to customs control, although a form of customs declarations would be adhered to in order to allay suspicion that we were doing anything unlawful. It was essential to keep the whole operation secret.

Having got our aeroplane, our job was to see how high we could go and still obtain clear pictures. For a start I obtained three Leica cameras from Germany, the ones with large rolls of film usually used for bird watching. We fitted them on to a specially made frame, one pointing directly downwards and the other two pointing out at an angle so as to get as much coverage as possible. I then had to get a hole cut in the bottom of the fuselage. This was not an easy job because it affected the stress of the fuselage itself and I had to have the job specially done by an aircraft factory with the utmost secrecy, since it was essential that as few people as possible knew of our efforts.

The plane was now ready to start experiments. It was Sydney Cotton's secretary who volunteered to lie flat on her tummy and operate the three cameras at given intervals, which we worked out to coincide with the height and speed at which the aircraft was flying. I suggested to Cotton that he should start off at 8,000 ft., take a series of pictures, and then move up about 1,000 ft. at a time until we had reached the ceiling of the Lockheed. We would then develop the films and find out at what height the condensation prevented us getting a clear picture. By this time it was early in 1939 and the weather was cold. On our first day up we were therefore not very optimistic. However, when we developed the three rolls of Leica film, we found that we had been taking perfectly clear pictures up to nearly 20,000 ft. Just how we had accomplished it we did not at first realise, but it was exciting, to say the least.

The next day we decided to have another go. The engines had been running up for some minutes and had nicely warmed the cabin when we crawled under the belly of the aircraft just before take-off to make quite certain that the small flap sealing off the camera hole which we could slide backwards and forwards from a control in the cockpit was in proper working order. It was then we discovered that, with the engines running, warm air was coming out of the heated cabin and flowing beneath the camera lenses. Here was the explanation and the secret of our success. It was as simple as that. I find it almost impossible to describe my elation at this chance discovery. Both Cotton and I realised that this was something of fundamentally supreme importance, not only for our own proposed operations over Germany but for the whole future of aeronautical photography; but we realised also that we had stumbled on a secret which must be kept. I decided there and then that I would tell no one until we had carried out full-scale experiments with RAF camera equipment.

Despite the fact that the Leica pictures had been clear, they did not show all the small detail we really required, so I went now to the RAF Photographic Department to ask for the loan of some of their latest cameras and equipment which the Chief of Air Staff had promised me. Group Captain Laws, who was head of the Photographic Department, was wonderfully co-operative. He supplied me with two separate cameras and several different-length lenses, and we spent a busy evening filing off all the RAF numbers and indications on this equipment in case we got caught. Better still, the RAF had produced a device for automatically timing the taking of the pictures according to the height and speed of the aircraft. This had an indicator in the cockpit to show that the cameras were working properly, and one of the cameras was duly fitted into the aircraft. The opening in the belly was camouflaged as an emergency fuel release and I had a special cover made for the cameras in the form of a spare fuel tank, so that anyone looking under the floorboards would have no reason to suspect what was going on. Now we were ready.

The results were marvellous: absolutely clear photographs taken from over 20,000 ft., overlapping so that they could be used with stereo and showing every detail. It was after these results that we decided to make a thorough test in the Mediterranean. With the aid of the Air Ministry I had extra tanks secretly fitted in the passenger compartment and arranged with Georges in Paris that Cotton should fly directly to Malta and then across to Algiers, where he would be welcomed by the French authorities and given permission to fly up the coast to Tunis. I did not want to go as far east as Cairo as there might be too much speculation as to what we were doing. The plan was to cross over from Tobruk to the north Mediterranean coast and, with the tremendous range that we now had with the extra tanks, to try to photograph the Italian bases both in the islands and on the mainland; then to turn back to Algiers. By this time I had recruited an additional young Canadian pilot, Bob Niven. He was actually a Reservist for the RAF but they agreed to let him come as co-pilot. We fitted out Sydney Cotton with papers saying he was a film tycoon doing a survey for possible locations for film making. It was as good a cover as anything else. I had to warn the authorities in Malta to keep it quiet that he had flown direct from the United Kingdom; they were naturally very intrigued by the whole subject.

The result of this trip in the early spring of 1939 was fantastic. Flying almost unnoticed at 20,000 ft. Cotton photographed every Italian naval and air base on the North African coast and then did the same along the northern Mediterranean. Dockyards, harbours, aerodromes—everything was photographed in detail. I had told the Air Ministry that we were going to do some experiments, but I had not given them any idea of the scope, and it was only when we got all the photographs back and had them printed that I was able to hand over complete sets to the directors of Intelligence of all three services and to Georges Ronin. At first they could not believe it, but when the explanation came the excitement was intense. Requests came pouring in from the Admiralty, the War Office and the Air Ministry for photographs of aircraft factories, dockyards, anything we could get over Germany.

Now that we had the technique, I had to organise the method. We decided to boost up the British side of Cotton's commercial film development company and increase its potential, so that those on the German side were enthused and encouraged with the possibility of building up their side of the production too. Cotton started making regular trips to Berlin. The first time the hatch in the belly was kept safely closed and was without cameras. Soon the Germans got used to seeing the Lockheed coming into Berlin. They had no doubt had a good look at it the first time, and now, with the camera installed under the cabin floor, the Lockheed became operational for espionage.

It was, incidentally, Cotton's German development company contact in Berlin, who was also an electronics expert, who managed to obtain details for us of a new type of acoustic mine which the Germans were developing; a mine which was set off by reverberations from the propellers of a passing ship. The Admiralty were delighted to get this information. Experiments were immediately put in hand to try to counter this potential menace, and as a result of our pre-knowledge many lives were later saved.

Cotton had found it difficult to fly directly over the targets because one could only see out of the aircraft at an oblique angle at the side of the pilot's seat, so he invented a new form of 'tear-drop' moulded Perspex window with a bulge in it which allowed him to see straight down to the target beneath him. It was a great success. He also varied his route to Berlin, refuelling at Hamburg or Frankfurt or some other aerodrome which would give him a 'run' over certain new aerodromes or aircraft factories we wished to photograph. So long as he kept around 20,000 ft., the Germans didn't seem even to suspect that he could be using a camera.

In order further to allay any suspicion, Cotton took the aircraft to the Frankfurt Air Show in the summer, leaving the camera in. The Lockheed was the centre of much interest since the executive aircraft had not yet made its appearance in Europe. And here Albert Kesselring crossed my path, unknown to him, for the last time before the war. He was very intrigued by this twin-engined American aircraft and asked Cotton whether he could take a ride in it. Cotton willingly agreed, and when they were well up over the Rhine he gave Kesselring the controls, at the same time switching on the cameras because there were various interesting areas close to the Rhine which he thought might be worth photographing. Kesselring was enthusiastic about the aeroplane. When he saw the green light flashing in the cockpit which indicated that the photographs were being taken, he asked Cotton what it meant. Cotton told him that it was a flow indicator for the fuel and as long as the green light was flashing, fuel was running smoothly to the engines. This seemed to satisfy Kesselring. When they landed back at the aerodrome, he thanked Cotton for a very enjoyable ride.

The Lockheed was in constant use throughout the whole of the 1939 summer up to September. Often Cotton took it over to France with some well-known people for an apparent holiday in order to keep up the pose of the wealthy 'tycoon' with his own aircraft. Most of the summer we were concentrating on photographing aerodromes and aircraft factories, and where possible, armament factories and dockyards as well. The German aircraft factories continued to park their newly constructed aircraft out on the tarmac and if one kept a close watch on these it was possible to judge the production of the factory concerned—information which was vital to the RAF at that time. Aerodrome construction seemed to follow a very stereotyped pattern, just as I had seen in my earlier flights over Germany.

By the summer of 1939 the RAF was studying our new technique closely. When I had dumped the five hundred perfect photographs of all the Italian installations in the Mediterranean on the desk of Archie Boyle at the Air Ministry, his first remark had been, "What am I supposed to do with these?" However, he very soon collected together all the people who knew anything about photographic interpretation and they trained others in this highly skilled procedure. It was this nucleus of people who were able to form the great photo interpretations centre at Medmenham in Buckinghamshire after war broke out.

I had also discovered from a friend in the Royal Air Force Club that there was a remarkable new machine in existence called a 'Wilt', which was built in Switzerland and was now being used in London, by an aerial survey firm, for three-dimensional examination of overlapping photographs. The firm had originally imported the machine in order to make a topographical survey in Persia. The owner allowed us to test it out; we found that we could not only measure with extreme accuracy the width and length of objects on the ground, but also the height, which of course was absolutely invaluable when it came to identifying warships by the height of their masts or factories by their chimneys, indeed, any object where height could give identification. I tried in the summer of 1939 to get the Air Ministry to order the only other one in existence that I knew of from Switzerland, but the civil servants at that time thought it was too expensive. However, the moment war seemed inevitable, they relented and the machine was installed at Medmenham.

An over-ambitious extrovert is perhaps not the best choice for a secret operator. During the summer of 1939 Cotton had done a really great job taking photographs over Germany and his results were producing ever more requests from the service ministries. However, in August a back door approach was made to him by Ian Fleming, a member of the DNI (Director of Naval Intelligence) Office to get Cotton to work for the Admiralty, where he would be given the rank of Captain and all the assistance and cash he wanted. Cotton casually told me he thought of taking the job, despite the fact he was still on my payroll and the aircraft and all the equipment belonged to the Secret Intelligence Service. I naturally advised the Air Ministry, and as a result a violent row broke out between the Chief of the Naval Staff and the Chief of the Air Staff, not only because of the underhand way in which Ian Fleming had tried to entice Cotton, but also because there was a definite agreement between the services that the RAF alone were responsible for aerial photography. The Chief of Air Staff took the matter to the Prime Minister, who rightly ruled in favour of the RAF. But the affair was too much for Cotton's ego and he now declared that he would work on his own directly with the various directors of Intelligence. I threatened to ground the Lockheed aircraft since not only was this a breach of faith with me and the Air Ministry, but also such random operations might well end in our losing the secret of our precious breakthrough as well as the aeroplane.

But Cotton was impatient to cash in on his new image. Just at the end of August, apparently encouraged by his friends in Berlin, he produced a hare-brained scheme to fly Goering from Berlin to London to meet Halifax in an effort to avert war. In his new-found glory he took his idea over my head to Stewart Menzies, who, in turn, was always prepared to try to get a bit of kudos from Downing Street. Presumably not understanding what it was all about, Chamberlain gave permission for the flight, and unknown to myself, Cotton set off for Berlin. Menzies himself never had the courtesy to tell me. I

200 The Nazi Connection

dared not try to contact Cotton personally, but I managed to get a signal to the Air Attaché in Berlin asking him to send Cotton back if things looked like getting too hot. I knew quite well it was a hopeless mission from the start, but of course it had got Cotton once again closer to Downing Street.

It happened that at this precise moment the DNI sent me an urgent request for a photograph of the German fleet, which was thought to be at anchor in the mouth of the Elbe. Winston Churchill, at that time the First Lord of the Admiralty, wanted to know exactly where the main German warships were. I managed to get hold of Bob Niven and told him to make ready the small Beechcraft three-seater aircraft I had acquired for communications purposes, and I finally persuaded a young, very gallant passport photographer, who normally supplied us with both real and false passport photos, to go off with Bob Niven with one of the Leica cameras. These two flew across to Holland and up the Dutch coast until they could see the German warships anchored in line in the mouth of the Elbe. As they flew nearer, two German fighter aircraft came up and started firing shots across their nose. They turned, but at that very moment the sun shone on the ships and the photographer took five long-range oblique pictures. It had been touch and go. There is, in fact, no truth in Cotton's story that he took the pictures on his way back from Berlin. He had only been allowed to leave Berlin if he agreed to fly at 500 ft. on a given course to London, nowhere near the Elbe and certainly not high enough to see it. Needless to say, the DNI was delighted with the pictures that had been taken. On Cotton's return I warned him that I was now going to seek Air Ministry authority to ground the aircraft. The Air Ministry were already asking me to pass over to them the whole outfit so that they could adapt the technique for the Air Force, who were proposing to start it up as a proper RAF unit. I was glad to do this for I felt that Cotton in uniform would have to do as he was told.

The new RAF unit which was to be set up was to be called the Photo Reconnaissance Unit or PRU. Wanting to play a more active role, I asked if I might be given command of it. I knew that it was bound to be of great importance in the future, whereas it would be well-nigh impossible to find and operate agents in Germany once war had been declared. I was told in no uncertain terms that it was not a job for a Reserve officer. However, the regular officer who took it over made a wonderful job of it, ending up as an Air Marshal, and I was able to make up for my disappointment when in April 1940 I was asked to organise one of the most fascinating jobs of the war, 'Ultra'—of which more later.

Cotton was transferred to the newly formed PRU with the rank of Wing Commander and the authority to adapt our techniques to this new unit. Two Spitfires were wheeled out of Air Marshal Dowding, Commander-in-Chief of Fighter Command, with the aid of Air Marshal Tedder. After they had been totally disarmed, cameras were fitted in the wings with heat from the exhaust carried beneath the lenses. The results were terrific.

Painted eggshell-blue and flying unseen at 30,000 ft., there was little that escaped the eyes of these Spitfires, whether it was over western Germany or over Belgium, where we had been denied any information regarding their aerodromes during the phoney war of the autumn of 1939 and spring of 1940. It was these same Spitfires which spotted the concentration of German tanks ready for the breakthrough in the Ardennes. But the information was disregarded by the French General Staff as had been all other indications of the German *Blitzkrieg* in this area.

Alas, the success of the unit went to Cotton's head once again, and just before the fall of France he could not resist poking his nose into politics. He tried to get the Home Office to let him fly the old Lockheed into Britain with a bevy of frightened French politicians aboard instead of looking after the evacuation of essential equipment and personnel. No doubt the Frenchmen had been willing to pay well for the flight to the UK, but this was too much even for the Air Ministry. Cotton was relieved of his job and thereafter the PRU flourished and expanded under a competent RAF Wing Commander.

When the United States came into the war and the secret of high-level photography was passed on to them, Elliott Roosevelt was put in command of the American PRU in Europe. I doubt if there was any corner of Western Europe and North Africa which was not recorded, and in due course the PRU activities were extended to the Pacific and South-East Asia; all of this with hardly a casualty.

Thus it was that a project, originally worked out in Paris between myself and Georges Ronin, had, by an absurdly simple discovery, become the forerunner of all spy planes. At last I was rewarded by the knowledge that no longer would RAF fighters have to escort RAF photographic machines on suicidal missions.

14
War

After the abdication of Edward VIII, Baldwin retired as Prime Minister, admitting that he had been wrong in his assessment of the growing threat in Europe. Chamberlain succeeded him. Much has been written about that unfortunate man, so I will only sketch my own brief impression. It seemed to me that he saw himself as completely self-sufficient: he thought that he alone knew how to deal with Hitler. He sold Czechoslovakia down the river in 1938, but his reasoning behind this may have been influenced by a growing conviction that morale in France was no longer to be relied upon. This the Francophiles in the Cabinet would not believe. Nevertheless, this underlying fear of imminent French collapse may well have induced Chamberlain to go to Munich to meet Hitler to try to find some way of avoiding immediate war over Czechoslovakia. Only then did the real value of the bluff we had used against Hitler pay off, in greater measure than we had ever contemplated, and in a way which we did not fully appreciate at the time.

Right up to 1938 Hitler had believed that he could secure British neutrality. His détente with the RAF must have convinced him of this, otherwise it was a most extraordinary course of behaviour for him to show the potential enemy the whole of his new and powerful Air Force while expecting to go to war almost immediately. Towards the end of 1938 Hitler must have realised that it would have to be total war, first in Europe and then in Russia. He made this decision only to find that his Air Force had been wrongly designed for a total war against Britain, if Britain was to withstand defeat on the continent. His twin-engined bombers could not carry a useful bomb load and enough petrol to reach our western ports; they just hadn't the necessary range. They could not disrupt our shipping in the Atlantic nor blockade our western ports, nor could they cut off our food supplies. Moreover, his fighter aircraft did not have the range to escort his bombers more than a short way into southern England—proof that they had not been designed with Britain in mind.

There were wild reports coming from agents still operating in Germany that Hitler had panicked and ordered a doubling and even trebling of the Luftwaffe; but we knew this was impossible due to the shortage of raw materials, and we calculated the amount of oil required to support such an enormous fleet of aircraft would be out of the question. It was reported, too, that Milch, who with Udet had been responsible for the aircraft programme, had been sacked.

I cannot really believe that Chamberlain, after his first meeting, fully trusted Hitler. Surely he must have discovered that the Nazis were playing for time just as much as he was; that they needed the Czech arms factories and a defendable buttress in the south-east against any surprises from that quarter.

It has been said that Chamberlain was pushed against his better judgement into making the 'peace in our time' declaration in the heat of the paper-waving moment. This I cannot believe of such an over-meticulous politician. Whatever anyone says about Munich, it did give us a breathing space of twelve months in which to clutch desperately at the lost opportunities of the past five years. Nevertheless the expansion of the RAF, which had been authorised in 1935, and the success of the Spitfires built in 1939 just, and only just, gave our pilots the edge that beat the Luftwaffe in 1940.

The story of the last two years before World War II is the story of the Government in London being either unwilling or unable to 'see the wood for the trees'. The entire basic policy of the Germans for the immediate future had been put before them: massive rearmament, the determination to become a world power alongside the British Empire and America; the overlordship—either politically or, if necessary, militarily—of Europe (with the exception of Britain); and finally the great conquest of the Russian Communists.

This was the wood; these were the stakes of the game we had to play, a game we should have tried to win with all the brilliance of a master chess player. Instead, we bumbled and stalled our way through meaningless treaties and bits of paper and dramatic meetings on unattainable objectives. These were the trees, which seemed to blind the politicians of the 1930s to the Nazis' real and relentless objectives. On these politicians lies the blame for our near defeat and they can claim no credit for our eventual victory.

I still maintain that instead of engendering feverish and useless diplomacy over each successive Nazi move—the re-occupation of the Rhineland, the move into Austria and the occupation of Sudetenland—we should have tackled the 'wood' at its roots.

What did we really want? Surely the destruction of the two most disruptive totalitarian forces of the twentieth century—Nazism and Communism. Could we have diverted the 'conqueror's madness' of Hitler away from Europe if we had put in process a rapid expansion of our fighter aircraft, with fleets of mobile self-propelled anti-tank cum anti-aircraft guns like the German 88 sufficient to blunt the progress of any *Blitzkrieg?* Could we and the French have hinted at neutrality if Hitler would leave Western Europe alone and go East?

I believe the French would have gone along with us. The question is whether Hitler would have fallen for the bait and been sufficiently satisfied to keep the bargain. As one who knew Hitler personally and had recognised his pathological hatred of the Communists and his fanatical determination to destroy them, I believe it might have been possible. In any case the

fate of the Jews and most of Eastern Europe could hardly have
been worse.

Those nurtured on the balance of power in Europe argued
that once Germany was in a position to organise the Russian
masses, it would be the end of this mythical balance and of
freedom for all of us; and besides, our honour would not allow
us to abandon even temporarily those smaller nations who relied on our aid. What aid? We had seen the Baltic States swallowed up by Russia; we had raised no finger at the rape of
Austria and we had sold Czechoslovakia down the river at Munich. I do not believe that any foreign nation can 'conquer'
Russia or, at least, keep her conquered. Russia, like China, simply absorbs conquerors or freezes them out, and a Russo-Ger-
man conflict in 1940 would, in my opinion, have resulted in
early German victories followed by a long-drawn-out resistance, culminating in a stalemate of frozen exhaustion which
would have made both the dictators ready to accept the Atlantic Treaty. Could we have taken the risk?

By the end of 1938 the chance had gone. All indications
were that if the Maginot Line could be by-passed around the
north, which seemed an inevitable probability to those who
knew the strength of the German armour, then there was little
doubt that there would be complete defeat in France.

America had been assiduously wooed by the Nazis; a large
section of the population and the press were definitely Germa-
nophiles. The Germans had every reason to suppose that America would stay out of a war in Europe. They proved right, of
course, until Pearl Harbor enabled Roosevelt to persuade
America that the war was global.

In March 1939 the Nazis seized those parts of Czechoslovakia
(Bohemia and Moravia) which they had not been given under
the Munich Pact. There was ample evidence coming out of
Germany that the Army was preparing to bring forward their
operations to rectify the Danzig Corridor position in September
1939. And now the British Government, without any means
of backing up a military threat, resorted to a diplomatic one:
they made a Defence Pact with Poland and Roumania which
everyone knew could not be implemented. This finally set us

on a collision course. Those of us who could, made plans to take a last holiday with a deadline for everybody to be back in London by mid-August.

I spent a week in the Alps above Chamonix where a party of French air scouts, boys of sixteen or seventeen, were studying air currents in the mountains. They played happily with their balloons and did not appear to have the slightest idea of what was in store for them. The Maginot Line complex had made them complacent. I went on to Normandy in order to be a little nearer home and flew back to Heston in the Lockheed from Dinard.

I was on duty in the office that first weekend of September when at about 2.00 a.m. on the Sunday morning the duty secretary brought me in a telegram. I picked up my green scrambler telephone. "Vicky, get me the Cabinet offices on the scrambler, please. Hello, is that you, Cox? May we scramble, this is Zero C speaking? Just to let you know, the first bombs fell on Warsaw a few minutes ago. Yes, that's all, don't stay up too late." As a matter of fact I knew that Cox would be spending most of the rest of the night on the phone to the various Cabinet ministers.

As I replaced my telephone and lay back on the camp bed in my office, the tension of the past few months seemed to relax a little. The ghastly inevitability of this moment had grown step by step over the past six years, and now the Second World War had begun. It would be total war, for my experience with the Nazis during the whole of the thirties had given me no hope that civilians would be left out of it. This had been reinforced by what had happened at Guernica in Spain and I knew that the five-hundred- and thousand-pound bombs manufactured for the German bomber force were certain to be used. We had known the approximate date for some months past from various competent sources, so that there was no sense of shock; now that it had finally happened I found my thoughts ranging back over the past decade. It would not be a repetition of World War I, for the Nazis would never allow themselves to get bogged down in the West as Stalin hoped. How could we cope with the might of the Germans? Could it have been avoided? Why had we failed so utterly both in diplomacy and in rearmament to deal with the gangsters of Berlin? One thing was certain, it had not been for lack of information.

The unearthly wail of the air-raid siren had proclaimed the new war, a poor substitute to the herald's trumpet of former days. Another generation of Britain's 'contemptible little Army', tough, determined men, backed up by a few tanks, guns and Bren-gun carriers, had arrived safely in France. There was no 'Tipperary'; someone had forgotten to write one.

It has been said that the comment of the Foreign Office after the declaration of war in September 1939 was that it was satisfactory to know that the correct protocol had been accurately and faithfully carried out. There seemed to have been left over from the Middle Ages an aura of solemn magnificence and grand occasion about declaring war, whereas in 1939 it was surely the simple admission of failure to deal with the German menace from the start. By September 1939 we had stabilised our estimate of German air strength at a figure of 3,000 first-line aircraft with large reserves of both machines and personnel. We also knew the types and performances of most of the German aircraft. After their losses in Poland, Norway and France, they were able to field some 2,700 aircraft for the Battle of Britain against our 1,700.

But at this point, just when we most needed information about the timing of the German operations, someone betrayed one of our few remaining networks in Germany, and two of our best agents disappeared. They were almost certainly shot. As it turned out we were to have six months of cold war breathing space before the hot war started: we knew that once the shooting began most of our remaining agents would either have 'gone to ground' or deserted us.

It was a strange turn of fate that at the end of the war a senior German Intelligence officer to whom the traitor had sold the names of our agents, while being interrogated in England, identified the culprit amongst the interrogating staff. The man was duly court-martialled and his thirty pieces of silver were no longer any use to him.

But now in September 1939 the outlook for Secret Intelli-

gence looked pretty bleak, and most of us felt that if Britain
was to survive we would need a miracle.

In July 1939 the Polish Secret Service had told us that for
several years they had had a brilliant spy in a top-secret German
cypher machine factory. In consequence, it had been possible
to reconstruct some replicas of the highly complicated, electri-
cally operated cypher machine which was to be used throughout the German armed forces; so this was to be the answer
to their *Blitzkrieg* communications. The Poles told us that they
thought the time had come for us to have one of these machines
to see if we could make head or tail of it. They had already
learned something of the mathematics of its operation. It
looked like an impossibly complicated machine which worked
with drums, rather on the lines of the fruit machine, the drums
revolving and proliferating the letters of the signal so as to
turn it into complete gobbledegook. The key to the cypher
was the way in which the drums were set before the signal
was sent, so that certain letters were in front. There were
five revolving drums in the wartime machine and the sequence
of letters was changed every day. We duly collected the machine from Warsaw and our backroom scientists studied this
apparently unbreakable cypher machine in the hopes of finding
some solution to an insoluble problem. It soon became evident
that the task of discovering the daily keys to this machine was
an enormous one, running into millions of mathematical per-
mutations every twenty-four hours.

All the most brilliant mathematical brains in the country,
mostly from our universities, were co-opted and brought to
Bletchley Park, a country house some thirty miles from London. And here in September 1939 they declared all-out war
on the problem, believing that if man could invent a cypher
machine of such complexity, he could invent another machine
to solve it.

In November 1939 the heads of our Intelligence organisation
in Holland were enticed to the German frontier with the promise of a plot by certain anti-Nazi generals to assassinate Hitler.
It was a trap. They were hustled across the frontier and
captured.

When we in the Intelligence Service had reached our nadir,

in December 1939, an amazing document was dropped through the British Embassy letter box in Oslo. Known as the Oslo Report, it contained scientific details of most of the German secret projects such as the V-1 flying bombs, acoustic mines, radar, rockets and even a projected jet aero-engine. It was an invaluable present from an obviously anti-Nazi scientist, but it was so far ahead of our own research at that time that it was thought at first to be a hoax. Always, Intelligence information has to be most carefully evaluated before it can be of much use; sometimes it is premature knowledge which cannot be acted upon until more is disclosed. But once you know that the Germans are capable of building rockets, then you can start looking for rocket sites; when you see strange buildings in aerial photographs whose use you cannot make out, you can start putting all the miscellaneous collection of facts collated over the years together and maybe come out with the right answer. Much Intelligence work consists of endlessly sifting and sorting information, keeping it in the back of your mind in reserve so that it can be brought out when needed. But still a miracle was needed if we were to make up for all the nonsensical delinquency of our rulers in the 1930s and eventually foil the world-conquering ambitions of the Nazis. Perhaps a real crisis in our chance of survival might throw up some more fertile minds than the ones we had watched rumble through the 1930s.

In April 1940 the brains at Bletchley made their first small breakthrough with the German 'Enigma' cypher machine. Just four little signals concerning personnel in the Luftwaffe had been decyphered. Had the miracle arrived?

It was a very small success but it was enough to make me wonder how on earth we should be able to handle the flood of German cyphered signals which would clog the ether if and when the hot war started, and if by that time or even some time later we were really able to read the principal German signal traffic. Such a vast mass of priceless information would obviously require a special organisation to cope with it and to maintain the absolute secrecy of our success. The whole idea made me grateful that I had visited Germany and known the Nazi leaders over the past eight years. I had some idea of the way they thought and acted and certainly a very good idea of the enormous power of their Army and Air Force, and I knew the scope and magnitude of what we should be up against. I was also aware of the type of warfare that would be waged. Unlike so many people who thought it would be 1914 all over again, I knew that it was going to be more of a scientific war, fought with speed and extreme violence, and that the ability to read German secret signals might be the only real form of Intelligence that we should be able to get. The details of the *Blitzkrieg*'s strategy, the memory of all those concrete installations in East Prussia, the driving fingers of Reichenau across the restaurant table and the vast network of aerodromes and factories in Germany made me realise that even if eventually we were only going to be able to read a tenth of the signals flowing from all the main Commands, then someone would have to build up an entirely new branch of our Intelligence system. I explained all my views to my Chief and managed to persuade him of the potential size of the problem which might soon be upon us.

In April my Chief gave me permission to set up a completely new organisation for the translation, distribution and complete security of the decoded signals at Bletchley where the cryptologists worked. Through April, May and June of that year we were getting enough signals to help us in the Battle of France and the first moves in the Battle of Britain; and then by August and September the miracle gradually emerged, and during the crucial time of the Battle of Britain we were able, with the help of the brilliant radar achievements of Sir Robert Watson-Watt and above all the determination and sacrifice of our pilots, just to tip the scales in our favour to beat the Luftwaffe's attempt to clear the skies of the RAF, the necessary preliminary to an invasion of Britain.

Now my time was fully employed on this new and vital Intelligence, which was christened 'Ultra'. By 1942 our 'brains' had constructed the first computer: it occupied the whole of a good-sized room, but it enabled us to find the keys and read all the important signals from Hitler on down for the rest of the war; a story I have told in my book *The Ultra Secret.*

Looking back over the years 1930 to 1945—at the frustrations of the early days, at the slow acceptance of my Intelligence information, at the extraordinary experience of working inside Germany in the strange world of the Nazi dictatorship reborn, alas, under a contaminated star, at my experiences of meeting Hitler and his henchmen and of carrying through the bluff of my Nazi sympathy during the 1930s—I found my initial aggravation turning into a more positive attitude of frustration and alarm, woefully unshared by the rulers of Britain.

I gained, however, a real sense of achievement when I discovered and perfected the technique of very high-altitude aerial photography which added so enormously to our wartime Intelligence and which compared so favourably with my earlier experiences of photography in the First World War. My whole experimental unit was taken over and adapted by both the Royal Air Force and the United States Air Forces and operated throughout the war almost without loss of pilots or aircraft.

However, I suppose the crowning satisfaction of my fifteen years' work in M16 culminated in my wartime association with Winston Churchill and all the principal Allied Commanders during the Second World War. I fulfilled my responsibility for the absolute security both of the distribution and the application of Ultra Intelligence so that the enemy never knew during the whole of the Second World War that we were reading his most secret signals.

Author's Note

In 1968 I wrote my first account of the years described in
The Nazi Connection, but as head of the Air Section of M16
in London my methods of obtaining secret information were
somewhat unorthodox, and there was much I could not write
about.

Since the publication of my book *The Ultra Secret* in 1974,
which disclosed important new information about wartime Intelligence, much more has been revealed about the secrets
of the Second World War, and I have now been able to write
of my experiences with the Nazi leaders in Germany in a
broader context.

F. W. Winterbotham

Index